THE GREATEST GAME

Also by Stephen Alter

NON-FICTION

The Cobra's Gaze: Exploring India's Wild Heritage
Wild Himalaya: A Natural History of the Greatest Mountain Range on Earth
Becoming a Mountain: Himalayan Journeys in Search of the Sacred and the Sublime
All the Way to Heaven: An American Boyhood in the Himalayas
Amritsar to Lahore: Crossing the Border Between India and Pakistan
Sacred Waters: A Pilgrimage to the Many Sources of the Ganga
Elephas Maximus: A Portrait of the Indian Elephant
Going for Take: The Making of Omkara and Other Encounters in Bollywood

FICTION

Death in Shambles: A Hill Station Mystery
Birdwatching: A Novel
Feral Dreams: Mowgli and His Mothers
In the Jungles of the Night: A Novel About Jim Corbett
Guldaar
The Rataban Betrayal
Renuka
Aranyani
Aripan and Other Stories
The Godchild
Silk and Steel
Neglected Lives

FICTION FOR YOUNGER READERS

If You Were a Tiger Cub
How the Cobra Got His Spectacles
A Little Lost Elephant
Great Indian Children's Stories (ed.)
The Phantom Isles
Ghost Letters
The Cloudfarers
The Secret Sanctuary

THE GREATEST GAME

Being the Further Adventures of Kimball O'Hara

a sequel to
Rudyard Kipling's *Kim*

STEPHEN ALTER

ALEPH BOOK COMPANY
An independent publishing firm
promoted by *Rupa Publications India*

First published in India in 2025
by Aleph Book Company
7/16 Ansari Road, Daryaganj
New Delhi 110 002

Copyright © Stephen Alter 2025

The author has asserted his moral rights.

All rights reserved.

This is a work of fiction. Names, characters, places, and incidents are either the product of the author's imagination or are used fictitiously and any resemblance to any actual persons, living or dead, events or locales is entirely coincidental.

No part of this publication may be reproduced, transmitted, or stored in a retrieval system, in any form or by any means, without permission in writing from Aleph Book Company.

For sale in the Indian subcontinent only.

ISBN: 978-93-6523-456-5

1 3 5 7 9 10 8 6 4 2

Printed in India

This book is sold subject to the condition that it shall not, by way of trade or otherwise, be lent, resold, hired out, or otherwise circulated without the publisher's prior consent in any form of binding or cover other than that in which it is published.

in memory of my cousin
Tom

Author's Note

Kim, Rudyard Kipling's only novel, was first published in 1901 and it has remained in print ever since, becoming both a bestseller and a classic work of English literature. The book has many admirers and detractors, for it is unabashedly of its time—a story of British colonialism in India with a vocabulary that is both richly embellished and often derogatory. No apologies are sufficient for some of the racial stereotypes and prejudices that Kipling presents in the novel. Yet, even the foremost scholar of Orientalism and a critic of the imperial gaze, Edward Said, praised *Kim* on many levels. In his introduction to the Penguin edition in 1987, Said writes:

> The variously qualified pleasure we can derive from reading *Kim* today, therefore, is that in it we can watch a great artist blinded in a sense by his own insights of India... (*Kim* is) a great document of its historical moment, as well as an aesthetic milestone along the way to midnight 15 August, 1947, a moment whose children have done so much to revise our sense of the past's richness and its enduring problems.

The novel you now hold in your hands makes no pretence of being a scholarly sequel or even a commentary on the Raj. It is simply an effort to spin the yarn a little further and follow that clever, mischievous young boy into an ambiguous future.

ہزاروں خواہشیں ایسی کہ ہر خواہش پہ دَم نِکلے
بُہت نِکلے میرے ارمان لیکن پھر بھی کم نِکلے

Hazaaron khwaashein aisi ki har khwaaish pe dum nikley
Bahut nikley mere armaan lekin phir bhi kam nikley

Thousands of desires have I cherished; for each I would have given my life.
Many of those yearnings were requited, but still they were too few.

—Mirza Ghalib

∞

He sat, in defiance of municipal orders, astride the gun Zam-Zammah on her brick platform opposite the old Ajaib-Gher—the Wonder House, as the natives call the Lahore Museum. Who hold Zam-Zammah, that 'fire-breathing dragon', hold the Punjab, for the great green-bronze piece is always first of the conqueror's loot.

—*Kim*
Rudyard Kipling

1

Lahore. 18 March 1947. Dusk brings with it stray breezes from the north, dispelling some of the day's oppressive heat. Summer has begun early this year, as if to make up for the cold winter we just had. A wheeling flock of pigeons fills the amber sky. Kicking my motorcycle to life, I can smell wet earth, where a bhishti with his goatskin waterbag has laid the dust in the forecourt of the Masonic Lodge. My worthy companions tried to persuade me to stay for another drink before curfew, but their conversations were full of rumours about Radcliffe's Boundary Commission, cricket, and the cost of a passage home to England, none of which I cared to discuss.

The Norton's engine sounds ragged but after I adjust the timing lever, it settles into a steadier, throaty roar. Switching on the headlamp, I circumnavigate a crescent of flower beds bordering the driveway and head out the gate, turning left across Charing Cross and onto the Mall Road. There is no traffic, only an empty tonga going in the direction of the walled city. Those who heed the evening call to prayer are in their places of worship, while followers of other creeds know better than to wander about at this hour, because of the recent violence the city has seen. Studying me with regal omniscience is the late, lamented empress Victoria, beneath a domed pavilion, her statue cast in bronze.

Seconds later, a sharp clang of metal rings out and the Norton shudders as I feel a burning sensation crease my thigh. The crack of a .303 follows an instant later. It's true what they say: you'll never hear the gunshot that kills you. Instinctively, I shift gears and give the Norton full throttle, as a second shot is fired. This one passes over my right shoulder, drilling the air just south of my ear. Lowering my head, I swerve back and forth across the empty road. A third bullet comes after me, but by now I am well out of range and all I hear is the distant report of the rifle, fired in frustration. The shooter must have positioned himself behind a hedge to the left of the Victoria Memorial, somewhere in the shrubs and shadows.

Heading towards Regal Crossing, I race past a line of European shops. Their display windows are lit up for evening customers, though the road remains deserted. Ranken & Co., Civil and Military Tailors, where I got an ill-fitting suit made some years ago. Cutler Palmer & Co., Wine Merchants, whose prices I can't afford. Smith & Campbell Chemists, offering cures for everything from hangovers to syphilis. And J. D. Bevan, who sells grand pianos, of which I have no need. They all go by in a blur, as I accelerate away from my would-be assassin, dodging a pariah dog that foolishly tries to cross my path. Nobody is in pursuit and the gunman must have escaped in the opposite direction, though I'm not taking any chances. By now, I can feel blood on my trousers and, glancing down, see a dark wet patch, six inches above my knee. The bullet grazed my leg and struck the air filter mounted on the Norton's petrol tank. All of this, I will confirm later, but for now I am grateful to be alive and happy to be heading into the familiar labyrinths of Anarkali Bazaar.

Here the shops are busier, as people hurry to buy provisions before the 7 p.m. curfew. Unlike the larger, European shops with their bright windows and neatly painted signs, most of the stalls are open to the street and lit by kerosene lanterns. Selling dry goods out of gunny sacks and heaps of vegetables, the merchants haggle with their customers. A goat's carcass, flayed and partially dismembered, hangs from the rafters of a butcher's shop while the aroma of roasting kebabs wafts out of the shadows where a charcoal brazier glows and sends up clouds of fragrant smoke. Gearing down, I weave through the cyclists and pedestrians, as well as a few stray cows. Though some of the people glance in my direction with hostility in their eyes, I feel safer here than anywhere else in the world.

Up ahead, an arched gateway is plastered with Congress posters bearing pictures of Mr Gandhi, appealing for peace. An advertisement for a magician, The Great Mustafa, is also pasted there, and other notices offering the best prices for dried fruit and nuts from Kabul. A colourful hoarding announces a new film at Imperial Talkies—*Abida*, starring Noor Jehan. I drive through the gateway, manoeuvring between a handcart piled high with onions and a woman in a faded black burqa, who seems to be deaf to the insistent carping of my horn. A few electric bulbs glimmer inside open doorways and a subtle yet cloying perfume fills the air, the mingling odours of incense, opium, and tobacco. Turning into a narrow gulley, I circle around to the back of a decaying brick building and park the Norton beneath a canvas awning. As I swing my leg off the motorcycle, a stabbing pain makes me wince, though I know I'm not badly hurt. Blood trickles down the inside of my thigh, while I fumble with my cigarette case and find a match. Lighting a Cavender's Navy Cut, I can see that my hand is shaking, the flame wavering in the dusty gloom at the foot of the stairwell.

I've been shot at three times before and wounded twice but never like this, without any warning, an anonymous bullet at twilight. Lahore has always had its dangers but until recently it was a peaceful city. Ever since last August, when Mr Jinnah put out a call for direct action, the troubles started and now it's hard to know whom you can trust. Of course, there's always been resentment towards the British, and anarchists of all stripes have targeted policemen, army officers, and other officials. As I make my way painfully up the stairs, favouring my injured leg, I wonder who the shooter could have been and whether his motives were personal or political.

Champa is in her chambers, curled up on a divan and painting her toenails a livid pink. When I enter through the curtained doorway, she smiles indulgently but her expression changes as soon as she sees the wound on my leg.

'Hai bhagwan! What happened?' she cries, swivelling around and getting to her feet.

'Someone tried to shoot me,' I reply, the cigarette still clamped between my lips, as Champa calls out for help and lowers me onto her divan.

'Bring another lantern,' she instructs the two young women who appear, 'and a chilamchi of water.'

After pulling off my shoes, unbuckling my belt, and opening the buttons on my fly, she removes my trousers.

'Slowly, slowly,' I try to reassure her. 'It's not that serious.'

Holding a lantern in one hand, Champa examines the wound, where the bullet has ploughed a neat furrow through meat and skin. Blood is seeping out and several drops fall on the patterned floor tiles. Before I've finished my cigarette, however, Champa has cleaned me up. Taking a small glass vial, she breaks the neck and pours a yellowish liquid into the wound. The pain makes me curse and for a moment my head spins like a phonograph. Folding a wad of cotton wool inside layers of gauze, she presses it down on the wound and tightly wraps another roll of gauze around my thigh. Then straightening the injured leg, she places my foot on a silk cushion and makes me lie back.

'Now, I need a drink,' I insist, 'if you don't mind.'

One of the girls brings a bottle of Dyer Meakin's whisky and a cut-glass tumbler, which I fill halfway to the brim. The alcohol goes down quickly, scorching my throat but easing the pain and steadying my nerves.

Champa shakes her head when I offer her a sip of my drink.

'Who would have wanted to kill you?' she wonders aloud, her hand stroking my forearm with unusual tenderness and anxiety.

'I wouldn't know,' I answer. 'I suppose I have more enemies than friends.'

'These days everyone is out for blood,' she says. 'Even our friends have become our enemies.'

'It's sure to get worse before it gets better,' I say, lying back and closing my eyes.

'Does it hurt?' she asks.

'Not any more. Only when I move my leg.'

She looks down at her half-painted toenails and shakes her head.

'Today I was saying to the girls, we must leave Lahore,' she murmurs.

'Why would you do that?' I ask, though I know the answer.

Champa looks at me with an impatient expression.

'Where have you been? Haven't you seen what's happening here?' she demands. 'For the past six months there's been nothing but bloodshed in this city, innocent people stabbed, mobs throwing stones. Right here in this mohalla, two houses were burned down. The smallest dispute turns into a riot. Yesterday, two people were killed near Taxali Gate, just because they argued over the price of garlic. Suddenly a mob gathered and beat them to death. And in Badami Bagh, a tongawallah was knifed after his horse knocked over a basket of tomatoes. Who knows when things will really explode? There's news of a massacre in Rawalpindi....'

I nod my head. 'Yes, but where would you go?'

Champa shrugs. 'Dilli. Lucknow. I know people there. No matter how much violence there is, women like us will always find patrons.'

'But Lahore is your home,' I remind her. 'Both you and I grew up on these streets. Why should we go anywhere else?'

'Because I'm a Hindu,' she replies. 'It's better to leave before they kill us. You're a Christian, you'll be safe.'

'Not much of a Christian,' I protest.

'You could always go to England,' she says, with a feeble smile.

'No, thank you,' I reply. 'It's a cold and miserable country.'

'How would you know, if you've never been there?' she responds.

'Jolly Old England.'

She laughs. 'At least you wouldn't have people shooting at you.'

'Maybe they mistook me for someone else,' I muse. 'It's happened before.'

Glancing across the room, I see my reflection in a full-length mirror on the wall. More shadows than light, this spectral image startles me because it brings back the last memory I have of my father, from when I was a very young child. Though I cannot remember his face, a vague recollection haunts my mind, of a dying man propped up on a sagging charpai in the one-roomed hovel where we lived. His emaciated body was almost naked except for a soiled and tattered pair of shorts. While I don't recall his features, I do remember the colour of his skin, white as bone.

My own complexion is somewhat darker, inherited perhaps from my mother who died of cholera soon after I was born. I have no idea what she looked like, though the woman who raised me after my father's death, told me that she had brown hair and jade green eyes. Wherever my skin is burnt by the sun, it turns a walnut tan. But lying here in my undershorts, my legs are pale as the gauze bandage on my thigh. I suppose the face that looks back at me from the mirror must reflect something of my father's visage, though he didn't live to be my age. I may have some black Irish in me, the blood of a shipwrecked Spanish sailor in my veins, perhaps. My eyes are grey with a trace of blue. Some have said I look like a Kashmiri, especially with my beard, now mostly grey, though it used to be a chestnut brown. Studying my dim reflection in the flickering lamplight, I realize how old I've grown.

Champa's room is full of mirrors. Sometimes I tease her, calling it a Sheesh Mahal. Looking glasses of different sizes hang on the walls, more than a dozen of them. Champa is vain about her appearance and likes to admire herself, pausing in front of the bevelled glass on the almirah door, which reflects her ample figure draped in layers of silk and satin, silhouetted against the lamplight. A few patches have turned black with mirror rot, as if the light itself has corroded and a bright crack runs across the lower right-hand corner. Even now, as she crosses the room, I catch her glancing towards the almirah mirror for the briefest moment, as if to confirm that she is still a desirable woman. Much older than her girls, Champa must be closer to my age than theirs, forty if she's a day. The full-length glass on the opposite wall, in which I see myself, has an ornate marquetry frame, inlaid with ivory and ebony, a gift from one of her admirers. On her dressing table are several handheld mirrors, two of them encased in silver, the others with carved wooden handles. Champa often picks one up and holds it close to her face, examining a kohl-rimmed eye, the rouge on her cheeks, or the gold and ruby stud that adorns her nose. She also wears shawls and chunnis embroidered with mirrorwork, their bright round facets like the glint of silver coins.

I can tell the girls are listening on the other side of the curtain. Three days ago, when I was last here, they told me their neighbours had warned them, saying that if they continued to entertain men in this house, they would burn it down.

'Have you had any more threats?' I ask, pouring another inch of whisky into my glass and lighting an accompanying smoke.

Champa shakes her head. 'Some of those same men have spent time in these rooms, enjoying our company. Now they disapprove of us....'

'Never underestimate the power of hypocrisy,' I mutter in English.

She gives me a quizzical look. 'What did you say?'

'Never mind,' I answer, stroking her hand, which she pulls away.

'You're not in any state for love tonight,' she scolds me.

'It's only a scratch,' I protest.

'Drink your whisky,' she tells me. 'I'll make you a paan.'

My leg has begun to throb, and she is right, there is no chance of making love, but that isn't why I came here.

Champa calls out to Munia, the youngest girl, asking for her paan daan. When she brings it into the room, Munia gives me a mischievous look. They know me well in this house of ill repute, which is the only place I can call home.

As I watch in silence, Champa prepares two betel leaves, smearing them with scarlet katha and white lime, then adding supari and strands of saffron. Her paan daan contains an array of secret ingredients, some of which she claims will make the weakest, most impotent man into Gama the Great.

'I'll need a place to sleep tonight,' I say.

'You can stay here,' she says. 'With the curfew, nobody comes at this hour and even if they do, the girls will make them comfortable in one of the other rooms.'

Pointing to my bandaged leg, I tease her. 'When did you become Florence Nightingale?'

'There was a time I dreamed of becoming a nurse,' she replies.

Despite the petulance in her voice, I can see that she is crying.

'Champa, what's wrong?' I ask, surprised. 'I've never seen you shed a tear.'

She wipes her eyes with the end of her muslin chunni and stares at me.

'I've never been afraid like this before,' she answers, handing me my paan, while she puts the other in her mouth. 'Every night, I wake up worrying, what will happen to us?'

We chew in silence, the clean, strong flavour numbing my tongue. 'I've added a pinch of opium,' she confesses. 'We'll both sleep well tonight.'

2

Twelve minutes late for my meeting with Dougal MacNeil, I see him waiting impatiently on the veranda at Faletti's, as I cut across the front lawn. A rust-coloured hoopoe flies up in front of me on black and white wings, then lands a few yards further on. MacNeil is a good man, except for his obsession with punctuality. 9.12 a.m. He scowls at his watch, as I work my way up the three shallow steps onto the veranda, trying to keep the weight off my right leg.

Two hours ago, I wakened out of a deep sleep and strange dreams of Kashmir. Hurrying back from Champa's kotha to my rooms in Gawalmandi, I had a quick wash. The bandage on my leg doesn't look as if it needs any attention, though the pain is now a steady ache that sets my teeth on edge. Hurriedly tying on a turban and wearing a pair of round, tortoise-shell spectacles, I have changed into a lawyer's black coat, striped trousers, and white bib, disguising myself as a venerable Sikh barrister at the Lahore High Court, which is just around the corner from Faletti's.

'Why are you limping?' MacNeil asks, gesturing for a waiter to bring us coffee. He is out of uniform but unmistakably a policeman in khaki shorts and knee socks. His sola topi sits on a footstool beside him like a tortoise with its head and legs drawn in.

'Someone took a potshot at me yesterday,' I answer, easing myself into a cane chair.

'What are you talking about? Why didn't you inform me?' MacNeil is a superintendent of police (SP) who heads up the Intelligence Bureau here in Lahore, and he expects to be the first to learn of anything that happens on his watch.

'Sorry. I got caught somewhere after curfew. Couldn't reach you... sir,' I add for emphasis.

'Someone tried to kill you?' he asks, as if I haven't made myself clear.

'That's my assumption,' I reply. 'Whoever it was, he was waiting with a three-nought-three, across the street from the temple.'

MacNeil is a mason too, though he wasn't at the lodge last night.

'Who was it?' he demands.

'I have no idea. Didn't get a look at him. I was too busy running away.'

He shakes his head in frustration. 'Are you hurt?'

I give him a pained look. 'A little. Superficial wound on my thigh.'

'Have you seen a doctor?' he snaps.

'In a manner of speaking, yes,' I reply.

'Not one of those native hakims, I hope,' he says. 'You'll get an infection straight away. I've known fools who lost a limb to gangrene, just because they didn't take care of a minor injury.'

For all six feet two inches and fifteen stone of him, MacNeil is a bit of a worrier, always nervous about his health and that of his subordinates.

'I'll be all right,' I try to reassure him.

He gives me a sceptical glance, then pays me a compliment.

'By the way, Sardar Sahib, your disguise is most convincing.'

'Hopefully, no one will recognize me,' I reply.

'I didn't want to meet in my office. Too many flies on the wall,' MacNeil says, then asks again, 'Any guess who it was that fired at you?'

'I suspect it was one of those Bolshie naujawans. They've had me in their sights for years. With all of this communal unrest, it's a chance to settle old scores while your police force is focusing on the riots.' This theory has been turning over in my head from the moment I reached Champa's place last night. It is the only explanation that makes sense.

'Possibly.' MacNeil nods and then falls silent as the waiter arrives with a pot of coffee and two cups, setting them on the table between us. A ceiling fan is spinning slowly overhead, rustling the air, which suddenly feels warmer than it did a minute ago. The hoopoe lands on the near side of the lawn, a foppish bird, fanning its orange crest.

'I was going to ask you to contact your sources, but under the circumstances....' MacNeil hesitates. 'Maybe Vincent can do that....'

'My sources are more reliable than Vincent's,' I remind him, then ask, 'What's the problem?'

MacNeil puts two sugar cubes in his cup and pours himself a black stream of coffee that looks as if it could be crude oil. I'm already itching for a whisky, but I help myself to coffee instead, adding plenty of milk and three lumps of sugar.

'We've been told there's a plan to blow up the railway bridge over the Ravi. Some new group of terrorists trying to prove themselves. We have two separate reports from different sources. Your informant should have some details.'

'If it's Sikhs or Hindus, then he probably isn't as well informed as he used to be,' I say. 'Nobody is talking to anybody except their own people these days.'

'Shite!' MacNeil mutters. 'I'll be glad to be out of this mess, as soon as I can, and back in the Highlands where I belong.'

'You've got at least one more promotion to go,' I flatter him.

He shakes his head. 'No. It's early retirement for me, heading home to Aviemore on the river Spey.'

'Cold place, I'm told.'

'Yes, but the salmon fishing is good. I'm not going to stick around to watch things fall apart in India. What about you?'

Taking a swallow of bitter coffee, I study the hoopoe digging for worms.

'Fishing never interested me. Depends too much on luck.'

'I meant, where are you planning to spend the rest of your life, O'Hara?'

'I know what you meant....' I shake my head. 'It's just that I don't have an answer.'

'You should try Australia,' he suggests. 'I'm told it's a good place to settle.'

'Too many kangaroos.'

'Then what about America?'

I shake my head. 'I'm not that eager for a change of scene.'

'How old are you?'

My coffee tastes like sweetened bile.

'Sixty, sixty-one,' I reply, 'Though the truth is, I've never been sure.'

'Time to start collecting your pension,' he suggests.

'Aye, but will His Majesty's government continue to pay me once they've quit India,' I wonder aloud.

'I wouldn't worry about that,' MacNeil says, glancing at his watch again and abruptly giving me my orders. 'Talk to your sources and ask if they've heard anything about the bridge. And make sure you see a doctor about that leg. Now, shall we go in for breakfast?'

This is a signal that all confidential matters have been concluded and whatever we discuss in the dining hall will be of a more public or personal nature. Faletti's is one of Lahore's better hotels, though it has a shabby formality I've never liked. The waiters are an arrogant bunch, especially when I don't look European. Most of the guests are boxwallahs, tourists, and other transients, which means very few people will recognize MacNeil and if they do, they'll assume he's meeting a lawyer about some pending case. The breakfasts aren't bad, and I like the sausages and bacon, which isn't something I can get in the bazaar.

'So, I suppose you'll stay on in India, won't you?' MacNeil returns to his original theme, after choosing a table in the far corner of the dining room. 'After all, this is the only home you've known.'

I shrug, wishing I could light a cigarette to steady my nerves for what I'm sure will be an extended interrogation. But being dressed as a Sikh, I've forsworn tobacco, until I shed this disguise.

'Come on, be honest with me, man. Are you more comfortable here at Faletti's,' he asks, 'or eating a mutton samosa in the Rang Mahal bazaar?'

'It isn't so much a matter of comfort....' I begin to reply but he interrupts me.

'Isn't it true that you grew up speaking Hindustani as a child before you learned English?' he asks.

'Yes, I did. A crude mix of Hindustani, Urdu, and Punjabi, the gutter-speak of Lahore,' I explain. 'As a boy, I had a gift for mimicry, imitating different dialects and accents, from the taciturn drawl of a Pathan horse trader to the haughty chatter of a Brahmin priest. I had a sharp tongue too and learned how to curse like a tongawallah.'

'And when did you learn the Queen's English?'

'I picked up a few words and phrases, early on,' I explain. 'But when I was eventually sent to Xavier's, they taught me how to read and write.'

'Xavier's?'

'St. Xavier's College in Lucknow. Almost got myself chucked out several times,' I confess, 'but they successfully turned me into a white man.'

'Really?'

'Or at least half white…as much as they could,' I admit.

He smiles. 'I hope you don't mind these personal questions. We've worked together for six years, isn't it? But somehow I don't feel I know you.'

'Well, there's not much to know,' I respond.

'Of course,' MacNeil mumbles into his moustache and takes out his pipe. He gestures to the waiter. 'We'll have some fruit first and more coffee.'

'Do you have any inside word on when the handover will take place?' I ask, trying to change the subject.

'As you know, Attlee and his socialists have decided that it must be concluded before July '48, which means at least another year of this bloody violence,' says MacNeil. 'Mountbatten is arriving next week to become the new viceroy and they say he's been given full authority to get the job done.'

'Is it true that India will be divided?' I ask, rhetorically.

'Yes, for sure. The Congress and the Muslim League will never come up with an effective compromise,' MacNeil replies. 'But I stay away from politics. My job is simple. Keep whatever peace I can, enforce the law and protect British interests.'

'You must be receiving a lot of intelligence on different factions inciting the riots,' I say. 'Probably takes up all your time these days.'

By now he's got his pipe fuming and squints at me with disapproval, through a cloud of smoke, as if I've crossed the line that separates conversation on the veranda from what we say inside this room. But only two other tables are occupied, both at the far end of the dining hall, well out of earshot.

'The minute we quell one riot another flares up,' he says in frustration. 'Sometimes I forget there are other threats to deal with.'

'It might help the situation if we knew where the borders will be drawn,' I say. 'Most of the Sikhs and Hindus displaced from the NWFP are now in Rawalpindi but nobody's sure if they'll be booted further on down the railway line. They're angry. They're desperate. And, from what I've heard, the Muslims are lashing out at them. Nobody knows what's going to happen.'

'Punjab will be divided. You can take it from me. And Mr Jinnah will get Pindi and Lahore,' MacNeil predicts, as two bowls of cut papaya arrive in front of us along with a fresh pot of coffee. Eyeing the papaya with disappointment, MacNeil complains, 'No mangoes?'

'No, sahib. Not yet,' the waiter answers, taking a step back.

'Not before May,' I interject, 'at the earliest.'

'By the way, I forgot that you prefer tea,' says MacNeil.

'Whisky, actually. But it's too early in the day,' I reply. 'No, coffee is fine. It's all the same to me.'

MacNeil laughs, filling both our cups. 'You know, O'Hara, I admire you. A man who reconciles the East with the West. Not many people are able to do that.'

'I've been called a "Friend of all the World",' I say as MacNeil picks at the papaya, which is overripe.

'And enemy of none?' he grunts.

'Not quite,' I remind him. 'The wound in my legs disputes that phrase.'

'You know, you have a reputation,' the SP says, looking me in the eye, 'for playing both sides. There are some officers in our department who don't trust you an inch. They claim that your allegiance is divided.'

'They can say what they like but my record speaks for itself. You've seen my file. I've served the empire for forty-five years, more or less, from the age of thirteen or fourteen.'

'Longer than anyone else,' he agrees.

'I was part of the Great Game until after the Kaiser's war,' I say, 'Colonel Creighton himself inducted me before I had a hair on my chin.'

'What was the Great Game like?' he asks with a smile.

'Devious. Full of treachery and betrayal. But we had a clear enemy then—the Russians. The Czar and all his Cossacks! Now the only adversary we have is ourselves.'

MacNeil points his pipe stem at me. 'You see, that's your problem, O'Hara. Too quick to express your ambivalence about British rule.'

'I speak my mind,' I say. 'Though I've been an agent of the empire for all these years, employed at different times by each of the services from the Survey of India to the Imperial Secret Service and your Intelligence Bureau. I've never betrayed that trust, even when I disagreed with policies and procedures. You can read my commendations. The arrests of seven Ghadar anarchists were based on information I provided.'

'Your resignation letter is also in your file, dated 14 April 1919. Four months after the Armistice.'

'And one day after General Dyer slaughtered more than a thousand innocent people in Amritsar, at Jallianwala Bagh,' I recall.

'Why wasn't your letter accepted?' MacNeil asks.

'The IB officer I reported to was Jack Kiernan,' I say. 'He held the same rank as you do, and he persuaded me to stay on. I was barely thirty and most people still believed that the British empire would last forever.'

'Why didn't Kiernan just tear up the letter instead of leaving it in your file?'

'Maybe as a warning, I suspect.' Pushing the bowl of papaya aside, untouched, I reach for my coffee.

At the same time, MacNeil heaves himself out of his chair, declaring, 'Let's get some real breakfast.'

We help ourselves from the chafing dishes on the buffet—eggs, sausages, bacon, fried potatoes, baked beans, and grilled tomatoes.

The waiter brings fresh toast with butter to the table, and I realize I haven't eaten for the past twenty-four hours. My appetite is almost a match for MacNeil's.

'Don't mind me prying, O'Hara, but you are a bit of a puzzle,' the SP muses between mouthfuls. 'I know you're able to transform yourself into a native, but are you acting or is it more than just a disguise?'

'I'm not sure I understand.' I balk at the question.

Raising knife and fork in his massive fists, MacNeil gestures impatiently. 'I mean, are you always aware that you're playing a role when you're wearing a turban like that, or is it just natural to become an Indian, even if you aren't?'

'I am what I am,' I answer cautiously, 'an Irish orphan who grew up on the streets of Lahore, though I've worn many masks over the years.'

MacNeil seems dissatisfied with my answer, as he cuts a sausage in half and thrusts it into his mouth, chewing thoughtfully.

'Do you dream in English?' he blurts out.

I shake my head. 'It depends, but I don't remember most of my dreams.'

He stops himself and smiles.

'Don't think I'm questioning your loyalty, O'Hara,' he says. 'It's just that I find it hard to believe that someone can change his identity so easily and effortlessly.'

'It's neither easy nor effortless,' I say. 'But I've learned how to do it over the years.'

'All right....' MacNeil blurts out, in frustration. 'Here's the question. Right now, at this moment, sitting here at this table having an English breakfast, are you pretending to be a native or are you actually one?'

I can't help but smile because the question seems to trouble him more than it worries me. I've never really spent much time wondering who I am, except when people like MacNeil insist on quizzing me.

'I know I'm not English,' I reply and then add, 'but with all due respect, neither are you.'

He laughs. 'Not a bloody chance of that. Call a Scotsman English and you're asking for a fight. But you are a Christian, aren't you?'

'I was baptized as an infant and there's a certificate to prove it, but I can count the number of times I've set foot in a church on the fingers of one hand.'

'Catholic, I assume,' says MacNeil. 'But by some accounts you're a Buddhist.'

Now it's my turn to laugh. 'That's a rumour that's followed me since my youth, when I accompanied a Tibetan lama as his chela, his devotee.'

'Was that a disguise too?' he demands, stabbing half a tomato with his fork and putting the whole thing in his mouth.

'In some ways it was, in others it wasn't,' I answer.

'Now you're being coy,' he says, waving his fork accusingly.

'My understanding is that one can be a Buddhist and a Christian at the same time,' I reply. 'But not every Buddhist can be a Buddha.'

'What do you mean by that?' He looks at me with suspicion.

'As you well know, I'm not entirely non-violent, nor am I free of material desires,' I say. 'And as far as I know, I haven't achieved enlightenment.'

'But you were a follower of this lama?' MacNeil's rusty eyebrows twitch.

'He was a wise man,' I say. 'And he made me understand many things that have guided me at points in my life. Not that I have always followed his teachings.'

'So, you're more inclined to be a Buddhist than a Hindu, Sikh, or a Muslim?' he asks, shovelling baked beans into his mouth with a spoon.

'I've found that every faith has some truth in it,' I reply, 'and a fair share of lies.'

'No, but let's say that you go out on the street, as you are now, disguised as a Sikh, then suddenly a Mohammedan mob surrounds you with murderous intent, what would you do?' MacNeil asks with a smug look on his face, as if this is the question he's been trying to ask from the start. Pausing for a moment, I considered the situation

MacNeil has described, which isn't entirely hypothetical.

'I suppose I would admit that I was white and take off my turban and shirt to prove it.'

'There you are!' MacNeil exclaims with delight, clapping his hands together, as if he's finally forced me to admit who I really am.

3

Kick-starting a motorcycle with a lame leg isn't easy but for half a pice, a street urchin in Gawalmandi agrees to help. One of several young ruffians that hang about near the crossing in front of my building, he reminds me of the boys I grew up with some fifty years ago. This morning, I took a tonga to Faletti's but now that I'm no longer in disguise, I prefer to use my Norton.

'What's your name?' I ask the lad, as he places a bare foot on the starter lever.

'Rasool Mohammed,' he replies, without looking at me.

'Now, don't do anything until I tell you,' I warn him, as I turn on the petrol tap and adjust the timing lever.

The boy is wearing a pair of torn knickers and a ragged tunic, with a cotton scarf wrapped around his head like a turban. He has a surly look on his face, though when I ask why he isn't at the madrasa, he smiles as if the answer is obvious.

'Have you never been to school?'

'Only for a couple of years,' he admits.

'Why did you stop?' I ask.

He shrugs. 'I couldn't remember what I was taught, and the maulvi beat me....'

'What about your parents, do they know you're loafing about like this?' I ask.

'My mother doesn't care as long as I feed myself,' he says.

'And your father?'

'He went away to Karachi and never came back,' Rasool replies impatiently, bracing one hand on the Norton's seat and clutching the handlebar with the other. He then stands up on the lever and tries to push it down with all his weight but nothing happens.

'I told you, not until I'm ready,' I scold him. Once he's hopped back down, I squeeze the decompressor. 'Now try.'

This time the kick-starter swings down under his weight and the

Norton gives an asthmatic cough. We try several times, as I twist the throttle and Rasool throws himself enthusiastically into the task. Finally, on the fifth attempt, the engine catches with a loud rumble and a puff of smoke from the exhaust. The boy looks up at me with a grin. We make a good team. Handing him a copper coin as a reward, I tell him that next time I need him, he'll get another.

Dr Cyrus Taraporewalla's Clinic is on Abbot Road, a ten-minute drive, though there is a Congress procession on the way, chanting slogans, and I have to stop to let them pass. The doctor is in and only two other patients are waiting. An elderly Parsi, who hardly says a word, Dr T has treated me for a number of ailments over the years. I prefer to go to him instead of the Civil Hospital, because he never asks unnecessary questions. He's also a fellow Freemason. When my turn comes, a nurse ushers me into the examination room and the doctor nods with recognition. I explain what's happened and he gestures for me to lower my trousers. Removing Champa's bandage, he studies the wound, which is crusted with dried blood, the skin around it inflamed. In a whisper, he tells me to lie down on the examination table, then sets to work with cotton wool and some kind of disinfectant that stings even more than Champa's ointment.

'It will need sutures,' Taraporewalla says, shaking his head. 'When did this happen?'

'Last evening, about six o'clock,' I tell him. 'Is it really necessary to stitch it up?'

He looks at me with a doleful expression and nods, then prepares a Novocain injection, which is jabbed into my thigh. Lying back and staring at the ceiling, I wait for the numbness to spread, as Dr T and the nurse get ready to sew me up. Though the pain is soon gone, I can feel the sutures tugging at my skin as if they're darning a sock. When the surgery is over, the nurse rebandages my leg and Dr T prepares another syringe.

'What's that?' I ask.

'Penicillin,' he mumbles under his breath and then makes me roll on my side, so he can stab the needle into my right buttock, which hasn't been numbed. I curse MacNeil for insisting that I see a doctor but am grateful for an envelope of painkillers that the nurse hands me before I leave. After swallowing two tablets, I limp out into the bright sunlight where the Norton is parked. It's 11.15 a.m. and for a moment, I consider going back to my rooms and lying down but decide that I should carry on with the rest of MacNeil's errands while the Novocain is still working.

Though I'm feeling a bit fragile after the surgery, a cigarette helps me recover and I drive slowly, holding it between my lips and letting the smoke snake into my lungs. Mushtaq Ali, an old friend, has a workshop near Mochi Gate, inside the old city walls. It consists of an open shed beneath a peepul tree, with a shallow space, like a built-in cupboard, at the back where he can lock up his tools and spare parts. Under the tin roof is an apron of spilled engine oil and grease, where he repairs motorcycles and other machinery like pumps and compressors. When I pull up, he is working on an Ariel Red Hunter 350, adjusting the tappets with a wrench in either hand.

'Salaam alaikum,' I greet him, and he replies with a mumbled yet pious response, raising one greasy hand to his heart. His hennaed beard is also streaked with grease and his salwar-kameez is more black than white.

'Whose motorcycle is this?' I ask, after his spanner boy helps me haul my Norton onto its stand.

'Some officer,' Mushtaq mutters. 'He sent it across with his batman.'

I can see a Gurkha orderly, lounging in the shade of the peepul.

'It looks as if it's in good shape,' I observe.

'Mijaz ke mutaliq,' Mushtaq complains. 'Temperamental.'

'Not like my ever-reliable Norton,' I say, leaning against it to keep the strain off my leg.

Mushtaq treats each vehicle he works on as if it has a personality, describing mechanical problems in human terms. For him a faulty carburettor is a broken heart that needs tender ministrations, while a spark plug can be either generous or stingy. Clutch plates are steadfast and loyal, Mushtaq asserts, except when they betray us.

'What's wrong with yours?' he asks.

'The air filter needs cleaning,' I say.

'Can't you do that yourself?' Mushtaq grumbles. 'Why come all the way here for a minor problem like that?'

'I don't have the right touch,' I reply. 'That's why I've come to you, ustad.'

Giving the right tappet on the Ariel a half-twist to the left, he stands up and wipes his hands on an oily rag that is even blacker than the stains on his shirt tails. The only clean fabric within sight is the white lace taqiyah that covers Mushtaq's balding scalp.

He starts the Ariel with a deft kick and the engine comes to life, its valves and piston throbbing with a faster, more high-strung tempo than my Norton.

'An officer's mount!' I shout, as he revs the throttle before letting it settle into a steady rumble.

'What did you say?' he asks.

'Army officers get to ride Ariels and Triumphs, while enlisted men are given Nortons and BSAs.'

Mushtaq smiles. 'So, there's caste even amongst motorcycles, is there?'

'A 350 cc engine with overhead valves is more responsive, makes it easier to escape the frontlines, while a 500 cc, side valve like this,' I pat the petrol tank on mine, 'is a steady thumper that plods its way forward, dutifully following commands.'

'Who told you that piece of wisdom?' Mushtaq laughs, beckoning to the batman.

'An Irish Tommy I met some years ago in Peshawar,' I say. 'He claimed his BSA had never let him down.'

'Motorcycles are like horses,' Mushtaq says. 'Each breed has its own character and reputation.'

When the Gurkha holds out a couple of rupees as payment, Mushtaq raises three fingers, insisting on more. The batman protests, but the mechanic shakes his head. 'Your sahib will be pleased with my work, don't try to cheat him or me.'

Reluctantly, the Gurkha gives him another coin and then drives off recklessly through the cluttered streets of Mochi Gate, while the spanner boy collects the wrenches and rearranges them carefully in a wooden tool chest.

I've known Mushtaq since childhood when we fought and played on the streets of Lahore, before it became a modern city. He always had a fascination for vehicles of any kind and I remember he knew the name of every car—Ford, Austin, Rover, as if it was his genealogy, though he was an orphan like me. By the age of twelve he was working as an apprentice to a mechanic at a military workshop in the cantonment, learning his trade with the best of them. He has a genius for resurrecting rusted heaps of steel and eventually he was able to set up his own workshop, here in the walled city. His reputation has spread by word of mouth. Though he has never sworn allegiance to the crown or carried a military rank, he insists that he has eaten the salt of the British Army, which is why he confides in me from time to time.

He also knows that I will never ask too much of him, only what he chooses to reveal. Mushtaq is a gunsmith too, though he does not advertise this talent and trade, working at home where he repairs and services weapons for those who remain in the shadows. He told me once that guns have no personality, they simply work or they don't, unlike the men who use them. Over the years, he has served anarchists and assassins, fixing a firing pin or filing the serial numbers off a revolver.

'Someone tried to kill me yesterday,' I tell him, as he picks up a screwdriver and stoops over the Norton.

He glances at me with narrowed eyes.

'Who?'

'You tell me,' I say. 'The bullet grazed my leg and it's now lodged in the air filter.'

He studies the neat round hole in the metal housing, then unscrews the bolts that hold the air filter in place. In silence, he pops open the cover and picks through the wadded folds of filter paper, which have been shredded along one side. Sorting through the mess, he finds the slug, an ugly stub of lead that was meant to kill me.

'Mashallah!' Mushtaq whispers. 'A three nought three. Are you badly injured?'

I shake my head, though the pain is beginning to return as the Novocain wears off.

With a fatalistic gesture, Mushtaq drops the bullet into my palm. After reassembling the air filter, he starts the Norton with a swift kick, more to cover our conversation than to check if it's in working order. His eyes are still as youthful as the companion I remember from childhood, though his features are creased and gnarled and his back is bent from leaning over too many broken machines.

'Can you find out who did it?' I ask, as he revs the engine loudly. 'Could be one of your clients.'

'No one has said anything to me,' he mutters. 'But I will learn more by tomorrow.'

'It won't put you in danger, will it?' I ask.

He shakes his head. 'They know who you are, and they know that you come to me for repairs. The few secrets you've shared, I've passed them on to gain their confidence. They think you are an indiscreet drunkard with a loose tongue, which is true, but beyond that they suspect nothing.'

The only person who might hear us is the spanner boy, but he is sorting through a box full of washers, as carefully as a bania counts his coins. If anyone is watching, it will look as if Mushtaq and I are discussing the Norton's infirmities.

'There is another matter,' I whisper, as the mechanic loosens a screw that regulates the mixture of air and fuel in the carburettor. The sound of the engine subsides into a gentler roar. He listens attentively, like a musician adjusting the pegs on a sitar.

Mushtaq does not look at me but I know he is waiting for me to continue.

'Rumours are circulating that someone is planning to blow up the railway bridge across the Ravi. Have you heard any news?' I ask.

He twists the throttle firmly and the Norton shudders on its stand. Before the noise subsides, he answers.

'I have heard the same rumours.'

'You know who's planning this?' I ask.

He leans a little closer. 'If the police conduct a raid and make arrests, they will assume that I am the one who betrayed them. These days nobody is above suspicion.'

'Is there anything you can tell me?' I press him.

'Very little. I do not know when it will be, only that the explosives were stolen from a PWD godown in Gujranwala, enough to blow up more than one bridge. That is something your people can find out, if they check the godown, but make sure it is done discreetly. Someone in the PWD is helping them.'

'How did you find out?'

Mushtaq glances at me and shakes his head, to indicate he can say no more.

'All right. I understand.'

'The only other thing I can tell you is that someone is arriving this evening on the Grand Trunk Express from Peshawar. If you watch the passengers getting down at the station, you might recognize who it is.'

'Thank you,' I reply.

Taking a four-anna coin from my pocket, I place it in Mushtaq's hand.

'It's not necessary,' he says, trying to give it back.

'Suspicions might be aroused if I didn't pay you for your work,' I tell him.

He smiles, as I keep the engine running and push the Norton off its stand, then gingerly climb onto the seat. My leg has lost all numbness now, throbbing with pain.

'Be careful,' Mushtaq warns me. 'The next bullet might find its mark.'

4

In need of some sympathy, I head across to Champa's place rather than returning to the solitude of my rooms. The painkillers that Dr Taraporewalla prescribed don't seem to be doing much good and I could use another pinch of opium, as well as a drink. It's half past noon, which is a slow time at the kotha, though I run into one of their customers on the staircase, a young Congresswallah in rumpled khadi, who looks at me with embarrassment and hurries past.

Champa seems glad to see me and asks about my leg. I explain that the doctor has stitched up the wound but the pain is worse than ever, exaggerating a little for desired effect. The bottle I drank from last night still has an inch of whisky, which I use to swallow the pellet of hafim, about the size of a pomegranate seed. While I wait for the drug to take effect, I ask her if she's still planning to abandon Lahore.

'What can I do?' Champa complains. 'The landlord came this morning before I'd even washed my face and he threatened to evict us, though I've been paying him rent for the past twelve years. He says the mullah next door is going to burn down the house if we continue to stay here.'

'I could get the police to threaten him,' I suggest, 'or hire a lawyer to file a case.'

'What good would it do?' she says dismissively. 'Those days are over when people respected the British qanoon. Law and order is no more.'

'When do you think you'll leave?' I ask.

'By the end of the month,' she says. 'I've already told the girls to begin packing.'

The poppy is doing its magic. Though I can still feel the ache in my leg, it hurts far less and the cushion under my head seems to have grown softer. Champa gets up from the divan and goes across to fix her hair in front of one of the mirrors on the wall, removing pins and letting her long, black tresses cascade to her waist, then brushing them slowly. I can see her eyes watching me as she does this, her mouth set in a seductive pout. The bangles on her arms clink and jingle with each stroke of the brush. Soon enough, my eyes grow heavy, the opium sucking me under as if I'm being swallowed by quicksand.

⁂

The sharp cry of a chukor partridge wakes me and I lie motionless in the dim shadows of an unlit room without any sense of where I am. The bird calls again, a repeated, chuckling cry. I realize that it is one of the pet birds that Champa keeps in a cage on her veranda. A heavy weight lies upon me, as if a thick cotton quilt has been drawn up to my ears, though the only thing that covers me is a thin muslin sheet. The air is warm and still, perfumed with traces of ittar. The hafim has soothed my pain and erased my anxieties, at least for now, while my eyes blink as I watch the play of late afternoon sunlight volleying back and forth between the mirrors that surround me.

I could lie like this for hours, but my mind is slowly regaining traction. Stretching my right leg, I feel the taut sutures biting into my thigh. On the table next to the divan is a packet of Cavender's where I left them, but as I reach out, they seem too far away. Brushing aside the sheet, I sit up slowly, unfolding myself from sleep. My hand touches the box of cigarettes. Drawing one out, I tuck it between my lips, then light a match, savouring the first sweet whiff of scorched tobacco. My wristwatch is on the table and as I study its hands in the half-light, it takes me a while to decipher the time. Five-thirty-three. I've slept more than four hours and my mouth feels as if it's stuffed with cobwebs, though the cigarette makes me cough and clear my throat.

The chukor calls again and one of the curtains sways aside, admitting Munia. She carries a candle that she places on the table, next to a clay surahi and a brass tumbler.

'I brought you some water a little while ago,' she whispers, 'but you were fast asleep and talking in your dreams.'

'What language did I speak?' I ask, hoping I'll get an answer to MacNeil's question.

'I don't know,' she replies. 'I didn't understand the words.'

'Where is Champa?' I ask.

'Didi has gone out. She said she needed to make arrangements for our departure and get train tickets.' The girl pours me a tumbler of water from the surahi and hands it to me, her glass bangles glinting in the candlelight.

'Do you want to leave Lahore?' I ask.

Munia looks away, her childlike features profiled against the flame.

'I don't care,' she says. 'Didi says that Dilli is a safer city. We are in danger here.'

The cool water has a clean, earthy flavour. I hadn't realized how thirsty I was, holding out the tumbler for her to refill.

'It's not as lively as Lahore,' I say. 'Many people find Dilli dull.'

'That doesn't matter to me,' Munia replies with a smile. 'I don't go out very often.'

'Like a bird in a cage?' I tease her. 'A little munia.'

She shrugs again. 'Is there anything else you need?'

Her watchful eyes glisten in the shadows.

'No, I'll be leaving in a minute. I have some work tonight,' I tell her.

'I've never been on a train before,' she says. 'What is it like? Does it go very fast?'

'Yes, and it makes a lot of noise—chuga chug...chuga chug... chuga chug. Outside the window, you'll see trees and fields race past.'

'I'll be afraid, if it goes too fast,' she says.

'Don't worry. You'll fall asleep on the train. It rocks you like a cradle and the next morning you'll wake up in Dilli.'

She nods and leaves the room, as I gather up my things and prepare to depart. As soon as I stand up, I can feel the ache again, though my leg is more stiff than painful. Descending the stairs, I lean against the wall for support. Outside, a clutch of four young men eye me with disdain, watching me leave the kotha. There's no one to help me start the Norton but fortunately, the engine catches on the first kick. Ten minutes later, I am in Gawalmandi, pulling up next to the neem tree beside my building and parking as I usually do, under a tin shed where my landlord keeps a stack of bricks and planks of wood, leaving just enough space for the motorcycle.

My rooms are on the ground floor, spartan lodgings but good enough for me. A charpai sits under the ceiling fan and, beneath it, a couple of tin trunks that contain what little I own. A second room lies beyond the first, where I have a kerosene stove for boiling water and a few supplies like tea leaves and sugar. It also serves as a washroom, with a single tap and a galvanized steel bucket for bathing. The latrine is around the back. Unlike Champa, I own only one mirror, which hangs from a nail, just high enough for me to see my face, as I apply colour. This evening there is no need for a bath. Opening one of the trunks, I find a bottle of country liquor and take a small tot, not too much, but just enough to bolster my courage and counteract the twinge of unease I feel as the opium wears off.

Half an hour later, when no one is watching, a stooped figure emerges and locks the door behind him, leaning on a battered crutch. I've used this disguise many times before and it makes me virtually invisible. A wretched beggar, I am dressed in tattered sackcloth that looks as if someone blasted it with buckshot. The crutch provides some support for my injured leg and adds to the image of an elderly cripple who bears the weight of poverty and despair on his shoulders as he walks the half-mile to the Railway Station. Whoever he passes receives a feeble cry for charity, as I hold out my hand pleading for alms and offering prayers for Allah's blessings in return.

Railway Road runs through the heart of Gawalmandi and I can still make out the tracks for the old tramline, though it went out of service years ago. Now there are just tongas, bicycles, and automobiles as well as the odd omnibus bringing passengers to the station. There used to be gaslights but now it's all been electrified and I hardly recognize this part of the city, with its new shops and eating houses.

Ahead of me looms the station, like a fortress with two tall turrets, each bearing a large, round clock, like a pair of spectacles, peering down on the chaos below. The crenellated walls and bastions make Lahore Station look more like a Victorian citadel than a railway junction, though the rush and tumble of passengers and baggage prove that this is a place where journeys begin or end, where people say farewell to each other or are reunited once again. Amidst the frenzied comings and goings, nobody pays attention to a stumbling old beggar, his head covered with a tattered burlap cowl.

Two Railway Police constables and an assistant station master are standing guard at the main entrance checking tickets, and making sure there's no trouble. People of every creed and caste are pushing their way inside, hurrying to catch up with red-shirted coolies carrying trunks and bistar bags on their heads. The babble of languages includes Punjabi, Pashto, Dari, Urdu, and Sindhi, as well as a few garbled tongues I don't recognize. It's sometimes said that the Indian Railways are the one place in this country where all religious and social divisions are erased. A Brahmin priest will sit next to a Jat farmer and a Sunni and a Shia will make room for each other in a crowded compartment. Only the English segregate themselves, in their first-class carriages, though they will tolerate a well-educated Parsi or a smooth-talking Bengali, if they must.

The entrance I use is a narrow gap between one of the pillars and a wooden partition that gives way to a firm push, like the flap on a letterbox. Once inside, I hobble across the main platform, dodging handcarts loaded with trunks. Because of the curfew, which will start three quarters of an hour from now, everyone is anxious to board their train. Six Gurkha soldiers, armed with Sten guns and khukris, saunter by, surveying the crowds for troublemakers. The British lieutenant accompanying them carries a slim baton under one arm. He looks as if he's no more than eighteen. I have always thought of this station as a circus or carnival and I used to come here for entertainment when I was a boy. The overhead walkways are like a high trapeze on which streams of passengers go back and forth. The thunder and whistle of trains arriving and departing punctuates a cacophony of cries and curses, laughter and wails. Crows and pigeons fill the air, flapping about and hunting for scraps. Platform hawkers shout over each other, selling everything from sweetmeats and sherbets to cigarettes and greasy kebabs. The Railway Police used to try to chase my friends and me off the platform as we begged and swindled but we would leap from train to train or jump down onto the tracks and hide beneath the carriages until they gave up.

The Grand Trunk Express is expected on Platform 6, but it is running ten minutes late. I make my way through the crowds, holding out a pathetic hand and collecting a few coins from pious travellers, mostly copper pice, with a hole in the centre like a washer. One of the passengers standing outside his carriage insolently hands me a half-empty bottle of Vimto. Though I take it from him, muttering words of gratitude and blessing, a minute later I toss it onto the tracks. Scanning the faces on the platform, I recognize no one.

Finally, I can hear the distant whistle of the train and see clouds of steam, illuminated by electric lights. The engine approaches the platform, a monstrous steel dragon with three glaring eyes and a blunt nose, riveted in place. Even now, at this age, I experience the same excitement I felt as a boy when a locomotive pulls into the station with a scream of brakes and the churning pulse of its coupling rods. Black clouds billow out of the chimney, and I can smell the sour, sooty odour of burning coal.

Positioning myself near the A. H. Wheeler bookstall at the end of Platform 6, I have a clear view of the passengers who disembark. Mushtaq gave me no hint of what I should look for and I have no idea what to expect. All he said was that I would understand, once I saw who it was. The minute the train halts, people begin getting off. A young Eurasian, carrying an attaché case steps down from a second-class carriage, followed by six white soldiers from a regiment I don't recognize. They march off in the opposite direction, as more passengers stream out of the carriages, families with children anxiously clutched by their wrists, women carrying bundles and boxes, men arguing with coolies, who leap aboard to unload luggage. One of the conductors, in a rumpled white suit, rings of sweat under each arm, surveys the crowd, as travellers try to squeeze on board before others can get off.

Fifty yards down the platform, the Tommies have lined up outside a first-class carriage, forming a protective square in front of the door, which hasn't opened yet. Two coolies almost run me over as they rush by pushing a handcart loaded with packages destined for the brake van. So far, I have seen nothing suspicious. A child is wailing and three holy men in loincloths, their bodies smeared with ash, pass by carrying tridents and begging bowls. I hold out a hand in their direction and they look at me with disdain, as if they are the only ones entitled to receive alms.

By now the first-class carriage door has opened and amidst the clamour and chaos on the platform, I see the soldiers stiffen. A senior officer, wearing a peaked hat with a red band and gold insignia, steps out of the carriage and returns a salute from his men. Several more Englishmen exit the carriage, all of them in uniform. Not wanting to be distracted by their presence, I focus on the passing crowd, hoping to recognize an anarchist among them and wishing Mushtaq had given me more of a clue. The soldiers are now escorting the officer towards me, pushing people out of their path. The crowd parts when they are a few yards away and I finally get a close look at the Englishman. He has a lean, pale face and light blonde hair under his khaki hat. The eyes are a fierce blue and his lips are fixed in a rigid expression, between a grimace and a smile. I recognize Brigadier Sir Denys Bromley-Pugh for I have seen him twice before. He carries himself with an arrogant aloofness, as if the platform were empty. Following at his heels on a leash is a fox terrier, a stern-looking dog, its white and tan coat carefully groomed and sporting a walrus moustache.

Though this isn't who I expected, I am certain it is the man Mushtaq intended for me to see, neither a terrorist nor a spy slipping into the city, but a British officer, whose presence in Lahore signals trouble of another kind. As I stand here bent and trembling, the soldiers march away, hobnails stamping in unison.

For several moments, my mind remains transfixed by the image of that cold and ruthless white face, until I am shaken out of my trance by shouts of panic from the far end of the platform, towards the last carriage on the train. Hearing a shrill whistle, I see people running in my direction. At first, I think a riot is starting. Others too have concluded the same and hurry past me, glancing over their shoulders. Hobbling towards the commotion, I lean heavily on my crutch. By now, most of the passengers disembarking from the G. T. Express have moved on and those that are boarding for onward destinations have squeezed into their compartments.

From what I can make out, there is no riot, though a knot of men has gathered in front of a third-class reserved carriage, gesticulating wildly. Two constables run past me, followed by a railway official. Another whistle shrieks—a repeated wail of alarm. By now, I can hear voices crying out in panic, someone speaking of murder. A Sikh passenger leaps down from the train, his eyes wide with fear. The reserved carriage has open windows, and I can see inside, through the bars. The second compartment from the rear appears to be empty, but the men on the platform are anxiously peering inside.

The crowd blocks my view and it is impossible for me to see what has happened. The constables are pushing their way into the carriage, though they make little progress because passengers choke the aisle.

Just then, I notice a steel ladder that provides access to an overhead tank, from which the carriages are filled with water. Hoping that nobody will notice a crippled beggar clambering up like a monkey, I drop my crutch and begin to climb. By the time I reach the sixth or seventh rung, I can see over the heads of the crowd and into the carriage. All of the interior lights are on and the first thing I notice are streaks of blood smeared on the walls and wooden seats, after which I count four bodies, two of which are slumped on the floor, the other pair on the lower berths. Even from this distance, I can tell that their throats have been slit.

5

Moving about this city after curfew can be a risky venture, especially when the police have orders to shoot any violators on sight. However, knowing the byways and back lanes of Lahore since childhood, I am able to safely make my way to MacNeil's bungalow in the Police Lines. Now, my problem lies in how to approach him, with two armed sentries at the gate. If they spot me lurking near the house, I know they won't hesitate to open fire. Climbing over the perimeter wall is not an option. MacNeil has a vicious Alsatian named Macduff that patrols his yard. While I am trying to puzzle through this problem, two jeeps approach with their headlights on high beam. An hour ago, I briefly spotted MacNeil at the Railway Station, just as he was arriving to inspect the dead men on the G. T. Express. Of course, there was no chance of speaking to him for the police quickly evacuated the station.

Crouching beside a culvert roughly thirty yards from the gate, I wait for the jeeps to pass by. The first vehicle has five policemen in it while MacNeil and his driver are the only occupants of the second jeep. They stop for less than a minute as the two sentries open the gate, just enough time for me to slip out of the shadows and climb over the tailgate of the SP's jeep. Open at the back, it has bench seats on either side. The sentries are blinded by the headlights while the roar of the two vehicles allows me to steal aboard undetected. The driver releases the clutch, and we follow the other jeep to the main portico of the bungalow. The moment the engine is switched off, I put on my best Scottish accent: 'Mony a mickle maks a muckle!'

The driver immediately whips around, reaching for his pistol, but MacNeil puts out a hand to stop him, recognizing one of the call signs we've used before.

He then glances back at me and sees that I'm dressed as a beggar. Shaking his head in disbelief, he reassures the driver and the other policemen, who have surrounded the jeep, that I'm not a threat.

'Bring him into my daftar,' MacNeil orders.

The policemen lower the tailgate and haul me out a little more roughly than necessary, making sure I'm not armed. Leading me into the house, they take me to MacNeil's study, where he and Macduff are waiting. The dog glares at me and begins to growl but his owner issues a sharp command and the Alsatian lies down meekly on the floor next to the desk.

'You can leave us now,' MacNeil tells his men, who retreat with baffled expressions.

I remain standing until the SP waves me into a chair and then fetches his pipe.

'What the hell do you think you are doing, O'Hara?' he lashes out at me with irritation and anger. 'You could have got yourself killed.'

'I took a chance,' I reply.

'You certainly did,' he snaps, as he fills his pipe.

'I was at the Railway Station when the Grand Trunk Express pulled in,' I explain, brushing the cowl off my head and straightening my back. 'I would have tried to speak to you there but they cleared us all out.'

His pipe is now lit and it lets off almost as much smoke as a fire-breathing locomotive.

'What the hell were you doing at the station?' he demands.

'Following up on the information you requested,' I answer, glancing across at the decanter of whisky on a table, next to the bookcase. He catches my eye.

'All right, I suppose we both need a drink,' he consents, rising from his chair and pouring three fingers into his glass and mine. Then over his shoulder, he asks, 'What sort of information?'

'My source confirmed that someone is planning to blow up the Ravi Bridge....'

Accepting the whisky as gratefully as I receive alms, I invoke God's blessings.

'Did he tell you who it is?'

I raise my glass. 'No.'

MacNeil frowns, takes a sip and fondles his pipe.

'Nothing else?'

'Explosives have been stolen from a PWD godown in Gujranwala,' I tell him. 'Some of the staff are complicit. My source has requested discretion. Unless your men tread lightly, he's afraid he might be exposed. Perhaps someone in the PWD could order a routine inspection and after they discover that the dynamite's missing, the police can investigate. That way it won't seem as if anyone's been tipped off.'

MacNeil grunts reluctantly. He's not a man who likes to be told what to do.

'That's all?' he enquires with a look of disappointment.

I nod. 'It seems they're ready to move ahead soon, which is why I thought you'd want to know right away.'

Most of my whisky has disappeared and I know that MacNeil won't offer me another, so I hold back.

'Why were you at the station?' he asks.

'Another matter altogether,' I answer. 'I'd heard that someone was arriving from Peshawar. Though I thought it might be one of the conspirators, it turned out to be the last person I expected.'

'Who?' MacNeil prompts me impatiently.

'Brigadier Sir Denys Bromley-Pugh and his brownshirts.'

The SP nods and swears under his breath. 'Aye, we got word the bastard was coming to town. It's all we need, in the middle of this trouble.'

'Do you have any idea how long he'll be staying?' I ask.

'No,' says MacNeil, 'But I suspect he'll be here for a week at least.'

I wait a couple of beats to see if he'll elaborate but MacNeil seems lost in thought.

'If it's not confidential.... Why is he here?'

'No, it's not a secret,' MacNeil says, waving his hand. 'Bromley-Pugh's sister, the governor's wife, is celebrating her birthday on Monday. He's here for the party and staying at Governor's House but I'm sure he's also going to meet with his chums, dreaming up some kind of mischief.'

'I'm surprised the army tolerates the likes of him,' I say.

'He's got friends in high places, including the royal family,'

MacNeil explains. 'Bugger caused all kinds of trouble during the war and they posted him to India just to get him out of the way. Anyone else would have been cashiered.'

I finish my whisky and begin to make a move, but MacNeil surprises me.

'Hang on, O'Hara. Help yourself to another drink,' he says. 'It isn't often I raise a glass with a barefoot beggar like you.'

The lead crystal decanter is heavy and I use both hands to pour the whisky.

'How's your leg?' he asks, after I sit down again.

Pulling up one end of my tattered dhoti, I show him the bandage. 'Eight stitches.'

'Still no idea who it was?' He reaches down to scratch Macduff's ears.

Shaking my head, I reply, 'I've asked around but nothing so far.'

MacNeil studies me, as if he thinks I'm concealing something.

'Did you see the dead men in the carriage at the station?' he asks.

'From a distance, yes,' I reply. 'Do you know what happened?'

'We're still piecing it together, but it seems there were two Afridis in the compartment. One of the Hindu passengers made a remark that offended them. When the train stopped at a signal, just before arriving at the station, the Afridis pulled out knives and cut the throats of all the Hindus and Sikhs in the compartment. After that they jumped off the train and disappeared into the night.' MacNeil lifts both hands in a gesture of frustration. 'At least that's what several witnesses reported.'

'It was a reserved carriage. You should be able to get their names,' I suggest.

'Possibly, but I'm not sure what good it will do,' he answers. 'Once the word gets out there will be reprisals. More violence. More deaths. There are so many murders these days, we can't even begin to investigate them all.'

'Will the army have to step in?' I ask.

'They might order a flag march, if necessary. We'll extend the curfew tomorrow until 3 p.m. and then shut down again at 6. But the real question is whether the military will be able to maintain discipline. One regiment has already reported clashes between Hindus and Muslims in the ranks. If they start killing each other we're doomed. Right now, the only troops we can trust are the Gurkhas because they don't have a dog in this fight.' MacNeil lights his pipe again. 'What do you hear on the street?'

'A lot of fear and tension, but mostly uncertainty. Nobody is listening to Mr Gandhi, especially not the Mussalmans,' I say. 'Except for a few, they don't trust the Congress.'

'Neither do I,' says MacNeil. 'We arrested six more of their leaders yesterday.'

'I wonder what will happen when the handover takes place?' I say, '...when the British finally quit India?'

'I don't want to be around to watch,' says MacNeil.

'There are rumours on the street that the British are stirring up the conflict rather than trying to contain it,' I suggest. 'Divide and conquer.'

'Except it's divide and withdraw,' says MacNeil. 'I don't think anyone in the government is instigating riots.'

'Not even the likes of Sir Denys Bromley-Pugh?' I respond. 'He's been quoted as saying it's a good thing if Hindus and Muslims kill each other because it means fewer natives to deal with. Lightens the white man's burden.'

MacNeil nods. 'He's a racialist for sure. If it was just words, it would be one thing but he and his Brotherhood of Courage give every white man a bad name. When he was commanding his regiment in Quetta some years ago, I heard he had a Eurasian captain stripped and beaten just because he danced with one of the English officers' wives. And there's a rumour that he had a Bengali accountant flogged and then sacked because he quoted Shakespeare in his presence. They say he has a special hatred for wogs and can't tolerate any Indian who puts on airs.'

'I heard he's openly said that he regrets we defeated the Germans,' I add.

'Fuckin' Sassenach,' says MacNeil, downing the last of his whisky.

The Brotherhood of Courage is a group of officers within the Indian Army, who espouse a fierce racial nationalism, believing that only men of pure English blood who were born and bred in England have a right to rule the empire. They blame the Irish, Welsh, and the Scots, as well as their own country-born compatriots, not to mention the Eurasians, for letting India slip out of their hands and they're suspicious of anyone who isn't a pure Anglo-Saxon. Bromley-Pugh is the leader of this cabal, which promotes arch-conservative values, unflinching loyalty to the crown, and a deep-seated hatred for Catholics and Jews. The Brotherhood has sympathizers in almost every officer's mess, though they keep to themselves and don't advertise their allegiance.

Several years ago, in 1943, before the Axis Powers were defeated, I helped crack a conspiracy to provide the Nazis with information regarding Indian troops that were being sent to fight in Europe and North Africa. MacNeil and I worked closely with military intelligence to uncover this ring. For several months I served undercover as a sergeant in a grenadier regiment that was preparing to ship off to Europe. As a result, we identified three young officers, two lieutenants and a captain, who were passing on information to a German spy. He was carrying a forged Canadian passport and staying in Lahore on the pretence of buying antiquities for a museum in Toronto. We exposed the plot just before the regiment shipped out. The three officers were court-martialled in secret. Bromley-Pugh interceded with the commander-in-chief, a distant cousin of his, and instead of being executed they were imprisoned for the duration of the war. After Hitler was defeated, the conspirators were quietly released.

As I set my empty glass on the side table and get to my feet, MacNeil rises from his chair and puts a hand on my shoulder.

'You know, O'Hara,' he says. 'In this outfit, you look a bit like Mr Gandhi.'

'I'd have to lose a few pounds,' I say, 'and some hair.'

'I suppose so,' MacNeil grunts. 'Though you're a master of disguise, I bet there's one role you haven't played.'

'What's that?' I ask.

'A blue-blooded Englishman,' he says with a look of distaste. 'I'm sure that would be a challenge for you, wouldn't it?'

He then presses a button on his desk and half a minute later his driver appears.

'Take him wherever he wants to go,' the SP orders.

By now it is close to midnight, and we drive in silence through the empty streets of Lahore. I am tempted to have the jeep drop me off at Champa's kotha, but think better of it and ask the driver to take me to Gawalmandi. I speak to him in Hindustani, which he seems to understand. Hobbling to my door, I find the key in its usual place, behind a loose brick in the wall. The rusty padlock opens reluctantly, and I enter my rooms with a sudden feeling of exhaustion and foreboding. Switching on a bare bulb over the slate counter where the kerosene stove presides in sooty eminence, next to a dented saucepan and several empty biscuit tins, I look around me with a realization that this is who I really am: an ageing, lonely destitute, living in rented quarters in a city that will soon go up in flames. After serving the British empire for almost half a century, this is what I have earned, the last dregs of a bottle of country liquor and a crooked charpai under a creaking fan. I consider removing my soiled rags and washing the stains off my face, but I'm too knackered and somehow it feels appropriate that I should lie down and fall asleep as I am, a stooped and injured pariah, who has crawled in off the street.

Extinguishing the light, there is some comfort in the darkness though I wish I had a pellet of hafim to ease me into sleep. Lying on this cot, wrapped in my burlap cowl, I wonder what I could have been if I had followed a respectable career. The boys I went to school with at Xavier's in Nucklau have gone their separate ways, becoming tea planters or working for Burmah Shell. Some are officers in the army, others are in the police service or the railways, respectably employed, with wives and children, perhaps even grandchildren. I have met a few of them over the years, though they don't recognize me, and I never let on who I am. Even if I did, what would I say? *Hullo, I am a secret agent.* Who would believe that? *A spy who lives in the shadows.* Go on, you're pulling my leg! *A poor white who scrapes by, running errands for higher ups....* That's more like it, a plausible reply. *A guttersnipe who bartered his soul for a lost cause.* Aye, now you're talking. *A drunkard who dreams only of the past and has no future.* There you are! I recognize you now, Kimball O'Hara!

6

The dinner jacket is a little tight under my arms and it takes me several attempts to successfully knot my black tie. This is the first time I've dressed for a formal dinner at Governor's House. The monkey suit with its sharkskin lapels was loaned to me by one of my worthy brethren at the lodge. He and I are about the same height and girth. Sadly, I had to shave off my beard, though I've salvaged a respectable moustache, waxed to a point at either end, while my silver hair is slicked down with pomade. Do I look like a gentleman? The mirror remains mute as I practise my accent, a plummy aristocratic drawl, enunciating the appropriate consonants and rolling each vowel on the back of my tongue. The face that stares back at me isn't as pale as I'd like, but there's nothing to be done about that. Too many years under the Indian sun.

MacNeil has arranged the invitation. My name on the card is Captain Leslie Townsend, RGS, Survey of India, and a founding member of the Himalayan Club. The Governor's ADC has been informed that I've just returned from a six-month expedition, exploring peaks and passes in the Eastern Karakoram. It seems the Governor likes to associate with men of action, 'the kind of chaps who've done something'. Fortunately, I've been to parts of those mountains, though it was twenty years ago, when I trekked from Leh into the Nubra Valley and then crossed back over to Skardu on my way to Gilgit by a circuitous route. Since my memory isn't as good as it used to be, this morning I got out an old map in the lodge library and mugged up on names.

Splurging, I've bought a packet of Pall Mall king-size and filled my silver cigarette case, which was a gift from the Wali of Swat for unspecified services rendered to his state. I don't use it very often because it's ostentatious but this evening it will make me fit right in, with matching cuff links and all. In another ten minutes, a vehicle is scheduled to pick me up. Splashing a little 4711 on my cheeks,

I remind myself that someone once told me it was General Franco's favourite cologne, which seems appropriate for tonight. Lighting a Pall Mall, I practise a few gentlemanly postures and phrases, honing the attitude and manners of a crusty pom who's spent most of his life in wild places but hasn't forgotten his manners.

MacNeil could have done better with the vehicle, a humble Austin 7, which carries me out of Gawalmandi and down Empress Road. At the gate of Governor's House, I present my invitation. The soldiers on duty inspect it, then wave me inside. A line of automobiles much grander than mine have pulled up ahead of us and I wait my turn as the evening sky darkens and the flying foxes begin their nocturnal sorties on ponderous black wings.

After stepping out of the car, I mount the steps, still limping from my wound, though Dr T removed the stitches this morning. One of the protocol officers checks my name on the guest list and announces my arrival. The Governor and his wife are chatting with someone important and acknowledge my presence briefly before turning back to their more eminent guest. I offer her ladyship my best wishes on her birthday, but she ignores me. Blonde and narrow shouldered, she looks older than her forty-three years. She has the same ice-blue eyes as her brother and shares his cruel profile. Setting off in search of a drink, I weave my way through the crowd as if I'm traversing the Baltoro Glacier, avoiding invisible crevasses. More than a hundred guests are milling about, and champagne is being served, though I find a waiter with a tray of whisky tumblers, who allows me to double up my drink by pouring one into another. If there's anything I know about the upper classes, they're allowed to be boors as long as they dress well and speak as if they've got a cockroach up their nose.

I recognize very few people, which is just as well, because I'm hoping that no one will recognize me. Across the room, I can see Brigadier Bromley-Pugh and several other officers laughing at a joke, but I bide my time. The evening is young and I'm sure we'll cross paths. Nodding and smiling, I nurse my whisky. A jazz band is playing in a corner of the ballroom and the voices around me are full of brittle bonhomie. You would never know there are riots and curfews in this city, or that all of this will soon come to an end. It is the twilight of an era, the curtain call of empire.

'Ah... Captain Townsend,' a hesitant voice stammers out my name and I turn with a world-weary smile to see a young officer of Skinner's Horse in dress uniform, with chainmail on his shoulders. 'Major Thomas Ewart, his lordship's ADC. We're so delighted you could join us this evening.'

'Thank you. It's very kind of her ladyship to invite a stranger to these celebrations,' I respond with casual courtesy.

'His lordship is very keen to meet you. He takes a special interest in the northern frontier, and has travelled throughout the mountains of Kashmir,' the ADC speaks with a lisp that makes him sound effeminate though he has the manly stature of a cavalry officer.

'Ah yes, the Vale of Kashmir....' I reply, then quote Laurence Hope. 'Pale hands I loved beside the Shalimar, where are you now? Who lies beneath your spell?...'

The ADC blushes and asks me if I've travelled much in Tibet.

'Only as far as Guge,' I reply, 'and the ruined citadel at Tsaparang.'

'Sounds very romantic,' he responds, with admiration. 'The back of beyond.'

'A dry and desolate place,' I say, 'but it has its charms.'

'Em...I wonder if I might introduce you to his lordship,' the ADC suggests.

'I would be honoured,' I reply, helping myself to another whisky from a passing tray and leaving my empty glass in its place.

The jazz band is playing Duke Ellington's 'It don't mean a thing, (If it ain't got that swing)', and several couples are dancing. The Governor is in conversation with an elderly man, who looks like a retired banker. We approach them through a milling throng of guests and the ADC presents me to his lordship, who shakes my hand vigorously.

'Ah, yes, Townsend, I was told you've just returned from the Karakoram,' the Governor says with a blustery manner. He is overweight with a mottled pink face and a toothbrush moustache.

'Yes, a bit of a jaunt but nothing too strenuous,' I respond.

'Did you get up to Gilgit?' he enquires.

'Yes, sir. Less than a month ago, I was there, before we came down the Indus.'

'Still winter, I suppose? Must have been damned cold. Any shooting along the way?'

'Several good ibex and a fine markhor. They descend to lower elevations this time of year, because of the snow.'

'Splendid sport! I shot a markhor in Kashmir, above Gulmarg. Would have been one for the record books but it broke a horn when it fell on the rocks. Damned shame,' says his lordship.

We chat about mountain shikar for a while, and then the Governor asks if I had any dealings with the frontier tribes and what they think of Mr Jinnah and his demands for Pakistan. I offer a few harmless, inconclusive opinions. He tells me that he firmly believes they will not accede to any form of democratic government.

'Headstrong buggers,' he says. 'Independent in every way. Especially the Chitralis. Brave men but nobody can tell them what to do.'

Out of the corner of my eye, I catch sight of the Brigadier heading our way, followed by a couple of his fellow officers, all of them in dress uniforms. His lordship beckons to Bromley-Pugh and introduces us, explaining where I've been.

Sir Denys eyes me with a distracted look, as if he's not impressed.

'Where exactly did you go?' he asks with a clipped accent.

I sketch out my route as he listens impatiently, his irises the colour of glacial ice and his taut features fixed in a haughty sneer. Casually, I mention meeting some of the Dard tribes in the Nubra Valley, and the Kalasha people in Chitral.

'They're as fair-skinned as northern Europeans, supposedly pure Aryans,' I explain.

A flicker of interest breaks through his supercilious demeanour.

'I've heard of them,' Sir Denys remarks. 'Someone told me they were descended from the Greeks, Alexander's troops.'

'Well, I'd say they were fairer than any Greek I've ever met,'

I answer. 'The women have the pinkest cheeks and eyes as blue as the turquoise in those hills.'

'The Moslems call them kafirs because they have their own faith,' the Governor interjects. 'Idolators and animists.'

'So, you believe they represent true Aryan bloodlines?' Sir Denys asks.

'I really couldn't say,' I respond, 'But I've read several ethnological monographs that propose that theory.'

'Perhaps we should kidnap a few of their girls,' Sir Denys proposes, winking at his comrades, who smirk at the idea. 'See if we can produce some thoroughbred stock.'

His lordship acts as if he's hard of hearing.

'Other scholars have suggested that they might be one of the lost tribes of Israel,' I add, with a shrug.

'But, surely they don't look like Jews,' Sir Denys retorts. 'These tribes sound as if they are a noble race, preserved from contamination in their Himalayan hideaway.'

He then goes on to assert his views on racial hierarchies, placing the Nordic and Germanic people at the top, an example of 'God's perfect children'. From there it is a slippery slope to the 'swarthy Spaniards and Italians', or the 'Eskimos and Asiatics, as well as American Indians, who stood in the way of progress and peace'. Sir Denys also contends that the 'Semitic races are an inferior lot'. And as for the Africans and Aborigines of Australia, he has nothing but contempt. 'Animals, really. Savages.'

I do not disagree though I find him more and more loathsome as he rants on with the self-assurance of an ignorant bigot who is simply parroting the prejudices he has heard from others of his kind. The Governor has obviously heard enough and excuses himself to speak with one of the high court justices.

Having baited the monster sufficiently, I then mention how I took a side trip up to the base camp of Nanga Parbat, at Faerie Meadows or Marchenwiese, where the German expeditions set off for their fatal climbs before the war. Hearing this, Sir Denys grows even more animated and excited, pointing an insistent finger at me.

'Nanga Parbat! Did you see it with your own eyes?' he asks and then continues without letting me reply. 'Schicksalsberg der Deutschen. The German Mountain of Destiny, where Willi Merkl and his bravehearts sacrificed their lives on the Silver Saddle. What a crusade! The cream of German manhood martyred on the Naked Summit!'

His fellow officers nod appreciatively, awed by the intensity of Bromley-Pugh's emotions. Clearly, I've touched a nerve.

Though desperately in need of another drink, I can't see any trays of whisky within reach, so I take out my cigarette case and offer Sir Denys and the others a Pall Mall. They help themselves and one of the junior officers lights mine for me. A sense of comradery unites us in a cloud of tobacco smoke.

'Are you in Lahore for some time, Sir Denys?' I ask, casually, blowing out smoke through my nostrils.

'Only two more days,' he replies. 'I'm heading down to Delhi on Thursday.'

'Advising the new Viceroy, I suppose,' I say with a cynical smile.

He laughs, a high-pitched whinnying snicker that ends with a sniff of disdain.

'No, Dicky would never listen to me. Nehru and the rest of those Congress bastards have got his ear,' Sir Denys says with disgust. 'Mountbatten has been sent to do Attlee's bidding. The Labour politicians in Westminster are all weak-kneed, spineless jessies. I don't know why we pander to these damned wogs. The government should have stood up to them long ago and let Gandhi starve himself to death.'

'Well, it seems the die is cast,' I respond. 'There's nothing to be done.'

'I wouldn't say that,' he disagrees, waving his cigarette about. 'Not everyone is willing to give up without a fight. Some of us are considering our options. With all of this rioting and chaos, there's a strong argument to be made for imposing martial law. It's clear that the Indians will never be able to rule themselves. Britannia needs to reclaim her position of power and reassert the values and morals of our empire.'

'I'll drink to that,' I concur, as I finally spot a waiter with whisky instead of champagne. 'Dicky Boy is sure to let the side down!'

'Good show, Townsend, we need more men like you, whose courage and convictions have been tested and proven true to the noble heritage of our Island Race.'

Each of us takes a fresh glass and Sir Denys offers a toast.

'To His Majesty the King Emperor, may we never betray England's honour and remain steadfast in our defence of the realm!'

Glasses clink and the whisky washes away some of the bad taste in my mouth.

A short while later, as the band begins to play Marlene Dietrich's 'Falling in Love Again', I slip out of the party and call for my vehicle. The humble Austin 7 is a comfortable change from the suffocating atmosphere of the ballroom. Rolling down the window, I inhale the night air of Lahore and then ask the driver to take me to Anarkali Bazaar. On the way, we're stopped at two checkpoints where I show my curfew pass. The bazaar is deserted and I get down near Qutab ud-Din Aibak's tomb, then slip through a narrow lane to Champa's kotha. Dressed in my dinner jacket, I must present a strange sight in this neighbourhood but the streets are empty and most of the windows are shuttered. Climbing the stairs, I knock softly on the door. At first, there is no reply, but after I rap my knuckles insistently, I hear Munia's hesitant voice from inside, asking, 'Who is it?'

'Qutab ud-Din's ghost!' I reply.

Seconds later, the chain rattles as it is removed from its hasp and the door is unbolted from inside. When Munia catches sight of me, she puts a hand to her mouth, gasping first and then breaking into giggles. She is holding a candle in the other hand. Out of the shadows behind her, I see Champa emerge from her room.

'What happened to you?' she says. 'What is this suit you are wearing and where is your beard?'

'Don't you think I'm looking smart?' I tease her. 'A real Angrez.'

Laughing, she leads me into her room, where a paraffin lantern is burning on the dressing table, its wick turned low. I can tell that Champa was getting ready to go to sleep. Munia comes in and lights two more candles, then departs with a knowing smile, as I shed my dinner jacket and unknot my tie.

'Is there any whisky in this house?' I ask.

'Only some brandy,' she says.

'I need a drop or two for medicinal purposes,' I plead. 'My poor heart is giving me trouble.'

Ignoring my remark, she asks, 'Where have you been?'

'Governor's House,' I tell her.

'No wonder you're dressed up as a joker,' she says, opening a cupboard and taking out a bottle. Placing it on the table beside her divan, she fetches two glasses and pours us each a generous dose. With a flourish, I produce my cigarette case and offer Champa a Pall Mall. Hesitating, she takes one for us to share. Lighting it with a candle, I snuff out the flame.

'Are you packed and ready to go?' I ask.

She draws deeply on the cigarette and then shakes her head.

'I can't get tickets for another month,' she says. 'The trains are all booked up. Everyone seems to be leaving Lahore.'

'There's been more trouble,' I say.

'I know,' she nods. 'Tomorrow they're lifting the curfew for only two hours and my landlord is ready to throw me out on the street. Every day, he comes and threatens me.'

The brandy is sweeter than I'd like but it soothes my nerves after an evening spent in the company of Nazi sympathizers. Reaching out, I stroke the back of my hand against Champa's cheek. She looks at me with an irritable frown.

'What if I get the tickets and accompany you and the girls to Dilli?' I ask.

She turns her head and exhales a stream of smoke.

'Would you?' she asks.

'Why not?' I say.

She takes a sip of brandy and shudders, then swallows the rest in one gulp as if it were castor oil.

'I think you're making promises you cannot keep,' she whispers, her fingers drifting up my arm and caressing the back of my neck.

'Have I ever lied to you?' I reply.

She smiles and stubs out her cigarette.

Finishing my brandy, I set the glass aside. As I lean back, Champa presses herself against me. Remembering all the years I've known her and imagining all the men she's held, I know there is no need for us to lie to each other or to speak the truth. Both of us are the same. We are what we are. Survivors of a shipwreck called life.

'Turn off the lamp,' she whispers.

7

Jadoo Ghar—a house of magic, as it is known to those in Lahore who do not understand what takes place within these walls. Lodge 782, the Masonic temple of Hope and Perseverance, is set back from the main road and has an austere, colonial façade. It is still referred to as the 'new temple' though it was built thirty years ago. The original lodge, in the heart of Anarkali Bazaar, a stone's throw from Champa's kotha, was a more ornate and mysterious structure, smaller than its successor but with a grandeur all its own. The blue walls and white Corinthian columns are one of my earliest memories, a strangely exotic yet recognizably European building, out of place amidst the clamour of an Oriental bazaar. The woman who did her best to raise me after my father died used to tell me in hushed tones, whenever we passed the Jadoo Ghar, that it was my birthright to enter its gates. Pointing to the leather amulet around my neck, she insisted that the documents it contained would permit me to pass through the heavy wooden doors that bore the carved symbols of a compass and a square.

At that age, I did not understand anything more than a vague sense of entitlement, for the woman usually spoke in riddles or nursery rhymes.

Kimball Kimball tera naam, chitta chehra, mera salaam!

She was often under the spell of opium like my father, though it hadn't killed her yet. I called her Ammi, even though I knew she wasn't my mother, a gaunt woman with fine, dark features, who loved me as if I was her only son. A maternal impulse guided her to protect me but there was also a careless irresponsibility about her that set me free at an early age. Every few weeks or so, she would vanish, abandoning me to my own instincts for survival. Each time she returned, Ammi would swear that she would never leave me again, though it was a promise she couldn't keep. What I remember most about her were the sing-song rhymes she mumbled in my ear, as the poppy numbed her pain.

Aggar baggar bambe bo. Assee nabbe poorey so.
Sew mein lagga dhagga. Chor nikkal ke bhagga!

Her fingers would tickle me gently as she recited the nonsense verse in a drowsy whisper and I would fall asleep against her breast. A few of these rhymes I'd learned on the street from my friends.

Illa pilla palla ho. Gorey ka mun kala ho!

Sometimes she sang lullabies in Hindustani and nursery rhymes in Punjabi. Scrubbing my head and shoulders, knees and feet, she bathed me with soap and water from a bucket, while singing:

Seer mundey godey per, godey per, godey per
Seer mundey godey per, godey per, godey per
Naaley ankh, naaley kan, naaley moo, naaley nak
Seer mundey godey per, godey per, godey per

Ammi disappeared for the last time when I was eight or nine and I never knew what happened to her, though I'm sure she must have pursued her addiction into oblivion, and I was left to fend for myself. By then I had a close circle of friends who looked out for each other on the street. More than one well-meaning memsahib tried to rescue me, but I knew better than to fall into their clutches and I hid my pale hair under an unruly turban and left my face smeared with dust.

Much later, after my journeys with the lama and my initiation into the Great Game, I shared the papers in my amulet with certain men I trusted. They verified my father's signature on the '*ne verietur*', as he called it, as well as my baptism certificate, confirming my identity, such as it was. Eventually, at the age of twenty, through a special dispensation, I was inducted into the Freemasons in 1913.

By then the original Jadoo Ghar was in a dilapidated state, with cracks in the walls and plaster peeling off the ceiling. This made it no less impressive and mysterious for me. I was told that the main hall had been fashioned and furnished to replicate King Solomon's Temple. In the centre of the ceiling was a mural of the sun and stars. At one end of the room, on the wall above a raised platform, was a bas-relief of the arc of the covenant guarded by the two figures of Solomon and Hiram, the king and his chief architect, who built the temple in Jerusalem. There were Egyptian motifs too—the winged eye of Horus, chariots and pyramids, as well as hieroglyphic emblems of fishes and birds, embellished with floral designs. For all its magnificence, though, the old lodge was about to collapse.

The new temple was completed a year later, after which whatever could be salvaged, including the ornate teak chairs with gilt patterns and the ceremonial tables, urns, candelabra, and tapestries, were shifted before the old Jadoo Ghar was demolished in 1914, razed to the ground, so that not one brick lay upon the other. Only the cornerstone was preserved and installed in the new building near Charing Cross. The old lodge had hand-pulled punkahs to stir the air in summer but the new temple was equipped with a swarm of long-stemmed electric ceiling fans that whirred together like a flock of birds. All of the Freemasons in Lahore and many from other parts of the world, including a Worshipful Master from the Great Lodge in London, convened for its consecration. Though I have never been one for pomp and ceremony, I found myself moved by this august gathering of men who pledged to serve humanity with 'hope and perseverance'. I remember thinking how proud my father would have been and Ammi too, seeing me standing there as the officers recited their vows and performed the ancient rites. My father had once stood proudly in their midst, shoulder to shoulder with civil servants, judges, and wealthy merchants, though he himself never rose above the rank of a colour-sergeant in the Mavericks. After cholera took my mother, he turned to drink and left the army, drifting into despondency and despair, but never forgetting his heritage as a Freemason, even as a destitute white in the one-room hovel where he died.

Though I've never aspired to rise through the hierarchy and the highest chair I've held is senior warden, I have always felt that I belonged within the fellowship of this secret society with its arcane rituals, codes, and conundrums. Our primary mission is to serve society through acts of charity and benevolence. Men of all races and faiths are welcome here, white and brown, Christians, Hindus, Parsis, Sikhs, and Muslims, as well as a few agnostics. We greet each other with dignity and affection, and I know what it means to be a 'Friend of all the World'.

With the extended curfew, the lodge is deserted. All of the chaprasis, malis, and other staff have been sent home. Only a pair of police sentries stand guard outside the main portico, facing the forecourt. MacNeil has a key to the back door. I turn on one of the lights and a fan above the bar. The spirits are locked away but we find two bottles of Murree Beer in the Frigidaire. I suppose if two secret policemen commit a burglary it isn't a crime, and we will settle our bill when the time comes. Until then, we are alone within the Jadoo Ghar, as discreet a place as any we can find.

'I almost didn't make it today,' MacNeil mutters. 'We've had to open fire on mobs three times in the past twenty-four hours. Six or seven killed and dozens injured. This plague of madness is infecting everyone.'

'I hear Rawalpindi is worse than Lahore,' I say.

'It's spreading to other cities too. Multan and Sialkot have also had violence....'

'Are the trains still running?' I ask.

'For the moment, yes, though the schedule has been curtailed,' MacNeil confirms. 'Several trains have been halted halfway between stations and passengers were stranded. At some places the tracks have been sabotaged, fishplates removed to cause derailment.'

'Any more word on the Ravi Bridge?' I ask.

'Your source was right. Two crates of dynamite were found missing from the PWD warehouse in Gujranwala. One of the sub-engineers has run away and he's the man we're looking for. Once we've got him in hand, he should be able to help us identify the conspirators. Meanwhile, we're keeping a close watch on the bridge.'

I notice that MacNeil pours himself only half a glass of beer, while he's more generous with mine, filling it to the brim. The SP is also carrying a revolver on his hip, prepared to step into trouble if it arises.

'It seems a strange time to blow up a bridge, when all of the other fires are raging,' I say, taking a pull at Murree's finest brew. 'You're sure it isn't something else?'

'Such as?' MacNeil eyes me with a suspicious look.

'Maybe someone is planning to blow up a mosque, or a gurdwara, or a Hindu temple. We're not the only enemy now.'

'Are you just speculating, or is this based on some new information?' he demands.

'Hypothesizing,' I reply.

After a pause, MacNeil asks, 'How was your dinner at Governor's House?'

'Very jolly,' I reply. 'His lordship wanted to know how many ibex and markhor I'd bagged and the general disposition of the hostile tribes on our frontier.'

'By the way, without your beard, you're looking half-civilized,' MacNeil compliments me. 'What about the Brigadier?'

'Splendid chap!' I reply, switching to the accent I used with Sir Denys. 'A blue-blooded fascist through and through. Gave me a lecture on the superiority of our Island Race and then got tears in his eyes as he extolled the virtues of German mountaineers. A fine, upstanding officer of the Third Reich.'

'The mangled bawbag!' MacNeil curses into his glass.

'For what it's worth, I think I made a rather good impression on him. He seems to think I represent the best of English manhood....'

'Now, there's a joke!' MacNeil laughs.

'Sir Denys is leaving for Delhi day after tomorrow,' I add.

'Any idea what for?'

'It seems they're planning a coup.'

'What?' MacNeil searches his pockets for his pipe. 'Are you mad?'

'No. He told me that the only way to pull the empire back from the brink is to impose martial law and forestall independence.'

'He actually said that?' MacNeil is now searching for his pouch of tobacco—Glasgow's finest Presbyterian Mixture.

'Not in so many words, but it was implied,' I affirm. 'And I'm sure he's not alone in his sentiments. There's a lot of disappointment with your prime minister and his labour party, who want to wash their hands of India, surrendering the Jewel in the Crown. Perhaps it won't be a coup, but influential elements in the army might just force the commander-in-chief's hand.'

'That would be treason,' MacNeil mutters as he stuffs his pipe and finally puts a match to it. Meanwhile, I've lit a cigarette. We smoke in silence for a minute or more as I study the antlers of a Kashmir stag on the wall above the bar and a wooden mantelpiece from the old Jadoo Ghar, which was rescued and installed on the opposite side of the room, decorated with pharaonic images and art deco motifs that incorporate a series of surveyor's pendulums along with bricklayer's trowels.

'Do you think we should file a report?' I ask, at last.

'Not yet,' says MacNeil. 'Other than cocktail party conversation, we've got no proof that Bromley-Pugh actually intends to carry through with this plan. I also wonder why he would tell a stranger like you, if he's seriously hatching a conspiracy to subvert the integrity of British India.'

'Not much integrity left to subvert,' I reply, allowing my cynicism to surface.

MacNeil gives me a severe glance. 'There you go again, O'Hara!' he says. 'You'll be the one pulled up for treason.'

After an appropriate pause, I announce: 'I'm thinking of making a trip to Delhi.'

He looks at me with a sceptical frown.

'Why? Are you planning to infiltrate the Indian Army?' he asks. 'Spy on our own military services?'

'Not exactly, but I should be able to get close enough to Sir Denys and his Jerry sympathizers to see if they are serious about this plan.'

'Are you going to travel with him?' MacNeil asks.

'No, he said he's going to fly down in an Air Force transport,'

I explain. 'But I shall take a train, as long as the Frontier Mail is still running.'

The SP pauses to consider my proposal.

'Be careful not to tread on too many toes in Delhi,' he warns me. 'If there's any misunderstanding, I'll deny all knowledge of your presence there.'

'Of course,' I reassure him. 'I'll be as discreet as possible.'

'We'll communicate by telegram. You can use the codes from last week,' MacNeil instructs me. 'Where will you be staying?'

'I'm not sure. Once I get there, I'll find suitable accommodation, probably at a hotel to begin with.'

'You'll need money, of course,' he acknowledges.

'I always need money,' I say, with a smile, finishing the last of my beer.

'Let me see what I can do,' he says. 'It won't be much but enough to cover your expenses for a couple of weeks. Off the books, of course, though I'll expect receipts as usual.'

MacNeil is a stingy Scot, but he's also adept at garnering funds from other operations, as well as dipping into cash that's been confiscated from criminal enterprises, to help cover the costs of my covert operations. That way there's nobody asking awkward questions. Once, during the war, he paid me with petrol coupons that had been seized from a smuggler, and I had to sell them on the black market to get reimbursed for my expenses. More recently, he supplied me with fake currency notes that were taken from a counterfeiter, which I used to bribe one of our suspects. A certain amount of moral ambiguity always accompanies these transactions, though I suppose it's all for the greater good.

'Anything else?' MacNeil asks, obviously impatient to get back to more pressing crises at hand.

'Actually, there is one more detail,' I reply, with feigned hesitation.

The SP raises a suspicious eyebrow. 'What?'

'I need a medal.'

His suspicion turns to annoyance.

'Are you joking? For what?'

'Not for me, personally, but for my alias, Captain Leslie Townsend. I thought it would be appropriate if he were to be awarded a Kaiser-e-Hind. It can be silver or bronze, not gold, bestowed by the Viceroy himself,' I propose.

'Have you lost your mind?' says MacNeil. 'How can someone who doesn't exist receive a medal for something he's never done?'

'Stranger things have happened, I'm sure,' I counter.

'But a Kaiser-e-Hind is given for public service, some sort of good deed,' MacNeil protests, 'not for just loitering about in the Himalaya.'

'Yes, of course, but if you recall there was an earthquake near Chilas this winter, about the same time Captain Townsend would have been somewhere nearby. If the Governor were to receive a report that Captain Townsend rendered assistance to the victims and rescued several survivors from the rubble with his own hands, then his lordship might be persuaded to forward a recommendation to Delhi.'

MacNeil's pipe has gone out, but I can almost see smoke coming out of his ears.

'You are a brazen impostor, O'Hara! No morals at all! A disgrace to the principles of Freemasonry.' MacNeil is enraged, but controls his temper, then asks, 'Besides, what purpose would it serve?'

I shrug my shoulders. 'Well, for one thing it would get me inside the Viceroy's House and it's the sort of commendation people talk about, which will provide me with introductions and access within the corridors of power.'

Rising to his feet and straightening his back, MacNeil shakes his head in disgust.

'Damn it, O'Hara. You're the most dishonourable man I've ever worked with. A Kaiser-e-Hind, good God!' he says, pointing me out the door. 'Shameless! Truly, shameless!'

∞

As I drive through the deserted streets of Lahore, the city has an eerie emptiness, as if all of its inhabitants have vanished into thin air. The throbbing sound of my Norton echoes in the silence, like a steady drumroll. At two separate checkpoints, I show my curfew pass. Being a European, both in dress and features, they let me carry on without any questions. It is growing dark and a flock of crows are quarrelling in one of the trees near my building while I can smell the charred odour of woodsmoke, or is it the pyres of riot victims burning on the banks of the Ravi?

Parking my motorcycle under the shed as I always do, I am distracted by thoughts of violent mobs converging on their prey, with cries of anger and fear. Being someone who lives beyond the pale, I cannot understand the psychology of killing a person because of his or her identity, the kind of senseless enmity that arises out of ignorant tribalism and brute politics.

After retrieving the key from its hiding place and unlocking my door, I push my way inside. Immediately, my instincts tell me that something is wrong, a sixth sense that warns me of danger. I am unarmed and the room is full of shadows. Reaching for the light switch next to the sink, I turn it on. A single bulb flickers and illuminates a chaotic scene. Someone has broken into my rooms, and I immediately see a shattered window on the other side of my charpai, which lies upside down, four wooden feet in the air. The trunks stored beneath it have been wrenched open and the contents, mostly clothes but also a few books and papers, are strewn on the floor amidst the shattered glass. My cupboard has been gutted too, disembowelled of its contents—empty cigarette tins, old magazines, and the kinds of valueless things one collects for no reason. I see that my sextant and bullseye lantern, which I haven't used for years, have been smashed beyond repair. The intruders are gone, having left by the same route they came in. It looks as if a riot has occurred inside my rooms.

8

Three special carriages and a brake van are coupled together on Platform 3, with a shunting engine attached, awaiting the arrival of the Frontier Mail. Through one of the reservation managers, who owes me several favours, I was able to get us six berths in a third-class three-tier sleeper. Hopefully, this is the last time in my life that I will have to travel in the company of five women. It took two bullock carts and a tonga to transport them and their luggage to the station. Eight coolies ferried the bags and boxes to our carriage and the brake van. Champa and the girls didn't want to leave anything behind, though I drew the line when it came to the larger pieces of furniture like the divan and almirah, which had to be abandoned.

The two chukor partridges in their wire mesh cage, as well as most of Champa's mirrors wrapped in velvet quilts for protective padding, her silver hookah and a folding wooden screen carved with elaborate patterns of grape vines, bundles of clothes tied up in sheets—all of these precious possessions were carried on the coolies' heads. After arguing with another family who had usurped our compartment and stuffing bags and boxes underneath and overhead, we finally settled into our seats, just as the Frontier Mail pulled up on the opposite platform. Minutes later, the shunting engine tugged us backwards then forwards, attaching us to the train.

Security at the Lahore Station is tighter than I've ever seen it before. Both armed constables and Gurkha soldiers are patrolling the platforms. Fortunately, the past two days have been relatively peaceful, and the curfew was relaxed this afternoon, which allowed us to empty Champa's rooms and leave for the station with just enough time to spare. The girls, especially Munia and Sarita, the two youngest, were weeping, while Champa showered abuse on her landlord as he watched them depart, a sullen yet satisfied expression on his face. On our way to the station, Kamla, the eldest girl, remembered that she'd left a box of bangles behind but I told her there was no going back. Whatever has been lost cannot be retrieved, not just physical possessions but memories too. Even I felt a strange sadness as we vacated the building, which had been my refuge for almost twelve years.

Dressed as a Hindu merchant, I am departing for Delhi with my wife and four daughters. My head is swaddled in a bleached cotton turban and my white moustache droops over my upper lip. The colour of my skin is a ruddy brown and I speak Punjabi. This morning, I told the girls to dress modestly, though they followed my instructions half-heartedly, unwilling to completely conform to their roles as my dutiful daughters. Sarita is still wearing a gaudy satin salwar-kameez and her chunni keeps slipping off her head. Radha, the eldest, has rouged her cheeks and lined her eyes with kajal. Champa too, looks less like my wife and more like an ageing film star, still glamorous yet a bit overblown, her lips stained with paan and a ruby stud in her nose.

I hear the whistle of the train and moments later we are jostled by the first slow tug of the engine. By now the aisles are full of passengers who have crowded into the carriage. An elderly couple commandeer a corner of my seat, though there is no possibility that anyone will be able to stretch out on a berth because of the heaps of luggage. Kamla has brought some food for us in a brass tiffin carrier and Champa offers me a glass of water poured from a pewter surahi. I would give anything for a whisky but the only bottle I brought with me is buried somewhere in a suitcase wedged under my seat, behind two other boxes of Champa's things.

Three nights ago, when I found that my rooms had been ransacked, I knew that I would have to abandon my lodgings. The rent is only a month overdue, and my landlord will be relieved to see me gone. Picking up a few clothes, both European and native costumes, I packed them into a duffel bag along with a couple pair of shoes and whatever else I might need in Delhi. The intruders failed to find my revolver, a Webley .38, that I kept in a hidden niche behind the cupboard. I was able to retrieve it and the precious documents I've carried since childhood, though none of them have any relevance now, except that they are my only link to my parents. These and a bottle of Dyer Meakin's, along with a few clothes for padding, fit into an old leather suitcase.

This is not the first time I have walked away from whatever charade of domesticity I have concocted. Though I've never married, there have been two women in the past who loved me and with whom I tried to create some pretence of cohabitation. But both of those relationships were doomed, and I left them with a sense of sadness and relief. This time there is no person to abandon. Though I am taking Champa with me, I have no expectations of seeing her again, once we reach Delhi. She knows this too and understands my need to run away from her and from myself.

The only thing I've left behind is my Norton. Mushtaq is keeping the motorcycle for me, parked at the back of his garage, amidst a heap of disassembled vehicles and other parts. I didn't tell him where I am going and he didn't ask. When I mentioned that my rooms had been broken into, he agreed that it was probably the same person who tried to kill me, though Mushtaq had no clues to his identity. Whoever it is, he clearly wants me out of the way. I can name at least three or four anarchists that I have exposed to the police, who might want revenge. They or their comrades have threatened me before, but I have always been able to stay out of reach.

As the train picks up speed, the rhythm of the wheels and the rocking motion of the carriage settles into a steady, pulsing tempo. A few cinders blow in through the window and I brush them off my clothes, then rummage in the pocket of my kurta for a packet of Cavender's. Lighting up, I let the smoke drift out the window and look across at Champa, who is sitting cross-legged on the lower birth. She is lost in her own thoughts, a strong-willed woman who has learned to survive by her wits and wiles. Though I can see she is distraught, Champa has maintained a calm façade, except when she cursed at her landlord, calling him a swine and a bhainchud.

Kamla is on the upper berth, staring at the ceiling while Sarita is sandwiched in between on the middle berth, which is crammed full of bedding rolls, as well as other bags and parcels. I can see that she is weeping. Munia and Radha are sharing the uppermost berth above me and whispering to each other, their words inaudible but anxious.

We have become refugees in our own homeland. All of the passengers on this train are either Hindus or Sikhs, no Muslims among us. Our journey is an escape from the hatred and divisions that have consumed Lahore. Of course, there were enmities beneath the surface long before this. As a boy, even amongst my friends, I understood the tensions between communities. We may have been orphans but we knew our lineage and caste. At the same time, it seemed harmless in a way, no more than hairline fractures that separated us, which have now shattered into fragments of bone. Inhaling the tobacco fumes, I try to think of other things—what awaits me in Delhi and my last conversation with MacNeil—but nothing can distract me from this feeling of being uprooted and torn apart by the hostility and terror that has spread like an epidemic, worse than cholera or the plague.

Night has fallen and checking my watch, I can see it is past eight o'clock. As a precaution, I have my revolver loaded and wrapped in a cotton scarf inside my jhola, which contains a few personal accessories that a Hindu merchant might carry with him on a journey like this, a diary and fountain pen, three handkerchiefs, and a case containing a pair of spectacles that both he and I require, when we inspect our tickets and reservation forms. I don't think a conductor will attempt to come through this carriage—there is no room to traverse the aisles but also because everyone on this train is undertaking a one-way journey of despair. To check our tickets would be a cruel farce. Nobody is leaving Lahore by choice.

The train is a shaft of light tunnelling through the darkness. From one of the other compartments, I hear a man's voice calling out to tell us to shutter our windows. 'It will be safer that way if they attack!' Throughout the carriage, I hear the clapping of metal against metal as fellow passengers heed the man's warning. Throwing my cigarette out the window, I pull down the shutters and draw the chatkanis to secure it. After that, I do the same with Champa's window. She watches me with a vacant look that makes me realize how futile these precautions will be if a mob lays siege to the train. With the shutters down, the air is suffocating.

I can imagine the landscape we are passing through, the outskirts of the city and then, the fields of wheat and corn, a mango tope, and a dry canal. The sound of the wheels chattering on the rails tells me that we are passing over a bridge and a familiar scent seeps through the vents in the shutters, of village fires and burning dung. Though all of it is hidden in the night, I can picture every detail in my mind, for I have travelled this route many times before.

'Will you have something to eat?' Champa asks me, playing the dutiful wife. 'Kamla made some rotis and aloo saag.'

'I'm not hungry,' I reply. 'Maybe after we've passed Amritsar.'

'How far is that?' she asks.

'Less than half an hour.'

The old man at the end of my berth is listening.

'After that we will be safe,' he says to me.

'There's no telling, dada,' I reply. 'Who knows what lies ahead?'

He shakes his head. 'Yesterday, they burned a train this side of Amritsar.'

'Who burned it?' Champa asks. 'Mussalmans, Sikhs, or Hindus?'

'I don't know which direction it was going,' the old man replies. 'They just said that the whole train was burned and all of the passengers on it.'

'Where are you headed?' his wife enquires of Champa.

'Dilli,' she answers, 'and you?'

'Our son is posted in Ambala,' the woman replies. 'He's a revenue officer. He insisted we come and stay with him until the trouble is over.'

'You've left your home in Lahore?' Champa asks.

'What could we do?' the old woman replies. 'We locked the doors and gave the key to our neighbour, who promised it will be safe until we return.'

Seated at her feet in the aisle is a woman with two infants, her face partly hidden by her chunni, though she looks up at us with a bitter expression. Squatting next to her on the floor is her husband, holding a third child.

'Mataji, there's no going back,' she says, raising her voice. 'We have left everything behind. Let them do with it what they will. At least our sons and daughters are safe.'

'Where are you going?' Champa asks her.

'As far as this train will take us,' the woman says. 'The farther the better!'

Conversations between strangers have always been a part of train journeys I've taken in the past. Each person has his or her stories to tell and it passes the time, hearing family lore and amusing anecdotes. Someone in the compartment has a joke to recount, or words of wisdom, but tonight there is only fear in these voices and uncertainty, no sounds of laughter or transient companionship. Despite my disguise, I feel estranged from those around me, a traveller without a destination. Even within this overcrowded carriage, I feel entirely alone.

Slipping off my Peshawari chappals, I tuck my feet up under my legs, as Champa prepares a paan for both of us. She applies and arranges the ingredients on the betel leaf as if it were a sacrament. Despite the discomforts and dislocation of this journey, there is something reassuring about the way she assembles and folds the paan, handing it across to me and then tucking the second one into her cheek before closing up the paan daan. She has added no opium this time and only a measured amount of tobacco, but it helps settle my unease more than the cigarette did. Champa also produces a small brass spittoon for us to use.

An atmosphere of calm seems to have settled over our carriage, as we are lulled by the rocking of the train. Lahore seems far behind us now while Delhi is still impossibly far away. Two lights are burning on the ceiling and one of the small overhead fans is whirring softly in its cage. A blue night light glows above the aisle, casting an eerie glow. The old woman, huddled at the edge of my berth, is mumbling prayers under her breath. One of the three children seated in the aisle whimpers softly. Champa gestures for the mother to lay her on top of a bedding roll that is wedged between our berths. The girl, no more than three years old, stretches out and stares at me for a moment, before closing her eyes. When she grows up, she will have no recollection of this journey, no memory of her birthplace Lahore.

Then all at once, the train begins to slow down, with a sudden wail of brakes. One of the packages on the luggage rack above us is displaced, sliding off and falling beside Champa. Each of us is shaken by the sudden break in momentum. Kamla and Radha look down at me with fear in their eyes and Champa puts both hands to her face. Seconds later, the train comes to a halt and there is silence. Nobody speaks, as all of us listen. It could be nothing more than a signal that has stopped us. There is no hint of danger. Our carriage is at the end of the train, far away from the engine.

Reaching over, I unbolt the shutter and raise it halfway, peering out into the darkness. No lights are visible, except for a few faint stars above the horizon. I can hear voices now, far off near the front of the train. Then, I hear the sound of a horse galloping through the night, its hooves pounding the earth. Several horses pass by my window in a blur of shadows.

We hear gunshots and I recognize the loud, hollow reports of a twelve bore, both barrels fired, one after the other. This is followed by the sharper crack of a pistol, like a dry branch being snapped. Immediately, all of the lights in the carriage are extinguished. A woman cries out in fear but her voice is muffled. 'Khamosh!' someone says. 'Be quiet!' In the compartment next to us, two men are whispering but other than that, there is no conversation. Reaching into my jhola, I unwrap the revolver and keep my thumb on the safety catch. More gunfire crackles and we hear running footsteps outside, five or six men coming towards us along the tracks. It is too dark to see who they are, only a passing movement. They call out in Punjabi, cursing loudly. Someone begins banging on the door at the end of the carriage, shouting to be let in. 'Khol do! Kholo maakichud!' One of the horses is returning, cantering after the running men. Just as the rider passes our carriage, he fires twice, a bright flash from the muzzle of his pistol and two loud explosions. Several passengers cry out.

Towards the front of the train, more gunfire erupts. Leaning forward with my face pressed against the bars on the window, I can see flames now, somewhere near the engine, a bright blaze of sparks filling the air, like a brush-fire. Someone is yelling, as if he's been wounded, or it could be a rallying cry. The night is full of confusing sounds. More people run past my window. Two of them are carrying lanterns, which sway in the dark. A scuffle breaks out inside our carriage as one of the passengers tries to make his way to the door to escape, while others shout at him to sit down. One man keeps insisting that everyone must remain inside, his voice anxious and agitated, haranguing his fellow passengers. 'Khabardar! Khabardar!'

9

With the carriage doors bolted and the windows barred, it would be almost impossible for our attackers to break in. At the same time, there is no escape from the carriage if it catches fire unless someone opens one of the doors from inside. As we wait, I try to decide how best we can save ourselves. If even a few passengers were to panic, the aisles are so packed with people and luggage that many would get trampled. Our compartment is in the middle of the carriage and the only exits are at either end. With the lights off, I feel a claustrophobic sense of being trapped inside an overcrowded tomb. Peering out into the darkness, I can see flames and hear angry shouting mixed with cries of fear. Another round of gunfire breaks out and then, miraculously, our train begins to move forward again.

As we gather speed, a volley of rocks strikes the steel walls of the carriages. The crowd of men who tried to stop the train are now hammering on the sides with staves and pipes. Lowering the shutter so there is only a crack, I can see a mob holding lanterns and torches. Several rocks hit my window as we pass through a cloud of fire and smoke. Moments later, we are beyond the angry horde and there is silence, except for the reassuring rumble of the train. Lifting the shutter completely, I can see firelight from a village in the distance and stars in the sky. Suddenly, everyone in the carriage is talking at once, a babble of voices, released from the terror of the past half hour. 'Hai Ram! Hai Ram!'

After another fifteen minutes, we arrive at Amritsar. As our train pulls into the platform, I can see two constables rushing towards the engine. Nobody from our carriage gets down at the station. Four men with a stretcher go by, carrying an injured man. When a coolie passes my window, I call out to him and ask if he knows what has happened. He looks baffled and shakes his head. The train is safe, but it takes a while for the news to spread. Though our carriage remains in darkness, the platform is illuminated. I light a cigarette and pass it to Champa, who draws in a lungful of smoke and hands it back. Finally, another coolie in a faded red shirt, with a brass medallion strapped to one arm, stops next to my window and tells me what he has learned.

'A pile of dry branches and brushwood was placed across the tracks. When your train approached, they set it on fire,' he tells me. 'The driver had to stop but there were six armed policemen with him. When the mob tried to board the engine, the guards fired at them. Several men were killed. A few of the attackers had guns too and they fired back. One policeman was wounded. Finally, when the blaze burned down, the driver started the train again and they were able to pass through. You are lucky there was an armed escort, otherwise they would have set the whole train on fire.'

Gradually, everyone learns what has happened, as stories and rumours are shared from one compartment to the next. Ten minutes later, the lights in our carriage finally come back on. Champa sees me wrapping my revolver in the scarf and stuffing it back into the jhola.

'Would you have used it?' she asks, with concern.

'Of course,' I answer, 'but it wouldn't have done much good.'

'How many of them were there?' Champa wants to know.

'Maybe fifty. Maybe a hundred men. I couldn't count them,' I tell her.

'They would have killed us all,' she says.

'Maybe, though we're lucky the engine driver kept his head and the Railway Police were able to hold them off,' I say.

'What is it that makes people act like that?' Champa asks.

'Retribution. Revenge,' I say. 'Trains going in the other direction have been attacked and burned.'

'The world has gone crazy,' she says. 'Why should innocent people be killed for crimes committed by others, all in the name of religion?'

'Now you know why I don't believe in God,' I say.

On the upper berth, Kamla is feeding the chukor, sprinkling grains of millet through the bars of their cage. She looks at me and smiles.

We remain on the platform for several hours and I see the stationmaster and others going back and forth, along with police and

Gurkha patrols. At one point, needing to use the toilet, I get up and wade through the passengers seated in the aisle. Even the vestibule is packed with people, so that they have to move aside for me to open the toilet door. After relieving myself, I see my reflection in the mirror over the sink, an elderly trader from Lahore. The name on my reservation form is Lala Jagat Kapoor. Had I died a Hindu, nobody would have been the wiser for it and nobody would have mourned my death.

When I return to my seat, Champa has taken out the tiffin carrier. She serves me some vegetable and two rotis, keeping a little for herself and passing the rest up to the girls. I am tempted to dig out my bottle of whisky, but I would have to move everything aside and it is now well past midnight. Except for the blue nightlight, all of the bulbs have been switched off. Eventually, Champa falls asleep with her head resting on a bundle of clothes. I begin to doze off too but the sounds from the platform keep waking me, passengers calling to each other and vendors selling tea and snacks.

At about 4 a.m., the train begins to move again, with a slow shudder and the groan of couplings. No whistle warns us of our departure as we glide away from the bright lights of the platform and into the night. For a ways, we pass through the city. A few lamps are burning in windows but most of Amritsar lies in darkness. By the time we have picked up speed, the buildings are behind us and I can just make out fields in the dim light from a half-moon that rose an hour ago. Seeing that Champa is awake, I gesture for her to come and sit beside me, moving one of the bundles aside to make room. She crawls over the boxes and bedding rolls and settles her head on my shoulder.

'What time is it?' she asks in a whisper.

'Quarter past four,' I tell her, checking my wristwatch in the dim blue light.

The elderly couple at the end of my berth have both fallen asleep, slumped together and leaning on my duffel bag. Above us, the girls are silent, and I can hear snoring from the compartment next door.

'Are we safe now?' Champa asks.

'Probably,' I say. 'At least the worst of it is over. Though we're still in the Punjab, the trains that are going in the other direction will be the ones that are stopped.'

She is silent for a minute or two and then mumbles, 'When will you go back to Lahore?'

'I don't know,' I reply. 'Maybe in a month. Maybe in a year.'

'But you won't return dressed like this,' she says. 'You'll go back as a gora?'

'Or as a Muslim,' I reply.

She shakes her head. 'They will see through your disguise.'

'Why?'

Champa presses her cheek against my arm.

'I know the truth about you,' she says, suppressing a smile.

'What are you talking about?'

'Remember, you aren't circumcised,' she whispers.

I raise a finger to her lips and reply, 'Who's to know that but you!'

'I'm sure you'll find some other lover in Lahore, a Muslim tawaif, who will discover the truth and betray you,' Champa laughs softly, but then sighs with remorse.

'And what about you?' I ask. 'Your lover is waiting for you in Dilli.'

'He's even older than you,' she says.

'And a good deal wealthier,' I say.

Several weeks ago, Champa wrote to one of her past admirers, Seth Gopalchand Kirorimal who owns several textile mills in Delhi, explaining her plight. He replied enthusiastically by return post, offering to take care of her and the girls, providing accommodation for them in Delhi. Obviously, his amorous memories were aroused.

'Who knows where he will put us up?' Champa whispers.

'I'm sure the Seth has plenty of properties, or else he'll rent rooms for you somewhere in the city,' I reply.

'I've only been to Dilli once, years ago,' she says. 'I'm sure it's changed.'

'Did you visit Sethji then?' I ask.

'No,' she replies. 'I only entertained him when he came to

Lahore. It was someone else who took me to Dilli. A younger man who wanted to marry me.'

'Ah,' I say. 'And you believed him?'

She shakes her head. 'I knew better than that, but he put me up in a hotel near Chandni Chowk and gave me expensive gifts. He showed me around the city too. What is that gol chakkar called?'

'Connaught Circus,' I answer.

'Yes. It had just opened and there were many fancy shops and restaurants,' Champa recalls. 'He treated me well and we ate all kinds of delicacies that I'd never eaten before. Pineapple pastries. But the whole time I was there, I missed Lahore.'

'Has Sethji offered to marry you?' I tease her.

'No, he has a wife already,' she replies.

'But he loves you more,' I say.

'Love?' She laughs at the word. 'No. He must be eighty by now, but he wants to relive his youth.'

'There's no harm in that,' I reply.

'I'm sure he'll prefer one of the younger girls,' she says.

'Then you'll remain true to me,' I say.

She laughs again, one hand stroking my arm.

'Why should I?' Champa replies. 'When you'll be off in another's arms, one of the houris of Lahore. Or maybe you'll find an English memsahib who will take you home with her.'

'Little chance of that,' I say.

'So, you will choose to live in Jinnah's Pakistan?' she asks.

'Who knows?' I say, 'Once the British leave, then it will become clearer where the lines are drawn and what the future holds. Until then, I'll keep my options open.'

'But someone like you won't belong on either side of the border,' she says. 'Neither here, nor there.'

'What is there and what is here?' I whisper. 'Maybe I'll make my home on this train going back and forth forever.'

'And after we get off in Dilli, will I never see you again?' she asks.

For half a minute, I remain silent, not wanting to tell her the truth.

'I will find you one day,' I say.

'Liar!' Champa nudges me.

'Don't worry, you'll forget about me soon enough,' I whisper.

'I've already forgotten you,' she says.

'Then we'll meet again as strangers,' I say.

'If only that were possible,' Champa murmurs.

She soon falls asleep again, her head still pressed against my shoulder, and I sit here listening to the far-off panting of the engine and the rhythmic clatter of the wheels. Finally, the sky begins to brighten as we head east across the Punjab. Bright fields of mustard appear, as if the yellow daylight has touched the earth before the sun has even risen. A flock of cattle egrets rise from a shallow pond, as white as handkerchiefs, waving at me. The sooty odour of coal smoke drifts in the open window and I light a cigarette as surreptitiously as I can, trying not to wake Champa. For the duration of this journey, she is my wife and I feel a certain contentment in that conceit.

We stop in Jullundur for fifteen minutes and I buy clay kullads of tea for Champa and the girls, along with two packets of biscuits. It is only half past six in the morning, though it feels much later. From here we carry on to Ludhiana, though before we get there, our train halts at a small station called Phillaur because the tracks are being repaired. When we finally begin to move again, I can see the reason for our delay. The charred remains of another train stands on the tracks parallel to ours. It must have been burned some days ago, but the fire has caused damage to the signals and switches. A gang of labourers with pickaxes are working to restore this section of the line, while others are trying to detach the mangled carriages from each other. Some are only blackened with smoke, while others are nothing but twisted skeletons of steel. As we creep by, I can imagine the conflagration. All of our eyes are fixed on the gruesome remains, as if we are being shown what might have happened to us last night.

The platform at Ludhiana is deserted, except for a railway constable who passes my window and tells me that the city has been under curfew for the past three days. No one gets on or off our train and within a few minutes of stopping, the Frontier Mail proceeds. The city has a haunted look despite the morning light and the only person I see is a young boy crouched on a rooftop, peering at us as we pass by. Flocks of pigeons wheel over the city against a sky of blue enamel.

Witnessing the burned train has silenced almost everyone in our carriage and only a few hushed voices can be heard. The three children in the aisle next to us have grown restless, Champa hands their mother one of the packets of biscuits I bought. She takes it after protesting that it isn't necessary. Her tiny daughters watch us wide-eyed as they eat the biscuits hungrily. The air is warmer now, even when there is a breeze coming through the window.

We make slow progress and pass no other trains. In the villages along the route, people are moving about as if nothing has changed for them. A young girl is herding six buffaloes towards a canal, while a flock of goats are feeding off bushes along the embankment. At a level crossing, six bullock carts are lined up, waiting for us to pass. When we come in sight of the Grand Trunk Road, I can see two or three automobiles, as well as streams of cyclists passing in either direction. At intervals there are wells, with Persian wheels, operated by camels or bullocks, the water spilling from the buckets into muddy channels that irrigate fields of mustard and grain.

'What is the next station?' Champa asks, fanning herself with the end of her chunni.

'Ambala Cantt.' I know this station well.

'How far is it to Dilli from here?'

'Still three or four hours at least. We will get in late in the afternoon,' I explain.

'Though the train seems to be moving so fast, sometimes it doesn't feel as if we're making any progress at all,' she complains. 'Those trees outside the window, I'd swear I saw them an hour ago.'

'You must be impatient to meet your beloved,' I whisper. The elderly couple are now awake and listening in on everything we say.

'We will get down in Ambala,' the old man says, with a hopeful look in his eye.

'Our son will be waiting at the station,' his wife adds. 'How far is Ambala from here?'

'Another ten minutes, Mataji,' I reply.

'Is your son married?' Champa asks.

'Yes. He and his wife have a young child, three months old,' the woman answers. 'At least I'll be able to hold my grandson in my arms before I die.'

'You are blessed,' says Champa.

The old woman hesitates and then looks up at the berths above. 'Are none of your daughters married?' she asks.

I can see Champa flinch at the question.

'The eldest one is engaged, but with all the trouble....' I answer. 'God knows what will happen now.'

The old woman sucks on her toothless gums and shakes her head.

'Which part of Lahore do you live in?' she asks, her curiosity aroused.

'Anarkali,' Champa replies.

'In the bazaar itself?'

'Our mohalla was near Anarkali's tomb,' Champa replies.

'There's been a lot of trouble there, recently,' the old man interjects.

'It had its pleasures and its sorrows,' I respond. 'Do you know the verse inscribed on Anarkali's gravestone by the emperor Salim?'

The old woman studies Champa with a look of suspicion as I recite the couplet:

Ah gar man baz binam ruyi yari khwish ra
Ta qayamat shukr goyam kardgari khwish ra

'I don't understood Farsi,' the old man replies.

I translate the lines for him into Punjabi: 'Ah! could I behold the face of my beloved once more, I would give thanks unto my Creator until the day of resurrection.'

We are now passing through the outskirts of Ambala and I can see the first scattered hutments and the walls of a regimental centre.

'Anarkali was a whore,' the old woman says, with a cruel sneer. 'Who would compose poetry for a woman like that?'

'Come,' her husband says, as the train begins to slow down. He tries to wrestle with his bags but they are too heavy. Two men in the aisle next to him stand up and lift the couple's luggage over the heads of the other passengers. The crowd adjusts itself as the two old people stumble towards the door. The platform is busy with coolies running back and forth. For several minutes, the elderly couple stand by their belongings, looking lost and abandoned. But then, a middle-aged man comes rushing towards them, obviously their son. He leans down to touch his mother's feet.

'Churail!' says Champa, as she watches them through the window.

10

I first visited Ambala as a boy of twelve or thirteen, just before the turn of the century, when I accompanied Teshoo Lama on his search for the sacred River of the Arrow. It was here that I learned the meaning of the red bull on a field of green, my father's regimental emblem and colours. The lama and I travelled from Lahore along the Grand Trunk Road, where we met up with a Rajput noblewoman and her retinue. She was entranced by the Holy One's teachings and became his devotee. It was here too that I was inducted into the Great Game by Mahbub Ali, the Pashtun horse trader, and Colonel Creighton of the Survey of India. Later, after our adventures in the Himalaya, I came back to Ambala with Hurree Babu, the loquacious Bengali spy. Eventually, the lama found the river he was searching for, the Ghaggar, which flows past Ambala. Considered by some scholars to be the remnants of the sacred Saraswati mentioned in the Vedas.

Ambala is mostly a military cantonment. In recent years, an air force base was established here. A busy bazaar is spread along the highway and Ambala Cantt. is a railway junction from where the trains go up to Kalka and then on to Simla. Though there is nothing remarkable about Ambala, except perhaps the cathedral built for British troops, I have always recognized a certain lyricism in its name. Some say it is named after the Amba Devi temple located here. Others claim it was founded by a warrior, Amba Rajput. There are even those who say its name celebrates the famous mangoes of this region. The English spelling, 'Umballa', is inelegant and always makes me think of the umbrella that Hurree Babu carried to shield his complexion from the sun. I prefer the way Ambala appears in Urdu script: امبالہ

For me, at that early age, the Great Game evoked a heady romance, appealing to my youthful sense of duplicity and intrigue. As an enemy, nobody can compare with the Russians! The idea that they would swarm across the steppes to invade India by crossing the high mountains to the north was a terrifying thought, though it was as far-fetched as any fairy tale. How could the armies of the Czar drag their cannons over snowbound passes and how would the Cossack cavalry follow on horseback, let alone ford the Indus? The whole idea was so preposterous and yet, it kept the men who governed India awake all night and fuelled their nightmares when they slept. As a boy, I accepted the paranoid mythology of the Great Game, though I grew disillusioned with it soon enough, when I saw how foolish our fears had become. The threat to the empire was not from outside India but from within. While we were jousting with Russian windmills, it was the Congress party and other Indian patriots who were plotting the downfall of British India.

I say 'we' because I have always been a part of the game, a secret agent of the Raj who has served his colonial masters just as Hurree Babu and Mahbub Ali did. A subordinate to the machinations of power, my loyalties are to myself and to my closest friends, those whom I have learned to trust and love. Yes, 'love' is a word I don't use lightly but it is more than just a sentiment for me or a casual valediction on a letter to someone for whom I might express affection. But love of country has always seemed to me an absurd concept, almost as nonsensical as the love of God. Why should I care about divinity or national identity, when neither has ever done me any good?

My codename in the secret service was Q15, which was assigned to me by Colonel Creighton after we returned from pursuing two Russian spies in the Himalaya. I remember asking him, at the time, if there was any significance to the letter and the numbers. He shook his head and muttered something about picking it out of a hat. The truth is that we hardly ever used our codenames. It was merely a formality for internal communication, though, as a boy, I remember feeling a sense of self-importance, being given a secret identity like that.

After departing from Ambala, the Frontier Mail crosses the river Jamuna and leaves the Punjab behind. Approaching Saharanpur, the landscape changes in subtle ways, becoming a shade or two greener, with many more orchards and fields of sugar cane. Now that the old couple are gone, we rearrange some of our luggage to make space on the lower berths so the girls can clamber down to see the passing countryside. Kamla and Sarita sit by one window, Munia and Radha by the other. They keep pointing at things we pass along the way, a village mosque or a temple overlooking a tank of water, vultures feasting on the rotting carcass of a horse, a herd of cattle grazing in a patch of scrub jungle and peacocks feeding in a field.

'What is that?' Munia asks me, pointing to a tall smokestack.

'A brick kiln,' I explain. 'The clay is dug out of the earth and formed into bricks, then fired underground.'

She looks at me with a puzzled expression. 'I thought bricks were stones.'

I laugh. 'Yes, man-made stones.'

Munia and the others have spent most of their lives in the city of Lahore. Though mature beyond their years in matters of seduction and love, they have lived a sheltered life and know little of the outside world.

'And what are those?' Radha asks.

'Telegraph poles. Urgent messages are carried on those wires,' I say.

She looks at me with suspicion. 'How can a message travel along a wire?'

'Don't be foolish,' Champa scolds her gently. 'You received a telegram once, from that army officer who wanted you to visit him in Kashmir.'

'But that was written on a piece of paper,' she says. 'You read it to me.'

Champa looks at me helplessly. 'How should I explain?'

'That wire is like the string on a sitar, which vibrates to make sounds,' I explain. 'Except that the telegraph makes words instead of notes of music.'

'Who plucks the wire?' asks Sarita, equally sceptical.

'A man in the telegraph office taps on a key and an electric current passes through those cables. When the signal reaches its destination, the words are written down and delivered to you like a letter. A telegram travels from Lahore to Dilli within seconds,' I say. 'Much faster than this train.'

'I don't believe you,' says Radha. 'You are making it up, just like the time you told me that people can fly in ships with wings.'

'All right, don't believe me then,' I say with a laugh. 'You'll learn about a lot of new things in Dilli that you never thought were possible.'

'I'm bored,' says Munia. 'Why can't this train travel as fast as your telegrams?'

We pass a canal, where women are washing clothes at the water's edge. Several green and blue saris have been spread on the grass to dry. A little further on, an elephant stands beside a stone pavilion. The girls have never encountered a live elephant before, but they recognize the animal from pictures they have seen.

'It's twice as big as a horse,' says Radha, 'and look at the elephant's nose!'

As the girls laugh together, I realize that they are little more than children. Each of them has her own sad story. Either they were orphaned at an early age, like Munia and Sarita, or grew up within a brothel like Radha and Kamla. Champa took them in at different ages and taught them their trade. Their lives have been full of sorrow and the ugliness of serving the desires and demands of strangers. Yet, Champa protects them fiercely and if any man mistreats her girls, she abuses him and throws him out onto the street, threatening to expose his infidelities to his wife and family.

Though the girls flirt with me, I have never laid a hand upon them, and they treat me as an elderly uncle. In some ways, I suppose, we are a family though there are no blood ties between us, and we have no illusions about the relationships that are transacted. The old woman, who called Anarkali a whore, will never understand the code of morals and dignity that these young women hold onto like fragile baubles that mean so much to them. They pride themselves on their beauty and their manners, as well as the attractive clothes and jewellery they wear, but mostly they take satisfaction in their ability to manipulate men and earn a living.

Pulling into Muzaffarnagar station, we see a train travelling in the opposite direction, for the first time since we left Lahore. Its carriages are as crowded as ours and they go by so slowly that we can clearly see the faces of the passengers looking out the windows. They stare at us as intensely as we stare back at them. Some of their expressions betray fear and sorrow, others are blank with vacant eyes. No one is smiling or laughing, except for a child who waves to us. One of the girls waves back. His mother grabs the infant's hand and pulls him away from the window. We watch in silence, the two trains no more than ten feet apart. These people are also fleeing their homes and like us, they have no idea what the future holds. We could be them and they could be us. Once the train has passed, we stop at the station and some of the passengers from our carriage get down.

'Will all of the Muslims in Dilli leave?' Munia asks.

'I don't think so,' I respond. 'Not everyone.'

'But they have had riots there too, haven't they?' Radha says.

'Yes, there has been trouble in some parts of the city,' I confirm.

'Will we be safe?' Sarita asks, giving Champa a worried look. 'Didi, where will we stay in Dilli?'

'Don't worry. Everything has been arranged,' Champa assures her, though I know she is anxious about relying on her Sethji. 'Just make sure that all of our luggage is taken out of the carriage when we get down. Don't leave anything behind.'

'There is so much to carry,' Kamla says, looking up at the bags and boxes on the berths above us.

'A lot of the passengers will get down in Dilli,' I say. 'The train will stop for at least half an hour, even though we're running late.'

'Will you come with us?' Munia asks.

'No, but I will make sure that everything is taken care of before I leave,' I tell her.

'Where will you go?' Sarita demands.

'I have friends in Dilli,' I tell her. 'I'll stay with one of them.'

'Will they recognize you, dressed up like this, Lalaji?' says Munia, smirking.

'All of my friends are Lalas like me,' I joke with her.

'We know who you really are,' says Radha, under her breath.

'Oh, do you?' I reply. 'Okay, tell me.'

'Stop this nonsense,' Champa scolds her. 'Behave yourselves.'

'No, let her speak. So, who am I?' I insist. Nobody else in the carriage is listening to us and now that we are only an hour or two from Delhi, I'm not worried if someone suspects my disguise. 'Go on, tell me.'

Radha looks at the others and laughs.

'We think you are an actor. You play so many roles. Someday, I'm sure we will go to the cinema and see you on the screen,' she says. 'Am I right or not?'

I laugh and even Champa smiles.

'You're wrong,' I tell her. 'If I was an actor, why wouldn't I be on a stage or facing a camera with a film director telling me what to do? Why would I be on a train with you?'

'But you use make-up to darken your skin. Some days you are one person and other days someone else,' says Radha.

'I don't think you're an actor,' Munia says.

'No?' I ask her. 'Then what am I?'

'I know you're a spy, like in the films. Not an actor but a real jasoos,' she says, eyeing me cautiously.

'Why do you think that?' I ask with an encouraging smile.

'Because someone tried to shoot you and Didi had to clean and dress the wound on your leg. That wasn't acting, was it?' she says.

'No, but it doesn't necessarily mean I'm a spy. I could be a thief who tried to rob a bank and was wounded by one of the guards when I escaped,' I suggest.

'Stop it,' says Champa. 'What is the point of this conversation?'

'I want to know who I am,' I say, giving her a serious look. 'Maybe you can tell me.'

She looks at me with an annoyed expression.

'You're not an actor, or a spy, or a thief,' she says. 'You're nobody, like the rest of us. A faceless castaway who has no home and no identity any more.'

The tone of her voice silences us and I feel no urge to argue with her. Now that we are approaching Delhi, the journey seems to slow down and every minute feels like an hour. Outside the train, the landscape has a stillness that makes it look like a painting. The sun has moved from one side of the sky to the other. Its light has softened and grown warmer, filtered by a haze of dust. We pass through several small stations without stopping and in Meerut more of the passengers get off. Those that remain on board begin to collect their bags. Though the Frontier Mail goes on to Bombay, it seems as if most of the passengers will disembark in Delhi.

Eventually, we cross the Jamuna once again, over a trestle bridge of steel girders. Without solid ground beneath us, the sound of the train changes to a hollow, rattling noise. Through the window, I can see the slow-moving river and the sandstone walls of the Red Fort. Minutes later we enter the switchyards, and the air is thick with the smell of woodsmoke and burning coal. I tell Champa and the girls to get ready to go outside onto the platform and to send six coolies in to collect their bags, while I stay in the compartment to supervise. At first there is so much commotion, with everyone pushing to get out the doors, it takes them several minutes before they reach the platform. When the coolies arrive, I give them their instructions and soon a pile of trunks, bags, and boxes are heaped on the platform. Until now, there is no sign of the Seth and I can see Champa looking about anxiously. Finally, when everything has been emptied from our compartment, I follow the last coolie out the door and tell two of them to bring a handcart to the brake van. The railway clerk demands a bribe when I show him the receipts. I have no time to argue, handing him a folded note and pointing out the boxes and some of the furniture. By the time it is offloaded, the whistle blows twice and the Frontier Mail continues on its journey, the carriages almost empty now.

When I return, I can see that two young men have joined the women. They must be employees of the Seth, smartly dressed in waistcoats and trousers, wearing caps instead of turbans. Neither of them pays any attention to me, as I collect my leather case and duffel bag, signalling to one of the coolies to pick these up. Champa catches my eye and begins to say something, but I gesture for her not to speak. We do not say farewell, parting as if we were strangers. She smiles sadly, as I slip away into the crowd, following my baggage balanced on the coolie's head.

11

Though I have arrived on a third-class ticket, the attendant at the second-class waiting room is happy to allow me inside when I press an eight-anna coin into his palm. The coolie deposits my bags next to a lounge chair in one corner of the room and I pay him off. Railway waiting rooms are much the same at every major station—anonymous, transient spaces where travellers can rest and bathe before boarding onward connections. The dark wooden furnishings are simple and functional. Ceiling fans stir the air while most of the occupants ignore each other. A couple of Eurasians, who look as if they might work for the railways, are reading newspapers and smoking while a corpulent Hindu gentleman, his waistcoat unbuttoned, is asleep on a daybed against the wall under a tourism poster that depicts the Gateway of India in Bombay.

As discreetly as I can, I take a few toiletries out of my suitcase and a fresh change of clothes. Nobody pays attention to me, though one of the Eurasians glances up and gives me an irritated look, as if he doesn't think I belong here, dressed as I am. Two of the bathing stalls are occupied but the third is empty and I'm glad to see that no sweeper is on duty to witness my transformation. Once I'm inside the stall with the door latched, I remove my clothes. Thankfully, there is no mirror to reflect my naked figure and remind me of the physical dissolution of age. The overhead shower doesn't work but the tap is sufficient, and I give myself a good wash, scrubbing off the soot and grime of the journey, as well as the colour from my face. It always surprises me how quickly I can remove a disguise that has taken me so much longer to put on.

Using my turban as a towel to dry off, I dress myself in a pair of khaki shorts and a cotton singlet. Stepping out of the stall, I commandeer one of the washbasins for a quick shave. A gaunt man in a cotton lungi is performing ablutions at another washbasin to my right, vigorously scraping his tongue. Emerging into the main hall, I put on my socks and shoes, as well as a wrinkled bush shirt. In this way, the metamorphosis of Lala Jagat Kapoor into Captain Leslie Townsend is complete. Fortunately, nobody seems to notice, though the Eurasian, who glared at me earlier, studies me with suspicion as I quickly repack my bags. When I ask the attendant to summon a coolie, he gives me a puzzled look but asks no questions.

As I suspected, Champa and the girls haven't left the station yet. Their luggage is being loaded onto a pair of bullock carts, which the Sethji's attendants are supervising. I'm glad it's now their job, not mine. Keeping out of sight, behind a sandstone column near the main entrance to the station, I ask the coolie to wait while I light a cigarette and watch their preparations for departure. Though a part of me resists the idea of shadowing them, I can't, in good conscience, let them leave without knowing where they are going. As the five women squeeze into a Victoria horse carriage along with their most precious belongings, including the bird cage, I signal to the coolie and board my own tonga, explaining to the driver that he should follow them at a discreet distance.

The worst heat of the day has dispersed and a mild breeze tousles the horse's mane as we pass the Red Fort and Chandni Chowk, along a busy road that leads to Daryaganj. The white dome and sandstone walls of the Jumma Masjid rise above the uneven rooftops of cluttered markets. The sky is full of pigeons and pariah kites.

The tongawallah is a chatty, elderly man about my age. He asks where I've come from, and I tell him I've just arrived from Lucknow. When I enquire about riots in Delhi, he says there was an outbreak of violence in the old city, two days ago, but the army had a flag march and the police have now brought things under control. Today the curfew has been lifted.

After passing the stone archway of Delhi Gate, Champa's Victoria turns right and we follow it past the Ram Lila grounds where some sort of political rally is being held. Though I do not know Delhi as well as I know Lahore, I have wandered through these streets often enough. A short while later, we reach Ajmeri Gate and their carriage pulls up in front of a three-storey building that has a grandiose but neglected façade, with a hardware store on the ground floor. Lighting another cigarette, I watch the women get down and make a mental note of the place, as they are ushered up a flight of stairs. From what I can see, my erstwhile wife and daughters will have a secure roof over their heads. Hopefully, the Seth has provided them with comfortable accommodation, where he himself will enjoy their company. After this, I ask the tongawallah to drop me at a taxi stand nearby, then hire a cab to take me to Maidens Hotel, retracing our route through Daryaganj and proceeding by way of Kashmiri Gate to Alipore Road.

I don't have a reservation but when I present my card, the hotel manager accommodates me with a spacious room facing the swimming pool. The tariff will put a dent in the funds MacNeil advanced me but I hope I won't have to stay here any longer than necessary. The truth is, I've never enjoyed luxury the way some people do, wallowing in lavish indulgences. For me the greatest contentment is derived from humble privacy and self-sufficient comforts. I'll take a room in a dak bungalow any day over an over-priced doss house like this. But in my current role, I need to keep up appearances.

The first item of business is to have a drink, so I root out my bottle of Dyer Meakin's, which has miraculously remained unopened since Lahore, then call room service for a bottle of soda and a bucket of ice. After that, I draft a telegram to MacNeil, informing him of my arrival. It is addressed to Professor Percival Jennings in the Department of History at Punjab University. A friend of MacNeil's, he often serves as a conduit for communication between us. I don't bother using a code since the message will arouse no suspicion: 'Arrived Maidens Delhi Townsend'. The bearer who brings my soda and ice conveys the telegram form to the front desk for transmission. After he closes the door behind himself, I prepare my whisky and finish half of it before picking up the telephone.

When I dial '0' there is a faint buzz on the line until the switchboard operator answers in a bored voice. I give her the number: Delhi 89400. A clicking sound signals that she is connecting me to an outside line after which she dials the number. I've never been comfortable using a telephone because it seems strange to be talking into a void, and I always suspect that someone is listening in, but here I have no choice.

'Good evening,' a familiar voice greets me.

I wait for the staticky click that means the switchboard operator has disconnected herself before I reply.

'Hello, this is Captain Leslie Townsend. I'm calling from Maidens Hotel. May I speak to Mr Roger Monkman?'

After a pregnant pause, I receive a curt reply. 'I'm afraid there's nobody here by that name. You must have dialled the wrong number.'

'My apologies,' I respond, just before the line goes dead. Returning the receiver to its cradle, I close my eyes for a moment, as a wave of exhaustion from the journey passes over me. Finishing my drink, I put away the bottle and lie down on top of the bed. Checking my watch, I can see it is almost six o'clock. Before I know it, I've fallen fast asleep though it seems as if only a few minutes have passed before the persistent ringing of the telephone wakes me. This time, my watch tells me it is 8 p.m. and the windows are dark.

'Good evening, sir. I'm calling from the front desk,' a polite voice answers, after I pick up. 'There's a gentleman here to see you, with a parcel. May I send him up to your room?'

'Yes, please do,' I reply before hurrying into the WC to splash some water on my face to help me wake up. Before I've finished, there's a knock at my door. Combing my hair with wet fingers and trying to look somewhat alert, I open the door to find Srinivas Iyer smiling at me. He hands me a small package, as I wave him inside.

'Sorry, I fell fast asleep,' I apologize and shake hands.

A slight man with a serious, sincere demeanour, framed by gold-rimmed spectacles, Srinivas is about fifty, though his hair is jet-black and his features youthful. The pencil-thin moustache on his upper lip twitches when he speaks in an Oxbridge accent. He once told me that he has a doctorate in philology from Trinity College and is fluent in French, German, and Anatolian. His thesis was on the polemics of master–slave relationships in Nietzsche's early work. One of the most intelligent, erudite men I know, he should have been a professor instead of a spy, though the academy's loss is the secret service's gain. The two of us couldn't be more different, a Brahmin from the Coromandel Coast whose mother tongue is Tamil and a country-born Irish urchin from the back lanes of Lahore who had no formal education until the age of twelve or thirteen. Nevertheless, we have forged an unlikely partnership. Srinivas surveys the room, as if to make sure we're alone, while I gesture towards two armchairs positioned on either side of a small coffee table next to the window.

'How good to see you!' Srinivas exclaims, glancing outside, where lights have come on near the pool. 'But I have to say, this isn't the sort of place I was expecting to find you.'

'I've moved up in the world,' I explain.

'So it would seem!' He laughs softly. 'Last time we met in that filthy tea stall next to Minto Bridge.'

'You have to admit, the pakoras they served us were good,' I say.

'Delicious, but my stomach was out for the next three days,' Srinivas complains. 'I don't know how you manage eating off the street.'

'I developed a lifelong immunity at an early age,' I confess. 'Shall I order something here in the room or would you like to go down to the dining hall?'

'Thanks, but nothing for me. I can't stay long,' he says.

'Not even a drink?' I ask, though I know Srinivas is a teetotaller.

He shakes his head and then with a mischievous smile he asks, 'Aren't you going to open your package?'

Picking it up, I squeeze the parcel, then shake it, pretending to guess what's inside.

'A gift?' I ask.

Wrapped in brown paper, it has nothing written on the outside. Tearing the parcel open cautiously, I can feel a leather case and suddenly realize what it is.

'My camera!' I exclaim.

'Correct,' Srinivas says. 'Our boys found it right where you dropped it when you had to escape from the palace in Bahawalpur. That was a close call!'

Opening the case, I admire the Leica, which still seems to be in perfect condition.

'The Germans may have been our enemies, but you have to admire their precision-engineering,' I remark.

'I'm afraid we removed the film and had it developed,' says Srinivas apologetically. 'It contained some interesting photos, which I can't return.'

I shrug. 'As I remember, there were several compromising shots of the Wazir Sahib and his Swiss stenographer. Did I get the focus and exposure right?'

Srinivas nods. 'Perfect. Cartier-Bresson couldn't have done better. After we showed him the photos, the Wazir was very cooperative.'

Srinivas recruited me during the war. At the time, he was one of the few Indian officers in the Imperial Secret Service, a brilliant analyst but also a shrewd field operative. He interviewed me twice in Lahore and once in Delhi, assuring me that by keeping him abreast of any information I gathered, I wasn't betraying the Intelligence Bureau or the Punjab Police. 'We're all on the same side,' Srinivas insisted, 'though it's better if they don't know about our arrangement.'

To begin with, he simply wanted me to report on what was going on in Lahore, though after we worked together for a year, Srinivas gave me several special assignments in Punjab's princely states. A number of foreign agents had insinuated themselves into the courts, particularly Bahawalpur and Patiala, where certain members of the royal families had fallen prey to their influence. While MacNeil is an honest, diligent policeman, Srinivas is a covert genius when it comes to ferreting out treachery and deceit. Now that the British are preparing to leave, he is well positioned to head up whatever intelligence services are to be formed after India becomes independent. From rumours I've heard, he's close to Sardar Vallabhbhai Patel and has been consulting with him and other Congress leaders, though he is still technically on the ISS payroll. It must be a delicate balancing act but if anyone can pull it off, Srinivas will. In all of our conversations, he's been very candid about supporting the freedom movement, though he insists that his political views don't compromise his professional commitments.

'I never thought I'd see this camera again,' I say.

'Well, I'm sure you'll have plenty of reasons to use it,' says Srinivas.

I give him a sceptical glance. 'Are you sending me off on another wild goose chase?'

'It depends on what you've called me here to discuss,' he answers, evasively. 'Please go ahead. I'm all ears.'

As succinctly as possible, I explain to Srinivas how I met Sir Denys Bromley-Pugh at Governor's House in Lahore and fill him in on our conversation. I also explain how I decided to follow him to Delhi, though I leave out the fact that I travelled here undercover with Champa and the girls. After I share my suspicions that the Brigadier and his men are hatching some sort of conspiracy to undermine the handover of power in India, Srinivas leans forward in his chair and questions me carefully.

'Did he definitely state that they are planning a military coup?'

'No, of course not,' I reply. 'But I think they're certainly intent on sabotaging the handover of power.'

'And what do you hope to achieve by infiltrating their cabal?'

'I'll learn more details and find out how soon they plan to act,' I answer.

'Why wouldn't you just let me assign someone else to investigate,' Srinivas argues, 'rather than putting yourself at risk?'

'Well, somebody has to do it,' I reply. 'And I've already laid the groundwork.'

'We have well-placed informants in the armed forces,' Srinivas reminds me. 'And we've already got our eyes on the Brigadier.'

'I'm sure you do but my instincts tell me that I can get to the heart of it,' I say.

'Instincts?' Srinivas says with a smile, leaning back in his chair.

'You don't believe me?' I respond.

'No. No, not at all,' he waves a hand. 'It's just that I don't want you to be exposed. You're too valuable an asset.'

'Come on, don't patronize me,' I complain. 'This is the end of the line for me. I'm a washed-up spy who has nothing to lose.

The empire is coming to a close. Let me at least try to bring these bastards down.'

Srinivas shakes his head. 'It's not the end of the line. Once the British leave, we'll need men like you who occupy that uncertain space between history and the future, black and white. I can promise you that once India is independent, the country will need your services, unless of course, you're planning to go off to England.'

'So, will you be India's head of intelligence?' I ask him bluntly.

Srinivas waves his hand again, as if trying to get rid of a fly. 'Whatever happens, I will certainly be in a stronger position to handle our security concerns, if I can depend on you from time to time.'

I want to argue with him, but I let it go.

'Please, let me meet Sir Denys one more time,' I plead. 'If I feel any kind of threat, I'll pull back.'

'You really do hate this man, don't you?' he says with a prescient smile.

'It's not personal,' I reply, 'if that's what you mean but, yes, he represents everything I despise about England and its ruling classes.'

Srinivas points a finger at me. 'That's exactly why I'm worried,' he says. 'Because you can't be dispassionate and that means you won't know when to step aside.'

'Give me a chance,' I demand, 'I swear, I'll be careful.'

He looks at me for almost a minute and I can imagine his mind ticking over like a finely tuned chronometer.

'All right,' he agrees, at last. 'But, please be discreet. The easiest place to find Bromley-Pugh is at the Gymkhana Club. Most mornings, he likes to play billiards there with his chums.'

'Thank you,' I say. 'I'll take every precaution and keep you informed.'

Removing his glasses, Srinivas wipes the lenses with a handkerchief and then puts them back on.

'You haven't told me everything that happened in Lahore,' he says.

Puzzled, I shake my head.

'Let me jog your memory,' Srinivas says. 'Somebody tried to kill you. You were wounded in the leg three weeks ago.'

I take a long moment to respond.

'Yes,' I confess. 'It wasn't a serious wound, so I kept it to myself. How did you find out?'

'Do you know who it could have been?' he asks, ignoring my question

'No idea,' I say.

Srinivas rises to his feet and prepares to leave.

'Whoever it was, might try again,' he says. 'And I wouldn't assume they don't know you're in Delhi.'

12

'Kim!' exclaims the princess. 'Where the devil have you been hiding?'

We haven't seen each other for a decade, but she recognizes me immediately, though both of us have aged.

'Here and there,' I reply, kissing her pale hand, which bears three extravagant ring stones, one of which is an emerald the size of a quail's egg. Its colour matches her eyes.

Anastasia is the widow of the late Kanwar Manjeet Singh, whose elder brother was the Maharaja of Lunagarh, one of the Punjab Hill States. A small kingdom tucked into the foothills of the Dhauladar Range between Kangra and Chamba, Lunagarh owes its wealth to trade with Tibet, mostly shahtoosh and gold dust as well as salt, from which the state took its name.

'I thought you had forgotten me,' Anastasia cries, grabbing my wrist and pulling me onto the sofa beside her, before planting a kiss on my cheek.

'How could I forget you!' I reply.

'Very easily, I'm sure,' she says. 'You've always been a rogue, Kim, and nothing will change that, but I'm delighted to see you.'

Her voice still carries traces of a husky East European accent. Born in Odessa, Anastasia met her husband at a spa in Crimea, outside Sabastapol, where he had gone to get treatment for arthritis. Prince Manjeet Singh was thirty years older than her. Anastasia's strong yet nimble fingers loosened his joints as she massaged her way into his life. Always a beauty, she is blonde and fair-skinned but with a hint of Asia Minor in her features. The elderly prince, whose only vice was partridge shooting, had lost his first wife to typhoid several years earlier. According to legend, he proposed to Anastasia while she was manipulating his femoral head and acetabulum. As she likes to say, 'I had him by the balls and sockets!' They returned to India together and lived for a time in Lunagarh, where she bore him a son, the year before Manjeet died. After that, she moved to his family home in Delhi, Lunagarh House, on Alipore Road, where she still lives.

'Tell me what you've been up to!' she insists. 'What wicked conspiracies have you been hatching?'

'Nothing very exciting,' I say. 'It's not like the old days!'

'Of course, it isn't,' the princess agrees. 'Nothing can be like the old days.'

Anastasia was one of the Great Gamers, who has never been given the credit she deserves. Though Odessa was part of the Czar's empire, the princess inherited her hatred for the Russians from her parents who were Ukrainian nationalists. When she arrived in India with her elderly prince, suspicions immediately arose that Anastasia might be an enemy agent. However, when she spent her first summer in Simla, Lurgan Sahib discovered the truth and quickly recruited her as an asset. The fact that she was fluent in Russian and English, proved invaluable when certain diaries and other communications in the Cyrillic script were acquired by the secret service. Among various assignments, she was sent on a mission to Ladakh where she interrogated a man named Petrov, who claimed to be a scholar of Buddhism, gleaning wisdom from the Gwalang Rinpoche of the Drukpa Kagyu sect and his lamas. Through her skilful questions, Anastasia exposed Petrov as a spy and he was arrested when he returned to Kashmir.

Colonel Creighton once told me that she was the only woman he ever trusted. Coming from a devout misogynist like him, it was a supreme compliment, though Anastasia always made a point of pronouncing his name as 'cretin'. A headstrong, devious but brilliant spy, she has a complicated personality. Unlike many other European women who married maharajas and petty princelings, Anastasia adopted her husband's Hindu faith and Rajput culture sincerely and speaks perfect Kangri and Punjabi. She has always dressed in salwar-kameez or occasionally silk saris, though her perfumes are French and her lingerie, Italian.

Anastasia has never been prudish and there are rumours of affairs she had, after her husband died, with both English and Indian suitors, each of which she ended on her own terms. The only person to whom she is totally devoted is her son, Pratap, who is now a distinguished lawyer representing some of the large European business houses, as they navigate the uncharted waters of Independence and Partition. His name often appears in the newspapers as he negotiates the commercial consequences of Britain's departure from India. I've known Pratap since he was a boy, and he always calls me 'Kimuncle'.

'What can I offer you?' Anastasia asks. 'A sherry? Some vermouth?'

'Whisky, please,' I reply, though sunset is still an hour away.

The princess calls out to one of her retainers, who arrives a few minutes later with a decanter and two glasses. As I pour us each three fingers, Anastasia raises an eyebrow. There was a time when she could drink me under the table.

'God bless!' she says, raising the glass to her lips.

She must be in her late seventies now but seems as resolute and youthful as she was when I knew her best, during the Great War. I was in my mid-twenties and she seemed barely a handspring older, without a trace of grey in her hair. We were never lovers, though I was close to her in other ways, sharing my innermost fears and despair. Anastasia coaxed me out of my darkest spells of depression and nursed me back to a life of hope with her Slavic sense of humour and practical no-nonsense nature.

'Last time I saw you was in Simla, 1937,' she says. 'Just before the war. Am I right?'

'Your memory is as good as ever,' I reply.

'No, it isn't. I'm getting senile,' she says with a smile. 'But all that means is that I've forgotten my past sins and transgressions.'

'The absolution of age,' I concur.

'You've put on some weight, but it suits you, Kim,' she says, sizing me up.

'And you're as lovely as ever,' I compliment her.

'If you take away the wrinkles,' she laughs.

'How is Pratap?' I ask.

'A dutiful son, as always,' she says. 'But the dear boy works too hard and refuses to find a wife. I've given up on grandchildren.'

'Do you still go up to Simla?' I ask.

'Every summer. Swinburne Cottage is still there, with the same leaks in the roof and mould in the cupboards, but I look forward to my time in the hills and my Simla garden. Delhi has lost its charm. Too many bureaucrats.' She takes a swallow of whisky, then asks, 'Where are you staying?'

'At the Maidens,' I say. 'We're neighbours.'

'Wonderful!' she cries, putting down her glass and clapping her hands.

Finishing my whisky, I look at her with an apologetic expression. 'Anastasia, I have a favour to ask,' I admit.

'Naturally.... I knew this wasn't just a social visit,' she says with an indulgent smile. 'You would never have come here just to say hello. So, you're still in the game, Kim?'

'Not really,' I reply. 'But I'm here on work.'

'Tell me, how can I help?' she insists, leaning forward.

'Do you still play bridge at the Gymkhana Club?' I ask.

'Every Monday, Wednesday, and Saturday,' she says with a smile.

'Would you mind taking me there tomorrow as your guest?'

Anastasia shrugs and looks disappointed. 'Of course. But is that all? I was hoping you were going to ask me to accompany you on a secret mission to Kashmir.'

'For now, that's all the help I need,' I say. 'Though it is a secret mission, I suppose.'

'All right,' she says, her eyes brightening with interest.

'I'll warn you, it could be dangerous,' I tell her.

'Lovely,' she replies. 'Help yourself to another drink, if you'd like.'

Grabbing the decanter by the neck, I pour myself two fingers of whisky, conscious that my hand is shaking. She notices and catches my eye.

'Just a tremor,' I tell her. 'I'm growing old.'

Anastasia nods sympathetically.

'I'll be leaving for the club tomorrow morning at eleven. You can ride with me, but I'm afraid I can't fit you into my game. There are four of us who've been playing bridge together for the past six years and we've never missed a day!'

'Thank you. I wasn't planning to play cards,' I assure her.

'Why do you have to be so mysterious with me?' she pouts.

'I'll tell you when the time is right,' I promise.

'And what do I get in return for this favour?' she demands.

'Anything you ask, my dear,' I answer.

'Don't I get three wishes?' she asks.

'Only one,' I say. 'I'm not a djinn, after all, just a....'

'Okay,' she interrupts me. 'I want to know what really happened in Murree with that Belgian girl. The whole truth, Kim!'

I pretend to consider her request reluctantly, then smile.

'I'll give you a complete confession,' I say. 'But only after you've taken me to the Gymkhana tomorrow.'

'You cunning bastard! I don't know if I can trust you!' Anastasia laughs.

∞

The royal limousine of Lunagarh is a 1935 Cadillac Fleetwood that Anastasia won while playing cards with the Nawab of Rampur. Having lost more than five thousand rupees at rummy that day, the Nawab Sahib bet his car on the final hand and lost. According to Anastasia, she offered to drive him home from the club, but he was so cut up that he went out onto the street and hailed a tonga.

When it comes to building big cars, the Americans have an edge on everyone else. A Cadillac may not be quite as luxurious as a Rolls or Hispano-Suiza, but its V12 engine emits a growl that would make any other limousine cower in submission and the fenders look like dragon's wings. We settle into the back seat, as her chauffeur edges out onto Alipore Road. The princess is dressed in a chiffon sari, wearing several strands of pearls and matching earrings. Her hair has been freshly coloured to a creamy blonde that hides any hint of grey and her lipstick is cherry red. Compared to her, I look like a complete duffer, in a white summer suit that bags at the knees.

'Is this a disguise?' she asks as we drive off.

'Indeed,' I confirm. 'The name is Captain Leslie Townsend. I'm a mountaineer and explorer, just back from the Karakoram.'

'Your accent isn't quite right,' she says. 'You sound as if you're about to sneeze.'

'Well, as a matter of fact, I caught a cold in the Karakoram and it hasn't completely left me yet,' I reply, taking out a handkerchief and wiping my nose.

Anastasia throws back her head and laughs. She herself is a marvellous mimic and I remember one time the two of us went up to Srinagar, pretending to be a German countess and her Dutch manservant. We got invited onto a houseboat where Nicholas Roerich, the painter-philosopher was staying. Creighton was sure he was up to no good and we spent a very strange evening with him and his wife, during which he tried to hypnotize Anastasia. She played along and pretended to fall under his spell, rolling her eyes and reciting lengthy passages of verse from Pushkin's *Eugene Onegin*, which alarmed Roerich no end. He tried to snap her out of it, but she kept going, until I had to pinch her ears, which brought her back to her senses. Ultimately, we didn't discover anything suspicious about Roerich and it turned out that most of his journeys to Tibet involved astral travel. He had very little sense of geography, beyond the mystical realm of Shambala.

Circling Connaught Place, I can see how much New Delhi has changed, since I was here three years ago. It seems much busier and the trees along the broad avenues have grown taller from when they were first planted in the thirties. Though I've always preferred Lahore, Delhi looks greener than it used to be and the flower beds on the roundabouts are beautifully tended. When we cross Kingsway, I get a glimpse of the Viceregal Palace on its hilltop with the two wings of the Central Secretariat flanking the dome. Lutyens' architecture is too pretentious for my tastes. It seems absurd that the colonial authorities built such monumental structures less than fifteen years ago, and now Delhi will become the capital of independent India.

The Gymkhana Club has not abandoned its colonial antecedents quite yet, though there are plenty of Indian members. The Cadillac deposits us at the front entrance and the princess ushers me inside with a regal flick of her wrist. The club is relatively quiet at this time of day. After I've been signed in, Anastasia abandons me for the card room, where I see her exchanging kisses with her companions before settling down at their table. Biding my time, I head for the library and select the *Times of India* and *The Statesman* from the newspaper rack. The headlines are mostly about riots in Calcutta, as well as Lahore and Karachi. There's also a photograph on the front page of the Viceroy and Nehru, conferring over important matters, though it looks as if they could just as easily be discussing the weather.

After half an hour of distracted reading, I wander outside into the garden and find a comfortable wicker chair in the shade, from where I have a clear view of the lawn tennis courts. Four women are playing a game of doubles while one of the markers is helping a young man with his serve. A pair of bulbuls are bickering atop a bougainvillea vine that climbs a trellis fixed to one side of the main building. A striped palm squirrel is fidgeting about on the branch of a neem tree overhead.

Gesturing for a waiter, I order a beer. When he asks for my membership number, I tell him I'm a guest of the Princess Anastasia and he looks about awkwardly. Speaking to him in Hindustani, I explain that she's in the card room and he can ask her to sign for me. Though I'm probably breaking club rules, the waiter complies and after ten minutes my bottle arrives. Well-chilled, it produces a respectable head of foam, as I try to project the indolent boredom of an English sahib, pissing away the morning.

Being a sahib requires a special blend of arrogant indifference and condescension that is carefully cultivated by most white people in India. Though I've often been called a sahib, I've never aspired to that honorific. In fact, I hate the title because it carries a pronounced note of disdain. Calling someone a sahib suggests that he does not understand the world he lives in. At the same time, it implies a certain respectability that denies me the hidden pleasures of living beyond the pale. These stray thoughts drift through my mind, as the bubbles rise inside my glass, before evaporating into the warm, dry air.

After an hour has passed, I begin to wonder if Srinivas was wrong and whether I'm here on a fool's errand. The club is mostly deserted and the tennis games have ended, now that the temperature has risen into the nineties. I'm sweating even in the shade and decide to go in search of a cooler spot. Carrying the remains of my beer onto the veranda, I find a seat under a ceiling fan that is whirring like the propellor on a Spitfire. Before I've settled myself, however, I hear the sound of jackboots on floorboards. Through a window on my right, I can see five men in uniform heading towards the billiards room. Even though I cannot see their faces, there's no mistaking the erect posture of Sir Denys, as he marches half a stride ahead of the others.

13

I was taught how to play billiards by a Goan crooner in Peshawar. Ronnie Pereira used to play the piano and sing every evening at Dean's Hotel. During the day, he hung around the billiards room, always ready to earn a few extra rupees off anyone who challenged him to a game. During the twenties, I spent a good deal of time in Peshawar working undercover as a horse trader with my old friend Mahbub Ali, gathering whatever information I could about Russian exiles who had fled their country after the revolution. Some of them were former courtiers to the Czar and other aristocrats who had escaped overland through Persia and Afghanistan. By the time they got to Peshawar, many of them had lost whatever money they had and they were desperate, which meant they were often up to no good. A few Bolshevik agents also infiltrated their ranks, stirring up trouble. Ronnie and I became friends, and he would tip me off to any suspicious guests staying at Dean's. In his company, I learned both snooker and billiards, though I prefer the latter because it's a mental game of stratagems and countermoves, as well as an exercise in skill.

When I stroll into the billiards room, Sir Denys doesn't recognize me at first, though one of the junior officers spots me right away.

'Aren't you the chap we met in Lahore?' he asks. 'Bit of a mountaineer, I recall?'

'Yes, indeed. At Governor's House.'

'Turnball, wasn't it?' he says, offering me a cigarette.

'Townsend,' I correct him.

The Brigadier is in the middle of a game and I can tell that he is a mediocre player, not sharp enough to know when to go for a cannon or a pot. He also has a clumsy stroke, holding the cue stick as if it were a rifle with a fixed bayonet. 'Think of it as a foil,' Ronnie used to tell me, 'as if you're fencing. Every stroke should be decisive but elegant. Imagine you're fighting a duel with a beautiful woman.' Sir Denys, on the other hand, looks as if he is trying to disembowel a pig. I can tell that his opponent is a much better player, who is letting him win, missing easy shots while setting up the table to give the Brigadier an advantage. When they finish, Sir Denys wins by three points.

'Good game, sir,' I congratulate him, adding to the chorus of compliments, as Sir Denys waves his cue stick triumphantly.

A few minutes later, after lighting a celebratory cigarette, he squints at me.

'Do I know you?' he asks, cocking his head in an arrogant manner.

'Captain Leslie Townsend.' I extend a hand to shake. 'We met at her ladyship's birthday party in Lahore.'

For a moment, it looks as if he isn't going to shake hands with me but then he concedes with a weak grip.

'Ah…yes,' he mutters, suspiciously. 'The explorer. What are you doing here?'

'I came down to Delhi day before,' I say. 'Have to file my reports with the red tape-wallahs in the Secretariat. Wretched paperwork! It's the hardest part of any expedition.'

'Are you a member here?' Sir Denys asks.

'No, just a guest, but I thought I'd try to get in a game of billiards.'

Sir Denys looks at me as if I am challenging him. Then he gestures towards the man he has just defeated.

'You should play against Lieutenant Craven, here,' he suggests. 'Used to be a junior world champion before the war…but he seems to have lost his touch.'

The young lieutenant looks about twenty, though he has a brutish mug like a Staffordshire Bull Terrier, with ghostly white skin and a protruding jawline. He gives me a slack smile that curls into a sneer. Two other officers are playing at a second table, as I select a stick from the rack on the wall and chalk up. We agree to play to 300. Craven wins the lagging, his ball stopping less than an inch from the baulk. With a surly expression, he allows me to go first, obviously wanting to see if I'm any good.

I can tell that this time, he isn't going to hold back. After I get 62 points on my first break, he quickly racks up 110 before missing the pocket on an attempted in-off. One of the officers has taken charge of the scoreboard. Sir Denys is seated with the others, watching us with a distracted air. Trying unsuccessfully to listen in on their conversation, I almost miss an easy cannon, my cue ball barely kissing the red. Regaining my concentration, I reach 143 before I fumble a six shot. My opponent is now completely mute, focussing on the table with predatory intensity. Stalking from end to end and side to side, he executes his shots with a ruthlessness that seems almost savage. Finally, on 220, he attempts a risky drop cannon and sends his cue ball wide of its mark. After that, I catch up with him slowly, Ronnie's words in my ear. 'Impatience is your worst enemy. Never hurry a shot.'

As I close in on Craven, Sir Denys and the others fall silent, watching with interest. When a bold cannon puts me one point ahead, they rise to their feet and gather round. The former junior world champion has underestimated this old man. I take my score up to 267, when I muff a difficult pot. The bull terrier grins at me, as if he is ready to sink his teeth into my throat. I can tell he is a killer. Ronnie always said that billiards has a way of exposing a man's true character. This young officer has violence brewing in his veins. He doesn't appear to take a single breath, until he reaches 300. After he's won, Craven exhales loudly, then turns on me with menacing defiance. Shaking my hand, his palm is as dry as toast.

'Hard luck, Townsend, looks like you've met your match,' Sir Denys blurts out, as if he is the victor.

'Too good for me,' I concede. 'I'm glad I didn't wager on the game.'

The Brigadier slaps a congratulatory hand on Craven's shoulder.

'Well done, lieutenant!' he says, then looks at me. 'A steady hand and a sure eye. One of our finest marksmen too! You should see him with a revolver. He can hit a four-anna coin at thirty paces. Don't ever challenge him to a duel!'

'I'll remember your advice, sir,' I say, nodding, while Craven watches me as if he is already taking aim.

'Let's have a drink before lunch,' the Brigadier announces. 'Will you do us the honour of joining us, Townsend? I've got a private room booked.'

'Thank you, sir,' I accept. 'It would be my pleasure.'

The private room is off the main dining hall, a simple yet discreet lounge with wood panelling and leather chairs. A pair of ceiling fans are spinning softly, though the air is stuffy, as if the windows haven't been opened in years. Two bearers follow us in and take our drinks orders. I ask for a large whisky with ice.

Hearing this, one of the officers warns me. 'I'd suggest you have it neat. The club's ice machine broke down last week and they've been getting it from the bazaar. There's a good chance of catching cholera.'

'Whisky kills any germs,' I assure him.

Once we've been served, Sir Denys offers a toast to his majesty, the King Emperor, with a solemn, ceremonious gesture. All of us wait for him to take a seat and as he does, the Brigadier waves for me to join him on a leather couch. I can tell that he doesn't trust me. Drinking a gimlet, he holds the thin stem of the glass between his thumb and forefinger, as if he might snap it in two.

'Tell me, captain. Did you fight in the war?' he asks.

'In the Great War, yes,' I confirm. 'Mesopotamia.'

'Which regiment?'

'Seventh Gloucesters, part of Baldwin's Brigade.' I have prepared myself for these questions.

'The Turks were a feeble enemy, from what I've heard,' he sniffs.

'Not entirely, sir. They put up a solid defence at Chunuk Bair. But by the time we took Baghdad, they were a demoralized lot.'

'So, you never fought in Europe?'

'No, I'm glad to say, I didn't have to kill any Germans,' I explain.

'Why's that?' Sir Denys asks, raising an eyebrow and touching the glass to his lips.

'I've never been able to think of them as the enemy,' I reply.

He smiles and takes a sip of his gin.

'Even Hitler?' he asks.

I shake my head but say nothing, not wanting to appear too

eager to advertise my Nazi sympathies.

'Mark my words: history will redeem the Führer,' my host declares.

Raising my glass, I take a slug of whisky before agreeing, 'A great visionary. He loved the fatherland.'

Sir Denys studies me for a moment as if trying to read my mind, then asks, 'I can't quite place your accent, Townsend. Where are you from?'

'Manchester, sir, though I was raised in London.'

'Public school?'

'Sutton Grammar.'

'University?'

'I was never a good student,' I reply, shaking my head. 'Worked with my father for a year, then joined the army.'

'What did your father do?'

'He was a vintner,' I explain. 'We had a wine shop in Morden.'

'Which year did you join the army?'

'Nineteen fifteen. I heeded Lord Kitchener's call. The following year I was promoted from the ranks, a temporary commission for the duration of the war.' Again, I've done my homework because I knew that Sir Denys would be curious about my background. He still seems sceptical but some of the tension has eased.

'When did you come to India?' he asks.

'Soon after the Armistice. Having had a taste of the East during the war, I was keen to travel further. I applied for a position with Jardine Matheson in Calcutta and they hired me,' I explain.

'Good God, not a boxwallah!' Sir Denys exclaims in alarm.

'That job lasted only a year,' I reassure him. 'While in the army, I'd learned surveying and discovered I had some skill in draftsmanship. So, I joined the Survey of India and served mostly in the Himalaya, trying to fill in blanks on the map.'

He seems to accept my story, though he clearly isn't impressed by my pedigree. After another round of drinks, lunch is served, a bland but hearty menu of poached fish, mutton cutlets, roast potatoes, and string beans, with bread pudding for dessert. I notice that Sir Denys picks at his plate, hardly eating anything at all, while Craven, who sits to my left, feeds like a bull terrier that's been starved for a week.

After the meal is over and the plates have been cleared, everyone has a cigarette and the room fills with smoke. Sir Denys ignores me and I carry on a conversation with two other officers, who want to know about the Hindu Kush and the Karakoram. Finally, I decide it is time for me to take my leave and I shake hands all around. As I thank Sir Denys and say goodbye, he asks where I am staying.

'Maidens Hotel,' I tell him.

'I'd like to speak to you again, Townsend, on a matter of mutual interest,' he says. 'We'll be in touch.'

'Of course, sir,' I reply. 'It would be my pleasure.'

After that, I go in search of Anastasia, who is waiting outside the card room, ready to go home.

'Did you enjoy your game of bridge?' I ask, once we are seated in the Cadillac.

'I'm really not sure if I ever enjoy bridge. It's a distraction,' she sighs, 'which has become a habit. Sometimes, I wonder why I keep playing with the same three old crones. We gossip and quarrel, but I often feel an urge to throw down my cards and walk away before it's too late.'

'Too late for what?' I ask.

'For life!' she answers. 'I feel as if I'm just marking time before I die.'

'That sounds very sad,' I say. 'I've never thought of you as despondent.'

'I need another adventure, Kim. One last challenge before I lose my marbles.'

'Espionage isn't the same as it used to be,' I tell her. 'It's become a dirty, ugly business.'

'But you're still in the game,' she reminds me.

'I'm on my way out,' I answer.

'Who were those men you were with today?' she asks, glancing at me.

'Which men?'

'Come on,' she replies, nudging me with her elbow. 'All of the bearers at the club are my personal informants. They told me you had a private luncheon with Brigadier Bromley-Pugh.'

'Do you know him?'

'Only by reputation,' Anastasia replies.

'And what reputation does he have?' I counter.

'He's terribly well connected but a man of dubious morals and corrupt motives. I've seen him at the club often enough, though we've never been introduced. He's always surrounded by his tight little clique of officers. I'm told he's a bully and a fascist,' Anastasia looks me in the eye.

'That's correct,' I confirm.

'So, I'm wondering why my dear friend Kimball O'Hara is dressed up like a stuffy old Englishman and consorting with the likes of him. Of course, I concluded that you must be working undercover.'

I laugh but admit to nothing. While I trust Anastasia and value her discretion, it's always wiser to keep someone guessing, even if it's your closest companion.

'My dear princess, if only I could enlist you in an adventure for old times' sake,' I say. 'But I'm afraid it's nothing as exciting as that.'

'Don't treat me like a fool, Kim,' she scolds me. 'Since when has the secret service started spying on British military officers, and a brigadier at that? I'd say you must have something serious up your sleeve.'

'Just a routine investigation,' I answer, knowing she won't be easily dissuaded.

'Is he still a supporter of Germany?' she asks. 'I heard that he was trying to get some of the top Nazi officers pardoned, as part of a group that wanted to forestall the executions after the judgements at Nuremberg.'

'Could be,' I say. 'You seem to know a lot about him. Did the waiters at the Gym tell you all this?'

She smiles and gives me a coy look. 'Let's just say that I try to keep myself well informed. And I think I should warn you, he's a dangerous man.'

'Thank you,' I reply.

'No, I'm serious, Kim. I'm worried about you,' she says.

'Why would you worry about me?' I ask.

'Well, for one thing, you're not as young as you used to be,' Anastasia says.

'That's true,' I agree, watching the trees glide past the car window.

'And I've been your friend long enough, so I can be honest with you,' she says. 'You're drinking too much. It makes you sloppy and careless.'

I keep silent, knowing that she's right but not wanting to acknowledge her remark.

'You'll get annoyed with me, of course,' she says, 'but I think it's time for you to hang up your boots.'

'A short while ago you were asking me to include you in one last adventure,' I remind her.

'Wishful thinking,' Anastasia admits. 'I knew when to stop, and you should too.'

'As I said,' I tell her. 'I'm on my way out. This will be my last hurrah.'

'Bromley-Pugh is a wicked, sadistic man who has surrounded himself with vicious louts who wouldn't think twice about breaking your skull and leaving you to die like a dog in a ditch.' Anastasia puts a hand on my arm. 'You don't need to prove anything with these men. They'll be out of India soon enough.'

'Maybe not soon enough,' I say.

14

For most of my life, I've thought of myself as being invincible. It's only during the last few years that doubts have crept in, and I've begun to wonder if I'm now a vulnerable old fart. Srinivas's warning and my conversation with Anastasia have left me unsettled. More than the fact that someone is intent on killing me, it's disconcerting to know that I am being watched and others know my identity and whereabouts. I feel utterly exposed, as if a mask has been ripped off my face. Secrecy is a shield and I've always prided myself on being able to hide in the margins but increasingly I find that I am the one who is unaware of the threats that surround me. Instead of always being a step ahead of the truth, I've fallen behind. Anastasia is correct when she says I've grown careless and after her warning, I resolve to cover my tracks.

Settling my bill at the Maidens, I check out by 5 p.m., explaining to the manager that my plans have suddenly changed, and I need to travel to Bombay. He agrees to hold onto any messages or telegrams that arrive in my name, and I tell him that I will send someone to collect them in a few days' time. Though I ask for a taxi to drive me to the Railway Station, once I get there, I hop into a cycle rickshaw and ask the driver to take me to Chandni Chowk. Because of the recent troubles, a lot of police are on the streets but I am able to enter a narrow gully near the flower market unobserved, carrying my own bags. A decrepit haveli, which has been divided into a dozen or more smaller flats, stands at the end of the lane. By the time I reach the top of a narrow staircase, I am out of breath and wait a minute before knocking on the door.

It takes a while for someone to answer and I wonder, briefly, if the flat may have been abandoned. I haven't been here for three years. Eventually, though, I hear a shuffling sound inside and the door opens a crack, still secured by a chain.

'Who is it? What do you want?' a boy asks in Urdu.

'I'm a friend, here to see Idrak Hussein,' I reply, keeping out of his line of vision.

There is a pause. 'He isn't here.'

'Are you his son?' I ask. 'Yusuf?'

'Who are you?' comes the reply.

'Qasim Khan, a friend from Lahore,' I answer.

Again, there is a long pause, until I finally hear the chain rattle and the door opens outward onto the landing. As soon as the boy sees me, though, he tries to shut it again. But before he can, I wedge my suitcase into the gap. He backs away in terror as I enter the room.

'Don't worry, I won't harm you,' I assure him. 'Are you alone?'

The young man has the beginnings of a beard and bad skin, with pimples on his nose and cheeks. He looks no older than sixteen.

'Is anyone else here?' I repeat the question.

'My mother is inside. She's sick with fever.'

'Then, I won't disturb her,' I say. 'When is Hussein Sahib coming back?'

'We don't know,' he replies, reaching out and bracing himself with one hand on the wall, as if he might faint.

The windowless entry hall in which we are standing is a cramped space, containing two chairs and a steel almirah. The boy's lips are trembling, as if he wants to speak but can't form the words.

'Where has Hussein Sahib gone?' I demand.

'We don't know,' says the boy, finally finding his tongue. 'Abba went out four days ago to get some rations and he hasn't come back.'

'You didn't search for him?' I ask.

'There has been a lot of violence...a riot,' the boy says. 'We were afraid. My mother wouldn't let me go out.'

Pulling my suitcase and duffel bag inside, I close the door behind me then gesture for the boy to lead the way into the main room off the entry hall. It looks exactly the same as the last time I was here, simply furnished, with a low divan and two armchairs upholstered in red velvet. A threadbare carpet covers the centre of the floor. The curtains, made of pleated green fabric, are drawn and the lights are off. A stale odour of perfume and spices lingers in the air.

'Yusuf, you don't recognize me,' I say.

The boy looks puzzled.

'I'm Qasim, your father's friend. I stayed here three years ago for several months. You were half your height back then. We flew kites together from your roof. Do you remember that?'

He stares at me, confused and suspicious.

'But you're an Angrez,' he says, eyeing my clothes and cleanshaven face.

'I've had to change my appearance,' I explain, 'because of the trouble. But I can prove who I am.'

'How?' the boy asks.

He still isn't convinced though I can tell he is studying me and trying to recall the sound of my voice.

'Last time I stayed in that room over there,' I say, pointing to one of the doors behind the divan. It is closed. 'I bought you a game. Snakes and Ladders. We played for hours. Do you remember?'

The boy nods and a nervous smile creases his lips.

'Is the game still here?'

Stepping across, I open the door and see that the room is cluttered with stacks of books in Urdu and Farsi. On the top of one shelf, I spot the flat box, with a colourful cover. The boy steps forward and takes it down, opening it to show me the board and dice. Seeing this, I mumble a blessing in Urdu, 'Allah aap ko sehtmand rakhe.'

Yusuf has tears in his eyes.

'I need a place to stay, again,' I explain. 'First, I'll get you and your mother some food, then I'll go and search for your father. Please tell your mother I'm here to help.'

∞

Hussein Sahib is someone I've known since the 1930s, when I used to come to Delhi more often than I've done in recent years. He is a linguist and poet, whose pen name is Yaqzan, which means the awakened or enlightened one. We first met when I was trying to untangle coded signals from an Ossetian double agent who conveyed his messages in Farsi verse. We knew who he was and some of his contacts but neither I nor my colleagues in the secret service were able to decipher his poems, which appeared in a fortnightly journal published in Quetta, before the earthquake flattened that city. Yaqzan was one of the few literati in Delhi who was fluent in Farsi and I was deputed to solicit his assistance.

Back then, Yaqzan was unmarried and a carefree, high-spirited young man. We hit it off immediately and I spent many hours with him, as he puzzled over the couplets that contained secret information on Russian agents. Eventually, he cracked the code, discovering that the poems were plagiarized from the works of sixteenth-century Sufi poets. The key lay in the words that were added to each line. With Hussein's help we were able to expose three Russians who were operating as traders in Baluchistan, crossing back and forth across the border.

After that, whenever I visited Delhi, Yaqzan insisted that I stay with him. He is a lively conversationalist who has an opinion on every topic and loves to debate politics, poetry, or the comparative beauty of film actresses like Sulochana and Devaki Rani.

Leaving my bags in my room, I head out of the house and bring fresh rotis and a kullad of dal from a dhaba nearby, as well as some vegetables. Tamanna Begum, Hussein's wife, emerges from her room and I insist that she and Yusuf eat a little before I set out to look for Yaqzan. Though she seems to be in shock, Tamanna recognizes me and tearfully pleads with me to find her husband. The fact that Yaqzan disappeared four days ago during the riots, gives me a sense of foreboding and I am not hopeful.

It has grown dark outside and a few streetlights are burning. At a crossing near the flower market, four constables are standing together on duty. Two of them are Sikhs and the other two, Hindus. When I approach them, they look at me with suspicion, unsure of what a white man is doing out at this time of night. Greeting them politely in Hindustani, I explain that I have just arrived in Delhi and am searching for a friend of mine who has gone missing during the recent violence here in Chandni Chowk.

The constables are unhelpful and direct me to the main kotwali. When I get there, the police station is crowded, full of men who have been arrested for rioting and other crimes. When I finally find an officer who is willing to answer my questions, he looks as if he hasn't slept in a week.

'I'm searching for a missing person,' I explain.

'So is everyone else,' he replies in a humourless voice. 'It seems as if all of the inhabitants of this city have gone missing.'

'Where should I start looking?'

'Perhaps in a mortuary,' he says. 'Was your friend a Hindu or a Muslim?'

'Would it matter?' I ask.

'Not if he's dead,' says the officer rubbing the stubble on his chin.

'Where is the nearest mortuary?'

'There's one near Sabzi Mandi,' he informs me. 'But I wouldn't go there, if I was you. It would be better not to find your friend. In this weather, even with refrigeration, a body begins to putrefy within a few hours. You could ask at the Police and Civil Hospital, which is nearby. They might have names.'

I take a tonga to the hospital. By now, it's past eight o'clock. The street outside is empty, though there is no curfew, but inside patients and family members are sleeping on the floor. A squalid place, it smells of urine and phenyl. Eventually, I find a nurse and ask if they admitted any injured after the riots. She looks at me with a cold stare.

'No,' she replies. 'If we had kept any Muslims here, the mobs would have found them and they would have been killed. The only survivors might be at Lady Willingdon Hospital. They have "native wards",' she explains, using the English phrase. 'Or you could try St. Stephen's in Tis Hazari. That's closer.'

By this time, I have given up hope, yet I decide to take a tonga to St. Stephen's. The old stone building with brick archways looks deserted but when I enter, two nurses are standing near the reception area whispering to each other. This hospital is much cleaner than the other but it feels sterile and gloomy. When I approach the sisters, one of them tells me that visiting hours are over. I explain my reason for being here and they look at each other uncertainly.

Asking me to wait, one of them goes off down the hall. A short while later, a white woman appears wearing a doctor's coat with a stethoscope draped around her neck. A missionary by the look of her, she has grey hair and wears round spectacles with thick black frames. Speaking in English, I explain that I am searching for a friend named Idrak Hussein and I wonder if they have any Muslim patients injured in the riots.

'Are you a family member?' she enquires.

'No, just a close friend, though I've come on behalf of his family.'

Glancing around, the doctor whispers, 'Come with me.'

Leading me back down the dimly lit hall, she climbs a brick staircase to the first floor, where we make our way through another hall to a locked door with a sign that reads: No Admittance. The doctor opens it with a key that she takes from the pocket of her coat. Inside is a ward with twenty beds, as well as half a dozen mattresses on the floor. A single lightbulb is burning in a socket on one wall. One of the patients groans and there is a strong stench of human bodies. The room has no ventilation, and I realize immediately that these patients have been locked up for their own safety.

A nurse emerges from the shadows and the doctor speaks to her, then takes a clipboard and runs a finger down a list of names.

'Hussein?' she says.

'Idrak Hussein,' I say.

'No,' she answers. 'I was mistaken, there's nobody here by that name.'

'Would there be anyone named Yaqzan?' I ask.

She checks again, then nods, leading me to a steel-frame bed, painted white. The man who lies there has his head bandaged and both of his arms appear to be injured, but there is something familiar about him that gives me hope.

'He was unconscious for three days and only began to speak this morning,' the doctor says, putting her hand on his knee. The figure stirs under the sheet.

'Yaqzan,' I whisper, leaning close to his battered face.

'Kaun?' he mumbles.
'It's me,' I say. 'Kim.'

∞

Two days later, I bring Yaqzan home. He is still badly bruised, and one of his arms is in plaster, but the doctor assures me that he will recover from the concussion and other injuries. Not wanting to draw attention to his return, I wait until dark and hire a taxi from the hospital to Chandni Chowk. Though he is fully conscious now, I have to support most of his weight as we make our way up the stairs. His wife and son greet him with tears in their eyes. Laying him on the divan in the main room and propping him up against several pillows, I make sure the front door is latched. The city has been relatively peaceful for the last few days, but I know it is only a brief reprieve.

Though he is still in pain and his speech is slurred, Yaqzan is full of questions and holds my hand as he speaks, asking when I arrived in Delhi and the purpose of my visit. I tell him vaguely that I am here on work and explain that I need to stay for a couple of weeks. He seems pleased and asks his wife to prepare his hookah. When it is ready, Tamanna hands me the coiled pipe fitted with an ivory mouthpiece, yellowed by tobacco fumes. Holding it to his mouth, I watch as he sucks on it gratefully, the water bubbling inside the brass vessel. Its smoke is fragrant, with a hint of apricots.

Exhaling, Yaqzan mutters, 'So many medicines they gave me in the hospital, and this is the only drug I wanted.'

We don't speak about his injuries or his ordeal until the next evening, when I ask him if he remembers what happened. Yaqzan says the only thing he can recall was leaving the house and seeing a crowd of men coming down the street shouting abuse.

'I tried to turn back but something struck me on the head and I have no memory after that...nothing at all,' he explains, with a shudder. 'They must have thought I was dead.'

'Alhamdulillah, you are fortunate to have survived,' I say.

'It is like 1857 all over again,' he says. 'But instead of fighting the British we are fighting ourselves.'

'Do you think you'll leave Delhi?' I ask.

Despite his bruised face, I can see him give me an incredulous look.

'How can I leave? Where would I go?' Yaqzan says.

'I could arrange for you and your family to move to Lahore,' I suggest.

'Bhai, Kim, you've brought me back from the dead,' he complains. 'Now, don't break my heart. How could I abandon Dilli?'

'This violence is likely to continue for a while and once the British are gone, who knows what will happen?' I reply.

'Stop,' he says, trying to lift a hand. 'I will never leave this city.'

He then recites two couplets by Mir.

Dilli jo ek sheher tha, aalam mein intekhaab
Rehte thay muntakhab hi jahaan rozgaar ke

Us ko falak ne loot ke veeraan kar diya
Hum rehne waale hain usi ujde dayaar ke

Delhi, a city once renowned throughout the world
Where the rare and chosen few made their home

Looted by destiny, it lies abandoned and in ruins
I belong to that ravaged and forsaken city

'If only people quoted poetry instead of shouting slogans,' I say.

He winces at my remark and then begins to cough, a painful hacking that comes from deep inside his chest. Two of his ribs are cracked. I bring him a glass of water to drink but he waves it aside. 'Don't you have anything stronger?' he asks.

'You must be feeling better,' I joke.

'Or worse,' he said. 'It will help me endure the pain.'

From my suitcase, I fetch my bottle of whisky, and Tamanna Begum, who has been listening from the kitchen, brings two glass tumblers, though she gives us a disapproving look. Yaqzan doesn't drink very often but when he does, I know he's in a melancholy mood. As I pour us each a generous peg, he quotes Mirza Ghalib, inserting my name instead of the 'saqi' or cupbearer:

Peeta hun Kim, gham-e-duniya bhool jaane ke liye
Jannat mein kahan gam hai, vahan peene me maza nahi

I drink wine, Kim, to forget the travails and sorrows of this earth,
In paradise there are no fears or worries. Hence, no pleasure in drink.

He smiles at me with his broken teeth and swollen jaw, as I raise the tumbler to his lips. 'Today, you are, indeed, my saqi!'

15

The following morning, when I go across to the Maidens to collect my mail, I have changed my costume and complexion sufficiently so that nobody at the hotel recognizes who I am. Yaqzan has loaned me a grey cotton salwar-kameez and a cream-coloured turban, in which I look every bit like an elderly chaprasi, the faithful retainer of a sahib. When I present the manager with a note from Captain Townsend, requesting that the bearer be given whatever communications have arrived in his name, he hands me three envelopes and a pink telegraph form.

Returning to Yaqzan's rooms, I decipher MacNeil's cable in which he tells me that they suspect that the man who tried to kill me in Lahore was a European. He doesn't say how he learned this but orders me to return to Lahore as soon as possible. After reading his message, I open the three envelopes. The first is sealed with an imperial crest and contains a letter from the Viceroy's personal secretary informing me that on the recommendation of the Governor of Punjab, Captain Townsend is to be awarded a Kaiser-e-Hind bronze medal. Furthermore, as the government in Delhi will soon be moving up to Simla for the summer season, a ceremony is scheduled there at the Viceregal Lodge on 12 May 1947 at 4 p.m. The second letter is an anxious note from Anastasia, asking me why I haven't been in touch and saying that she hopes I am safe. She also reminds me that I still owe her a full account of what happened with the Belgian girl in Murree. The last letter I open is from Brigadier Bromley-Pugh, KGM, OBE. He asks me to meet him at No. 12 Cornwallis Road on 26 April, at 2.30 p.m., which, when I check my watch, is less than three hours from now.

This isn't the first time I have ignored MacNeil's orders and as I make up my mind to call on Sir Denys, I tell myself that I can always claim that I didn't collect the telegram until it was too late. If I don't show up for my meeting with the Brigadier, it will mean I have wasted hours of my time insinuating myself into his circle.

A good wash with Lifebuoy soap, under a tap at Yaqzan's flat, removes whatever colour there was on my face and I dress in the few remaining clean clothes I possess—a pair of white drill trousers and a drab cotton bush shirt. Summer has begun in Delhi and, as a white man, the only thing I lack is a pith helmet. The one drawback of this costume is that there is nowhere to hide a revolver on my person, so I must go unarmed. From Chandni Chowk to Cornwallis Road, a tonga will take three quarters of an hour and I time my departure so that I will arrive roughly five minutes late.

The midday heat is oppressive, and the horse is soon lathered with sweat, though the tongawallah assures me that he is a young gelding with plenty of strength and endurance. After winding our way through the crowded lanes of Daryaganj towards Ajmeri Gate, the congested streets of the old city finally open out into the broad avenues of New Delhi. At this hour of the day there is very little traffic, except for a few military jeeps and a battered Humber saloon, driven by an elderly Sikh, who toots his claxon impatiently, as he overtakes my tonga. Most of the vehicles on the road are bicycles ridden by clerks and cashiers, heading home from their desks in government offices. The radial road we pass along is well shaded with neem trees. For this brief stretch there is some semblance of coolth as the bright sunlight slants through the branches overhead.

Most of the bungalows on Cornwallis Road seem to be the official residences of military commanders as well as a few senior civil servants. Number 12 has a modest gate with no nameplate and a single military policeman on sentry duty, who stops us and asks my name. He then promptly opens the gates and lets us drive in under a low portico at the front of a gracious bungalow, framed by two large ficus trees with dense foliage. The tongawallah agrees to wait when I tell him that I won't be more than an hour. By then the horse should be rested and watered. As I get down, the animal eyes me with a look of premonition. Mahbub Ali always swore that horses possess psychic powers when it comes to danger and deceit.

Two liveried servants open the front door for me and three ceiling fans swirl the shadows in the hall. One of the brigadier's

ADCs, whose name I can't recall, greets me with a firm handshake. He leads me into a drawing room furnished with the spare, masculine aesthetics of a regimental mess. The officer asks me to take a seat, while one of the servants pads in with a glass of water, which I drain in a single draught.

Three minutes later, Sir Denys enters, accompanied by another officer whom I don't recognize. Both men are unsmiling and tense. After a hurried greeting, the Brigadier gestures for me to take a seat and launches into a short speech about the noble legacy of the British empire and the need for unwavering fealty to the King Emperor and his dominions.

'This is a critical point in history when the true mettle of our race will be tested in the crucible of adversity,' he declares, with a dramatic thrust of his jaw. 'Townsend, I must ask you to give us your solemn word, as a gentleman: whatever conversations take place within this room will not be repeated outside. We need your complete assurance that you will not speak of this to anyone,' the Brigadier insists.

I look at the three men with an innocent expression.

'Sir, I have no intention of betraying confidences,' I reply.

'Do you swear this, on your honour, as a God-fearing Englishman!' he demands.

'Of course,' I reply, startled by the intensity of his words.

'We need someone like you, who is not a serving officer but has a military background. A man of action and discretion. We represent the only hope for the future of British rule in India. Our aim is to restore the dignity of the King Emperor's realm.'

Though I am tempted to ask if His Highness is aware of their intentions, I bite my tongue and simply nod my head as he continues.

'We are a brotherhood of officers committed to our sworn duty to the empire, both as soldiers and subjects of the crown, who have banded together in a crusade to oppose native rule.'

'Well, I'm glad to know that someone is standing up to these Congress buggers,' I interject, when he pauses long enough for me to get in a word.

'Precisely! There are too many weak-kneed politicians and bureaucrats who want to cut their losses and go home. We mustn't let them surrender India as if it were an onerous burden they would rather not bear,' Sir Denys exclaims, his face flushed and beads of sweat trickling from his brow.

'But, if I may, sir. How do you propose to set a new course?' I enquire. 'From what little I know the die has been cast.'

The Brigadier's blue eyes flash for a moment, as if he still doesn't trust me, before he abruptly gets to his feet.

'If you'll excuse me,' he says. 'I have another appointment, but Major Stapleton here will brief you on the plan that he and some of the others have put together. It's imperative that I should not be directly involved, though I can assure you I will do whatever I can to support your efforts. Should you agree to help us, Townsend, from here on in, it will be better if you and I don't meet again. But good show and good luck!'

This time, Sir Denys shakes my hand vigorously before he and the ADC march out of the room, their jackboots clattering on the terrazzo floor. Once they are gone, I offer Major Stapleton a smoke. Though he declines, I light one for myself.

Running a pale hand through his treacle-blonde hair, which is noticeably thin, Stapleton looks as if he is more nervous than I. While they seem to mean business, the whole thing strikes me as an amateurish plot. The major's eyes are a soapy-grey colour and his teeth protrude slightly beneath his upper lip, which bears a downy moustache that droops over the corners of his mouth. Though he is in uniform, it doesn't fit well, his olive-green jacket bunching up at the shoulders.

'Captain Townsend, I must impress upon you the importance of keeping this entire discussion confidential....' he begins.

Raising my right hand, as if I am swearing an oath, I interrupt him. 'Not to worry, Major. I'm on your side.'

'Very good,' he nods. 'Essentially, we want to create a political crisis in which it will be quite impossible for the Viceroy to hand over power, a real jolt to the system that will give every member of parliament second thoughts.'

He pauses and glances around the room, as if to make sure nobody else is present.

'Go on, Stapleton,' I coax him. 'I'm listening.'

'We are hoping that you can help us carry out a secret mission to assassinate some of the top Congress leaders and make it appear to have been orchestrated by supporters of the Muslim League.' He speaks rapidly, as if he's memorized these lines.

Though I have prepared myself for something like this, hearing the words spoken in plain English, makes me wince. The idea that army officers would stoop to the level of anarchists, fomenting violence and bloodshed, when India is already on the brink of chaos, seems the most cynical and cold-blooded conspiracy anyone might hatch.

'Brilliant!' I exclaim, trying not to reveal my true emotions.

Stapleton smiles for the first time, then nods appreciatively. 'Thank you, Townsend. I think it is the only way forward, under the circumstances.'

'But how are you planning to carry out the assassinations?' I ask. 'Snipers? Poison?'

'No,' he shakes his head. 'We're thinking of detonating a bomb.'

'Ah! A bomb!' I react, trying to sound enthusiastic.

'One of our team is an engineer with the Madras Sappers. He's a demolition expert who assures us that he can build a bomb with material that won't be traced to the British Army, some sort of German plastique that was salvaged after the North African campaign, along with some Italian detonators.' Stapleton stops himself, though he's obviously enamoured of the explosive technology.

'And where and how are you planning to put this bomb in place?' I ask.

'That's where you come into the picture,' he replies. 'We need someone to recruit and supervise a dependable native, who can be taught to set things up. There will be a timing device, of course. Our primary target is Nehru.'

'Not Mr Gandhi?' I ask.

'We've debated that issue amongst ourselves. If we can kill

Gandhi and Nehru in one go, of course, that would be ideal. But if we have to choose one of them, Nehru is the more critical target. He's slated to become the first PM and he's got a close rapport with Mountbatten. If he and half a dozen others are blown up, you can be sure that the Viceroy will get cold feet.'

'More than likely, everything will blow up,' I remark.

'Exactly,' Stapleton agrees. 'And there will be no choice but to declare martial law.'

'Once the army takes charge, they'll set things straight!' I predict, hardly able to believe that these are my words. The plan is as audacious as it is misconceived and utterly stupid.

'I'm so glad you agree with our logic, Townsend,' the Major declares, looking relieved. 'I hope that means that you're ready to help us with this.'

'How could I refuse, when the future of British India depends upon it?'

Stapleton seems gullible enough and I begin to prepare myself for the difficult yet subtle task of collaborating with traitors while gathering enough evidence to expose their conspiracy. On the other hand, reminding myself of MacNeil's message, I wonder if I'm walking into a trap and perhaps these men intend to murder me, though if that is their intention, I'm not sure why they haven't done it already.

'On the eighth of May, there's going to be a Congress rally at Edward Park, opposite the Railway Station. It's also known by the natives as Dangal Maidan because the local wrestlers exercise there. Nehru is scheduled to address the gathering. The rally is illegal, so the police won't be providing security, just keeping an eye on the crowd,' the Major explains. 'The best thing would be for you to recruit a Muslim who can be trusted to plant the bomb discreetly and not open his mouth. Don't tell him what we're planning, of course, just say he'll be given instructions when the time comes.'

'I know just the man. A Hazara sirdar who's accompanied me on my expeditions. Loyal to the bone! He'll do whatever I ask,' I assure him.

'Splendid,' says Stapleton. 'That's exactly what we were hoping for, knowing your ability to lead men into tight places and come out of it alive.'

'Compared to the Mustagh Pass, this will be a walk in the park,' I reply.

'I say, did you actually cross the pass?' Stapleton eagerly wants to know.

'By the same route that Younghusband took but in the opposite direction, which is a good deal more difficult, I might add,' I tell him, while mentally warning myself not to embellish too much. At this stage, I wouldn't want any of my lies exposed.

'How long will you be in Delhi?' he asks.

'Another two weeks,' I tell him.

'Perfect,' he says. 'The sooner we set things in motion the better. Are you still staying at the Maidens?'

'No, I've moved in with a friend. But I think it would be best, after this meeting, if we didn't have any direct communications. Perhaps we could work out a dead drop somewhere,' I propose.

'Absolutely,' says Stapleton. 'Good thinking, Townsend. Wouldn't want anyone intercepting our messages.'

'I would suggest that you can leave written instructions for me at Empire Stores in Connaught Circus. The message can be placed in a narrow gap between the shelves, immediately to the right of where they stock packets of Darjeeling tea. You'll find it easily enough. Once you leave a message there, make a diagonal chalk mark on the front window frame of Wenger's confectionery to signal that the dead drop is active. I'll check it every day.'

The Major nods appreciatively, as he jots down the details in a small notebook that he takes from the inner pocket of his jacket.

'Should we use a code?' he asks.

'No need,' I say, 'as long as we keep things brief and to the point. Essentially, you can inform me when and where to have the bomb collected. And, of course, any other information, as necessary.'

'All of that will be explained,' he says.

'Perfect!' I reply. 'Then, I'll take my leave.'

'Thank you, Townsend. We're most grateful to you. I'm glad you're on board.'

We shake hands and Stapleton escorts me to the front door, which the servants throw open as we approach. Outside, the air is still as hot as a blast furnace. My tonga is waiting in the shade under one of the ficus trees. Climbing aboard, I signal to the driver that we can depart.

'Back to Chandni Chowk?' he asks.

'No,' I say. 'Alipore Road. Lunagarh House.'

16

Five and a half years ago, in October 1941, I was summoned to Delhi by Srinivas Iyer. Until then, I had been communicating with him mostly through an intermediary in Lahore to whom I dictated rambling and mostly innocuous reports about various incidents and individuals that might have been of interest to the ISS. My covert amanuensis was Sheila Ghulam-Massey, who excelled at shorthand as well as badminton, of which she was the Punjab Women's Singles Champion. Srinivas introduced me to her when I complained that writing reports was not my strong point. I've never been good at committing my thoughts to paper and much to the dismay of my masters at Xavier's, I hated reading as well. Tell me a good story and I'll listen for hours but don't ever ask me to open a book. Other than Urdu couplets, there's something about literature that strains my eyes and mind after forty or fifty words. The same goes for a pen or a pencil. My fingers cramp up the minute I try to compose a sentence, though I can express myself verbally without restraint.

Sheila ended up marrying an American professor at Forman Christian College and losing her security clearance, but that's a tale for another day. She is the one who passed on word from Srinivas that I should travel to Delhi immediately. Having just bought my Norton, I decided to drive the Grand Trunk Road, stopping overnight at a dak bungalow near Jullundur. Motorcycling in North India in October is sheer delight, when the air is clear and cool but not yet freezing and the sugar cane has yet to be cut, so the roads are relatively empty of bullock carts. The Norton behaved beautifully, chugging along at a comfortable 50 mph.

Srinivas and I were still getting to know each other at the time, and he had a somewhat formal manner that I attributed to his South Indian roots. We met at a bungalow on Aurangzeb Road, which was being used as a safe house in those days. When I arrived on my motorcycle, the military policemen on duty wouldn't let me inside until Srinivas came out and persuaded them to open the gate. I noticed immediately how they treated him with disdain even though they obeyed his instructions. While some of the senior officers in the secret service admired Srinivas's intellectual acumen, having recruited him straight out of Oxford, he suffered a lot of derision and prejudice from the other ranks.

As soon as we sat down, Srinivas got straight to the point. He wanted to know if I had any connections with the royal families in the Punjab. I told him that the only associations I had to any of the princely states was Lunagarh, through Anastasia. Srinivas then explained that he needed me to keep an eye on some of the younger royals living in Lahore, particularly two nephews of the Nawab of Bahawalpur and three minor princes from Patiala. Both states had large properties in Lahore and being from royal households they socialized mostly amongst themselves. In the elaborate and arcane ranking of princely states that offered fealty to the King Emperor, Bahawalpur and Patiala were entitled to 17- and 19-gun salutes respectively, which placed them high up the ladder but not quite on par with more important states like Kashmir and Gwalior, which were granted 21-gun salutes. Srinivas explained this briefly and suggested that it had always been a source of some resentment towards the British.

He then went on to tell me how he had received information that some of the younger princes in the Punjab seemed to have come under the influence of a German agent operating in Lahore. His identity had still not been established but it seemed that the younger royals were being groomed by the Nazis with promises that when Hitler won the war—which was a very real possibility in 1941—they would be rewarded by the Führer with greater influence and power than the British had bestowed upon them. Maharaja Bhupinder Singh of Patiala, who died in 1938, had ten wives and eighty-eight offspring. The Nawab of Bahawalpur, Sir Sadiq Muhammad Khan V, had only six children though his extended household consisted of numerous cousins, second cousins, and cousins once removed, all of whom felt a certain level of aggrieved entitlement, which the Germans hoped to parlay into an alliance with the Axis powers. There was even said to be a secret wing of the Hitlerjugend whose members consisted of a clique of disaffected teenaged royals.

Obviously, my job was to investigate the veracity of these reports and try to discover the identity of the German agent. On the face of it, the assignment that Srinivas offered me in 1941 seemed to be a relatively simple task but as I became enmeshed in it, Operation Übermensch (Srinivas couldn't resist paying homage to Nietzsche), kept me busy throughout the war. Even today, the wide-ranging conspiracy we uncovered continues to throw up a variety of loose ends and unconnected dots. Though Hitler was defeated in 1945, much to the disappointment of the discontented princelings, a network of Nazi sympathizers continues to operate in India. Sir Denys Bromley-Pugh and his brownshirts are only one part of the puzzle.

Juggling my commitment to the Intelligence Bureau in Lahore as well as the ISS was a challenge during the war but, fortunately, I have never had to keep office hours and the nature of my work means that I spend most of my time unsupervised. Nevertheless, if I was heading out of Lahore, MacNeil expected me to inform him and explain why and where I was going. Trips to Delhi were always relatively easy to justify but when I eventually had to make visits to Bahawalpur and Patiala, it required elaborate alibis.

Befriending the young royals in Lahore was not particularly difficult because they all had a keen interest in horseflesh, and I was able to fall back on everything that Mahbub Ali had taught me in my younger years. Posing as a horse trader was second nature to me and I still had contacts in the NWFP and Baluchistan, which allowed me to procure several handsome hirzai, a much sought-after breed developed by crossing an Arab stallion with a Baloch mare. Both nephews of the Nawab of Bahawalpur and the princes from Patiala were members of the Lahore Polo Club, where they spent a good deal of time. It soon became clear to me that the German agent was also a member of the club and there were several possible candidates, all of them Europeans with dubious pedigrees. Any Germans, Austrians, and Italians who happened to be in India when Britain entered the war, had been rounded up and placed in prisoner of war camps in Dehradun or Poona. But there were plenty of other foreigners drifting about.

As a native horse trader, I was permitted to hang around the stables at the club, though the rest of the facilities were out of bounds for me. Nevertheless, I was able to gather a good deal of information from the syces, who sat together and gossiped about their employers. Because of the war, most of the British officers who would have patronized the club, were off fighting in North Africa or on the Burma Front, so there wasn't a lot of activity in Lahore, at least not on the surface.

One of my prime suspects was a Rhodesian businessman named Gareth Dennison who had been living in India for the past ten or twelve years. Among other things, he owned an import–export company that traded in ivory and semi-precious stones. Dennison had three horses stabled at the Polo Club. His syce was a taciturn Shia from Multan, who revealed very little about his master, except that Dennison was divorced and in addition to horses, he was a collector of antique firearms. One day, however, he let slip that the Rhodesian was heading off to Patiala, accompanying two of the young princes. They had invited him to inspect the royal armoury, which contained a number of rare weapons. I decided that there might be some value in following along.

Rather than going as a horse trader, I decided it would be better if I travelled to Patiala as Michael Evans, a journalist with *The Statesman*. No disguise was necessary. Dennison and the princes travelled by train, using one of Patiala's royal carriages, while I got a berth in a second-class bogie. At Rajpura, just before Ambala, where the branch line cuts off to Patiala, I got down from the train with my bag and strolled along the platform to where the royal carriage was being detached. Dennison had stepped outside to have a smoke, since tobacco was forbidden in the Patiala carriage. I greeted him and asked for a light, after which we chatted for a bit. When I mentioned that I was going to Patiala, he suggested that the princes might allow me to join them in their private carriage. A special engine had been arranged to take us the fifteen miles from Rajpura. Soon enough, I found myself ensconced in a very comfortable saloon, with velvet upholstery and a crystal chandelier. The two princes were in their mid-twenties, tall, strapping young Sikhs with a haughty manner, though they had cordially invited me aboard when Dennison introduced us.

During the course of the thirty-minute journey, I told enough yarns to keep them amused and when we arrived at Patiala, they invited me to join them for lunch at the palace. I accepted, saying that I was going to leave my bag at the Circuit House, and I would drop by around one o'clock. So far, there was nothing suspicious about Dennison, who seemed to be an affable man without any clear political leanings. Though my plan seemed to be going smoothly, it was about to be derailed.

When I showed up for lunch, the two princes and Dennison were sitting outside on the lawns under a gulmohur tree drinking beer. Also in attendance was a man I hadn't expected to be there, Dr Victor Joubert, a South African veterinary surgeon who had a practice in Lahore and was much in demand for his expertise in horse-breeding and equine diseases. I recognized him immediately, but more importantly, he recognized me. When Dennison introduced me as Michael Evans from *The Statesman*, I could see the look of suppressed hostility in Joubert's gaze. He said nothing as we shook hands but excused himself a short while later and did not join us for lunch. Though I knew my cover was blown, I stayed on and kept up my banter with the princes, who had no idea what was going on. At around 4 p.m., when I took my leave, a black Vauxhall 12 saloon was waiting to take me back to the Circuit House. When I got into the back seat, however, Joubert was there with a small but very serious looking Beretta semi-automatic in his hand.

I now knew, with complete surety, the identity of the Nazi agent though it didn't look as if I would be able to convey this evidence to Srinivas or anyone else. Having no choice, I settled into my seat as the driver headed out of the palace gates. We didn't speak for several minutes until it was clear that we weren't headed to the Circuit House.

'May I ask where we're going?' I enquired, giving Joubert a tight smile.

His pistol remained pointed at my navel.

'What are you doing here?' the veterinarian asked, ignoring my question.

'Sightseeing,' I replied. 'This is my first visit to Patiala.'

Joubert moistened his colourless lips with the tip of his tongue and shook his bald head. His eyes were grey, the colour of tarnished silver.

'So, you're still with the secret service, O'Hara?' he asked.

'No, not at all. The Great Game is over. Hadn't you heard?' I answered, trying to act as if all of this was a misunderstanding.

'Stop being glib,' he snapped, his South African accent clearly discernible and adding a note of menace to his words.

The first time I met Joubert was in Swat, where an outbreak of equine influenza had infected most of the horses in the Wali's stables. This would have been 1923 or '24. I had driven up from Peshawar because there were rumours of a Bolshevik agent having crossed over the Hindu Kush, which turned out to be a false lead. Joubert was clearly not a socialist and we had several conversations, mostly about horses. Later on, he and I crossed paths occasionally in Lahore, where I eventually earned his enmity when I discovered that he was having a homosexual affair with a young Muslim League politician. It caused something of a scandal. Joubert himself was never named, while his lover was jailed for sodomy. I regretted the whole affair, and it wouldn't have become public knowledge except for the IG at the time, a straight-laced Yorkshireman named Withers, who decided to make a point of identifying the young freedom fighter. Joubert knew I was the source and never forgave me. Nevertheless, until this moment, I wouldn't have guessed that the horse doctor was working for the Germans.

'I hadn't pegged you as a Nazi agent,' I said. 'Do you really think these rajkumars will suck up to Hitler?'

The muscles around his eyes twitched, which confirmed my suspicions.

'Why would you accuse me of something like that?' he asked. 'You've always traded in lies, O'Hara, like the true bazaar rat that you are.'

'I should have known a Boer would have German sympathies, even if he has a French sounding name,' I said. 'Or are you doing it just for the money?'

'Not all of us are cheap bumboys for the Brits, like you,' Joubert said with a sneer. 'What is it that you work for, O'Hara? Honour? Duty? God Save the King? Do you really think the English care about your loyalty? To them, you're just a stinking Irish hoer.'

'At least I haven't pawned my soul to the Führer,' I replied. 'I bet they promised to tattoo a swastika on your ass. Or is it those Fritzies in Lederhosen that turn you on?'

'Be careful,' he said. 'I'll put a bullet in you sooner rather than later.'

'If it's inevitable, let's get it over with,' I said. His finger was on the Beretta's trigger but I knew he wasn't going to kill me in the car. Too much of a mess. He would stop somewhere and push me out, then shoot me in the back. My left hand was about eight inches from the pistol, but I didn't want to take any chances.

'You still haven't told me where we're going,' I said.

'You'll find out soon enough,' he answered.

After that, we both fell silent. A few minutes later, we joined the Grand Trunk Road and as we passed through Ambala, I wondered if I would ever see this town again. The Vauxhall had good suspension and most of the road was smooth, except for a few patches where repairs were underway. After an hour of driving, we came to the Upper Jamuna Canal. Joubert spoke to the driver for the first time, telling him to turn off onto the canal road. It wasn't difficult for me to gauge what he planned to do.

After we'd gone a furlong or so, the horse doctor ordered the driver, 'Stop here, under this tree.' The car slowed and pulled over in the shade.

'Get out,' Joubert said to me, gesturing with his pistol.

The canal was to our right and a dense line of tall moonj grass with feathery plumes grew along the embankment. Joubert was to my left, on the opposite side of the backseat. Outside his window was a strip of scrub jungle, mostly kikar trees, beyond which lay fields of sugar cane. Opening the door, I slid out of my seat and as soon as I got free of the car, I threw myself to one side and leapt towards the high grass. Joubert was taken by surprise but seconds later, he had flung open his door and stepped out. The first bullet he fired caught me on my right side, just above my hip. By the time he fired again, I was in the canal. At first, there was no pain, only a dull heaviness in my right leg, as I began to swim downstream, carried by the current. The water was cold and full of silt. Glancing back, I couldn't see Joubert but there was a thin vein of blood in the water, trailing behind me.

I knew I wouldn't last long in the canal. Up ahead were the arches on the motor bridge where the GT Road crossed over. Joubert was sure to be waiting there to finish me off, so I dragged myself out of the water and into the high grass. The bullet hole was just above my belt, but the slug hadn't gone through me. Stuffing my shirt tail into the wound, I tried to staunch the flow of blood, though the pain almost made me black out. Then I heard the car drive by and saw a cloud of dust as it passed. They were headed for the bridge, which gave me a chance to scramble out of the grass and across the canal road, heading for the sugar cane, which was seven or eight feet high. Pushing my way into the dense thicket, I stumbled several times, leaving bloodstains on the stalks and leaves. After struggling through the cane for five or more minutes, I stopped to think through my situation. Joubert would come back to find me, I felt sure, and the trail of blood would be easy to follow.

The field was about fifty yards wide and when I made it to the other side, I could see a rutted village road bordering the cane. Beyond that were more fields planted with mustard and wheat. About half a mile away was a village and I wondered if I could make it that far. The blood was still seeping out of the wound. Though it seemed to have slowed, I knew that if I ran or walked I'd probably die before I reached help. Dropping to my knees, I tried to control my breathing, which came in uneven gasps. Just then, I saw a buffalo cart coming towards me, driven by a Sikh farmer with a flowing grey beard and a loose turban. It seemed to take forever until he came near enough for me to stagger out, hailing him for help. The last thing I can recall was being hoisted into the cart and lying down on the straw and rough boards at the back.

17

'Well, to begin with, she wasn't Belgian....'

Anastasia gives me a sceptical frown as I continue.

'She was a Dane, though she'd grown up in Brussels as a child. None of that really matters, of course, because the girl had renounced her nationality when she came to India on a spiritual quest. After reading Nicolas Notovitch's *The Unknown Life of Jesus Christ*, she was convinced that our man from Nazareth spent part of his youth in Kashmir and was influenced by Buddhist and Hindu scriptures.'

'I remember, she called herself Sister Mariam,' Anastasia adds. 'But what was her real name?'

'Clara Mortensen,' I answer. 'She chose Mariam because she was convinced that the town of Murree was named after Mother Mary. I first met her there in 1923. She had befriended an Ahmadiyya family, and they let her stay in a couple of rooms at the back of their home. During the summers she would go up to Kashmir and lived in Srinagar near the tomb at Roza Bal. Sister Mariam was translating a Sanskrit text that she believed was the inspiration for the Sermon on the Mount. She even went up to Hemis monastery to interview the lamas whom Notovitch claimed had a secret Christian gospel in their library of holy books.'

'Notovitch was such a fraud!' Anastasia blurts out impatiently. 'A Crimean Jew, who passed himself off as a Russian aristocrat. He made it all up!'

'Of course, he did,' I agree. 'But do you think he was a spy?'

'I don't know. I never met him, though several people I tend to trust, insist he was a Czarist agent, spooking around Ladakh.'

'Sister Mariam was convinced he was a prophet!' I recall.

'Spies and prophets. Same thing,' says Anastasia with a laugh. 'But you're avoiding the most important part of her story.'

'Which is?' I ask, feigning ignorance.

'She got pregnant,' Anastasia says, throwing up her hands

impatiently. 'And she claimed it was an immaculate conception.'

'Well, there you are!' I say. 'The story comes full circle. Isn't it biblical!'

'No, Kim! You can't pretend you're innocent,' Anastasia wags a finger at me. 'You know the truth and you're going to tell me. You promised!'

'What's there to tell?' I protest.

'A lot of people, including Lurgan, believed you were the father of the child she bore,' says Anastasia. 'Now, I want to know the truth. A simple yes or no.'

'She was a pretty girl,' I admit. 'But I didn't sleep with her, if that's what you want to know.'

Anastasia glares at me, as if I'm lying.

'Honestly, Kim?'

'I'll swear on the King James,' I say.

'Then, who was the father?' Anastasia demands.

'She had a lot of Kashmiri admirers, though she presented herself as a virgin,' I say. 'Chaste and pure.'

'But obviously she wasn't, was she?' Anastasia insists.

'Probably not, though who am I to doubt her?'

'Kim, you're hiding something, I know it,' Anastasia scolds me.

'Why would I lie to you at this age?' I argue. 'If I had anything to do with that child, I would admit it, but I didn't. All I know is that a year or two after the boy was born, Sister Mariam married a Scottish missionary, who adopted the child as his own. They left India a few years later and lived happily ever after in Glasgow.'

We are sitting in the drawing room of Lunagarh House and for once I'm drinking tea instead of whisky. Anastasia looks across at me with an inquisitive glance.

'You must have sowed plenty of wild oats in your younger years,' she says. 'Do you know if any of them sprouted?'

'Well, I know the world is full of bastards,' I say with a philosophical smile.

'You never wanted to be a father?' she asks in a serious tone.

After thinking about it for a moment, I shake my head.

'No, not really. I would have been a terrible parent.'

'But if you knew that there was a child you'd fathered, wouldn't you want to meet up with him or her?' Anastasia isn't going to let me off so easily.

'That's a difficult question,' I reply, trying to sound as earnest as possible. 'I hardly knew my own father.'

'Don't you think it's a basic human instinct to want to have children?' she asks.

'Maybe, for some people,' I say, 'like you. You've got your son.'

'Wouldn't you want someone to look after you in your old age?' Anastasia teases me, though her eyes are still serious.

'Certainly not! I can take care of myself,' I reply.

'More tea?' Anastasia asks.

'No thanks,' I refuse.

'Am I making you uncomfortable, asking personal questions?' Anastasia enquires.

'Not really. But it's odd, you know. A strange thing happened to me five years ago, in the winter of 1941. It was the only time I've ever thought I might have been a father,' I confess. 'Though I swear I didn't impregnate Sister Mariam, I'm pretty sure I may have had a child with someone else.'

'Good God!' Anastasia exclaims, leaning forward. 'The sphinx is about to speak.'

'Mmmm,' I nod. 'But before I unburden myself, I think I need a drink.'

'You know where the bar is,' Anastasia says, impatiently. 'Help yourself.'

Rising to my feet, I begin my story. 'There are a lot of things you don't know about me, Anastasia, including the fact that I almost died in forty-one. A German agent named Joubert put a bullet in my gut and I was a goner, even though I escaped from him. If it wasn't for a Jat farmer who picked me up and then blocked traffic on the GT Road with his buffalo cart, until a motorist agreed to take me to the military hospital in Ambala, I wouldn't be alive.'

After filling my glass, I return to my seat as Anastasia watches me.

'It was touch and go, for several days. I'd bled a lot, but I suppose I was lucky because the bullet was lodged in my large intestine just below my spleen. An inch or two higher and I would have died within minutes of being shot. And if the slug had gone through me, I'd have lost a lot more blood.'

'My sympathies,' says Anastasia, when I pause to take a sip of my drink. 'But what does this have to do with your child?'

'Bear with me,' I say, as the whisky warms my vocal chords. 'After being shot, I was unconscious for three or four days, and I have no memory of what happened. But then, eventually, I opened my eyes and the first thing I saw was an angel.'

'Oh, come on, Kim! Don't expect me to believe that the minute you came out of a coma, you had a mystical epiphany,' Anastasia scoffs.

'No! It wasn't that, but believe you me, I was sure I'd died and gone to heaven....'

'Not much chance of that,' she says.

'The angel was a young nurse, dressed all in white, with a starched cotton cap that looked like miniature wings on her head. Her long, dark hair was neatly plaited and coiled in a bun. She was Indian but with a light complexion and grey-green eyes.' As I'm speaking, I watch Anastasia who is now listening intently. 'Of course, I had no idea where I was, though I gradually realized it was a hospital. For another day or two, I kept slipping in and out of consciousness. Each time I woke up this woman was there. My wound had become infected, and I had a fever. She wiped my head with a cool, damp cloth and moistened my lips with a sponge dipped in water. There were others too, attending to me, several older English nurses and doctors who came and went but most of the time the young woman looked after me on her own. Later, I learned that a surgeon had removed the bullet and sewed me up, though there was still a tube inside me to drain out the pus.'

When I stop to take another swig of whisky, Anastasia says nothing. She has listened to me many times before when I have confessed some of my innermost fears and darkest secrets.

'It must have been a week, at least, before I could speak. They were probably weaning me off the morphine because I only gradually became aware of my wound, as the pain surfaced. When I did begin to talk, the nurse and I communicated in Hindustani. I didn't want any of the European staff in the hospital to understand what we were saying. One of the doctors asked me my name and I said that I couldn't remember. The whole experience was like a hallucination or a warped dream. As some of my memories began to return, I worried that I was still in danger and kept imagining armed figures in the shadows. The only person I dared confide in was the nurse. Eventually, I asked her name and she told me it was Laila.

'For a while I wasn't even sure if she was actually there, or if she was some sort of apparition, conjured up by my fevered brain. Whenever I fell asleep, I had nightmares of being chased and often I woke up in a sweat, shouting or crying. Laila was always there to comfort me and I would whisper to her, asking if anyone else was around. They had me in a private ward, with a second bed that was unoccupied though I was convinced my assassin was lying there. Laila reassured me that I was safe and calmed my paranoid delusions. At one point, I tried to escape, pulling the needles out of my arm and crawling off the bed but I fell to the floor before I'd taken a couple of steps. Laila picked me up and helped me lie down again, fixing the sheets and pillows, checking my bandages and giving me an injection to calm me down.

'Finally, when they got the infection and fever under control, I became more lucid. Nobody knew who I was or why I'd been shot. The doctors kept asking if I was in the army and they said that the police wanted to speak with me. Slowly, as I got my wits together, I realized that I would soon be interrogated and I continued to pretend I was suffering from amnesia. At this point, I still felt sure that Laila was the only person I could trust. One day, I asked her for a pencil and a piece of paper, on which I wrote a brief coded message. "I need you to do me a favour, Laila, but you must not show this to anyone," I insisted. "Can you send a telegram for me? I don't have any money...but I promise I'll pay you back." She smiled and looked at me with those grey-green eyes, then nodded. "Your wallet is in the safe," she told me, "along with your watch. That's all you were carrying when you were admitted."

'She had a quiet, endearing manner and I could now see that she was neither an apparition nor an angel, though she was a lovely girl. I was still quite weak and helpless. She took care of everything: gave me my medicines, changed my bandages, handled the bedpan, bathed me with wet towels. In the evening after she sent the telegram for me, Laila came to check my bandages and give me my medicines. As we were talking, I asked her where she was from and about her family. She told me that she came from Kasauli. Her mother was a teacher at the cantonment school. Her father had been a drummer in a regimental band.

"How old are you?" I asked her.

"Twenty-four," she told me.

'Which year were you born?'

"1917, in July," she replied. By now, my mind was racing, trying to calculate backwards in time. The whole thing seemed so absurd, too much of a coincidence....

"Were you born in Kasauli?" I asked.

"Yes," she told me. "My parents still live there, though my father is retired."

"How did you come to Ambala?" I enquired.

She answered, "I just finished my nurse's training. This is my first posting."

'Though I wanted to ask her more, I could see that she was puzzled by my questions, and I didn't want to alarm her. After refilling the glass of water by my bed, Laila said goodnight and turned off the light. As I lay in the dark, there were so many thoughts going through my mind, realizing that she could be my daughter. I told myself that the next day, I would confirm her mother's name. However, I didn't get a chance. The telegram had reached my superiors and been decoded. At daybreak the next morning, two policemen were standing by my bed. I thought they had come to question me, but they told me they had been sent to take me to Lahore in an ambulance. I began to protest but there was nothing I could do. One of the doctors on duty reluctantly discharged me, after the policemen showed him their orders. I was placed on a stretcher and carried outside. Seven hours later, I was in Lahore.'

Anastasia cocks her head to one side, when I finish speaking.

'What was her mother's name?' she asks.

'Kavita.'

'And what were you doing in Kasauli?'

'I was there for a couple of months, keeping an eye on a man who worked at the Central Research Institute, where they produce vaccines for diseases like rabies. It was a red herring. I had a lot of time on my hands.'

'How did you meet this woman, Kavita?' Anastasia demands.

'I was out for a walk and so was she, two strangers crossing paths....'

'Where was her husband?'

'He'd been shipped off to France with his regiment,' I explain. 'Though I don't know why they needed a drummer in the trenches.'

'So, you seduced her?' Anastasia asks.

'She was lonely. So was I.'

'Of course,' she says with an understanding smile. 'But how can you be sure that this young nurse was your daughter?'

'I'm not exactly sure, but....' I hesitate. 'I was in Kasauli in November, 1916. Our affair didn't last very long, just a few weeks, because Kavita's husband was on his way home. At the beginning of December, she got word that he'd arrived in Bombay. I was about to leave. The timing was convenient.'

'I'd say so,' Anastasia agrees. 'Did you go back to Ambala?'

'To see Laila?' I ask, before answering my own question. 'No.'

'You didn't want to find out the truth?'

'At first, I did. But lying in the hospital in Lahore for a couple of weeks, I had a lot of time to think it over.' I try to explain, though the truth is, I don't know what I felt then or feel now. 'Of course, I knew I couldn't say anything to Laila about my suspicions. That would have been unfair, and she would never have believed me, anyway. Better to let things carry on peacefully and innocently.

Whatever happened between me and her mother will remain our secret. I've told no one but you.'

'And I won't tell a soul,' says Anastasia. 'Have another drink, Kim.'

'No thank you,' I say. 'I'm trying to cut back on the booze. But before I leave, may I use your telephone, a local call?'

'Of course, it's in the other room.' Anastasia waves a hand to direct me.

Excusing myself, I go and ring Srinivas.

18

Yaqzan's condition has improved considerably during the six days that he has been at home. Yesterday, I removed the bandage from his head. His injuries are healing well, though he is still badly bruised. Despite a haunting sadness in his eyes, he has grown more cheerful too. When I return home after visiting Anastasia, he is sitting on the roof watching the sun go down over his beloved Dilli. A second chair has been placed beside him in anticipation of my arrival. Soon after I join him, the Maghrib azan echoes across the rooftops. Several muezzins from different mosques nearby recite the call to prayer, their voices layered in sacred harmony. From where we sit, I can see the sandstone ramparts of the Red Fort and the minarets of the Jama Masjid, but most of what we look out upon is an uneven mosaic of lesser buildings, without symmetry or design, yet somehow joined together at this hour in complex geometric patterns beneath a rust-coloured sky. A flight of egrets wing their way towards the river, while flocks of pigeons circle restlessly overhead.

'I should pray,' says Yaqzan, once the azan has ended. 'But my injuries make it difficult, unless you will help me.'

'Of course, if that's what you wish,' I reply. His prayer rug is rolled up beside him and I unfurl it on the weathered bricks.

'Turn it a little to the left.' He indicates with his finger.

I help him rise from his chair. Once he is standing, he does not require any support but when it comes time for Yaqzan to kneel, I take hold of his arm at the elbow and assist him as he gets down on his knees. After he bows and touches his forehead to the carpet, I lift him back onto his feet. In this way, he completes his prayers, slowly, painfully but with determination and devotion. Finally, when he is finished, he drops into his chair again and watches the final embers of the day smouldering to ash on the horizon.

'I may be an irreverent poet, and a sinner,' he says, after a pause, 'but I still take comfort in my prayers.'

'I envy you that comfort,' I say.

'Don't you ever pray?' he asks with a smile.

'No,' I tell him, 'not really.'

'But you know the salat, don't you?' he asks.

'Yes,' I admit. 'And when it is required, I have gone through the motions, though I am not a believer.'

'Some would say that is blasphemy,' he responds.

'Perhaps,' I concede. 'But if it is so, then God will judge me.'

Yaqzan smiles and recites a couplet from Ghalib.

Na tha kuch to khuda tha kuch na hota to khuda hota
Duboya mujh ko hone ne na hota main to kya hota

If there was nothing, there would be God.
In that void God would be there.
Immersed in my own being, if I didn't exist, what would I be?

'I have never understood those lines,' I say, 'though you have quoted them often.'

'Perhaps I do not understand them myself. That is why I keep repeating this couplet, so that I might someday comprehend its meaning,' he says, then asks, 'Where did you go today?'

'Out and about,' I reply, offering him a Cavender's Navy Cut.

'Someday, I will be able to wander freely through this city again,' he says wistfully, as I light the cigarette for him, the flame from the match illuminating his injured features. Then I light one for myself and we smoke in silence.

After several minutes have passed, I tell him, 'I must go out again this evening.'

'Are you meeting friends or enemies?' he enquires, looking at me.

'A friend,' I say.

'I am jealous of your friendships,' he complains.

'He is not a true friend like you,' I say. 'But someone I trust.'

Though I have confided very little about my work, Yaqzan understands that I live a clandestine existence, changing my identity as required.

'By what name does he know you?' he asks.
'My Christian name,' I reply. 'Kim.'
'What about Qasim?'
'You are the only one who knows me as Qasim,' I say. 'Because you are the person who gave me that name.'
'And when will Kim become Qasim?' he whispers.
'Soon enough,' I reply.

∞

Srinivas is waiting for me outside the Regal Cinema just as the evening show lets out, a rerun of *Notorious!* with Cary Grant and Ingrid Bergman. It is half past ten and a sparse crowd disperses quickly into the night. We walk together down Parliament Street for half a mile, then come to a nondescript, double-storey building. It is unguarded and deserted at this time of night. Srinivas has a key to the front door, which admits us to a stairwell, cluttered with boxes and old furniture. Using a torch, we climb to the second floor. Srinivas opens a padlock that secures an iron grille, behind which is another door with a second padlock. We enter an office full of steel filing cabinets and cupboards, overflowing with files and stacks of documents.

'We'll have some privacy here,' Srinivas remarks, switching on a light.

'What is this place?' I ask.

'The building was an old warehouse, used for military supplies during the war. It was emptied out last year and is scheduled for demolition. We're using it temporarily as a records room.'

Picking up a file marked Top Secret, I flip through it casually. From what I can see, it is a list of individuals, with symbols and numbers written beside each name. One of these has been crossed out and the word 'deceased' is scrawled next to it in red ink.

Srinivas takes the folder out of my hands and carefully replaces it in a stack.

'All of these files are being sorted to see what should be kept here in Delhi, what should be burned, and what should be sent to London,' he tells me.

'Why wouldn't the British take them all?' I ask.

'That was the original plan,' Srinivas explains. 'But there are a lot of documents and reports that will have little or no value in London, though they could be very useful to us after independence. One of my primary responsibilities these days is trying to decide what we should keep and which documents should be destroyed.'

'What sort of files are these?' I ask.

'Those cabinets over there contain a tranche of dossiers informally known as the Durbar Archives. Initially, these were intelligence reports compiled on the rulers of princely states around the time of the Delhi Durbar in 1911. Since then, quite a bit of other sensitive information has been added to the original papers. Over time, it has become a repository for confidential profiles on the personal weaknesses, depravities, and debts of India's maharajas and nawabs, as well as their many indiscretions and vulnerabilities. I can assure you that it makes for salacious reading.'

I glance at him, as I begin to understand what's going on.

'So, you're planning to use these files to help keep the princes in line, once the handover takes place,' I suggest. 'Am I right?'

'Something like that,' says Srinivas with a smile. 'Roughly forty per cent of the territory on the subcontinent is in the hands of five hundred and sixty-five royal families. Their subjects account for twenty-three per cent of the entire population. It's not going to be an easy task to persuade them to accede power to a democratically elected government, especially since we're dealing with a preponderance of vain and callous men.'

'But all of them have sworn allegiance to the King Emperor. If he instructs them to accept the authority of India's new leaders, they won't have much choice,' I say.

'That's wishful thinking,' says Srinivas. 'It's going to take a great deal of diplomacy and tough negotiations to settle the matter, one state at a time. There's a Council of Princes that is negotiating the terms of accession, but not all the royals are willing to give up their power and privileges. Fortunately, most of them have considerable moral and financial liabilities. You'd be surprised how many of them have criminal cases pending against them in European courts, everything from shoplifting to murder. They've all been to Monte Carlo and the Riviera but they don't always play by the rules. Half of them have defaulted on loans taken out against their jewellery....'

'So, you're going to blackmail them, plain and simple,' I suggest.

'Sometimes the most important secrets are those we keep from ourselves,' Srinivas responds with a note of conscious ambiguity, as he takes a seat and directs me to another chair next to a table piled high with papers.

'May I smoke?' I ask, taking out a packet.

'Sorry. I'm afraid not,' Srinivas warns me, waving a finger and then pointing to several stacks of film cannisters. 'There's not just paper here but celluloid too. We don't want all of our precious information going up in flames.'

Putting the cigarettes back in my pocket, I ask the question that's been on my mind from the start: 'Why would you bring me here and show me all this?'

Srinivas waves his hand as if he wishes it would all disappear.

'Because I want to impress upon you the critical challenges we face. Independence and Partition are inevitable. It's going to happen. The question is who takes custody of the information that's been gathered by the ISS. If Jinnah's Pakistan gets created, as I'm sure it will, then they will demand a share of the spoils, whatever the Brits leave behind. I'm simply making sure that we keep whatever is in our best interests.'

'All right,' I say, 'But again, why me?'

'Only a handful of Indians are currently working in the secret service, and I don't know who all of them are. Naturally, the British have kept us each in our own separate pigeonholes.' He gestures with both hands to suggest a series of compartments. 'Eventually, when independence happens, the new government will establish a national intelligence service and we'll probably be the ones they turn to for leadership. I'm sure there will be a lot of backstabbing and competition. To be honest, right now, I don't know whom I can trust other than you.'

'Me?' I ask in disbelief.

'You've been involved in Operation Übermensch for the past seven years and have worked undercover in several of the princely states. I think you understand the dynamics as well as anyone, at least in the Punjab,' he says. 'Besides, you're one of the few people with a neutral perspective. Neither are you a native, nor are you a sahib.'

'Which means that I could betray either side,' I say.

'Yes, but I don't think betrayal is part of your nature, even though you are a slippery character, if you'll forgive me for saying so,' he adds. 'You almost lost your life when that veterinarian Joubert shot you in the back. A lot of men would have quit after that, but you went back to work, as soon as you could walk.'

'I was too old to change my occupation,' I admit. 'The only part I resented was that Joubert was never arrested. He got off scot-free when he should have gone to jail!'

Srinivas studies me for a moment, then leans forward.

'I'm sure you wondered about that, but I can assure you that your efforts weren't wasted,' he says. 'Again, I'm going to reveal something that I shouldn't, but I want you to understand how invaluable you are.'

I have to laugh. 'You're paying me a lot of compliments tonight, Srinivas. That makes me suspicious.'

'After you identified Joubert as a German agent, we were able to turn him,' Srinivas says. 'He didn't have much choice. Either we'd charge him with espionage, which meant he'd be hanged, or he agreed to work for us, supplying intelligence on the Germans and their collaborators in India.'

'Of course, I should have guessed.' I nod.

Srinivas points to a stack of documents on top of one of the filing cabinets.

'There's a whole set of files over there that prove how a number of princes were ready to throw in their lot with the Nazis. You'd be surprised at some of their names. And it wasn't just maharajas and nawabs. There are dossiers on British officers too.'

'Sir Denys Bromley-Pugh?' I ask.

'Yes, Joubert provided us with a lot of details about the Brotherhood of Courage. They were obviously part of the equation, courting the princes and the Nazis.'

'So, what happens now?' I ask.

'Of course, these files will ultimately be the property of India's new government but until such time, they provide me with leverage and, hopefully, protection. You see, other than my superior, I'm the only person who knows exactly what we possess.'

'By the way, who is your superior?' I ask, without expecting an answer.

Srinivas gives me an irritated look, as if I should know better than to ask.

'Is it Ulysses?' I suggest.

'Why would you want to know?' he retorts, regaining his composure.

'Curiosity,' I say. 'The truth is I often wonder if Ulysses even exists. Maybe he's just a fictional spymaster created to give the impression that someone's in charge.'

Srinivas smiles and shakes his head. Within the ISS there's always been a good deal of speculation about the identity of the head of operations, who is something of a phantom presence and is never named. In fact, he or she doesn't even have an official title, though I've heard various people refer to this exalted personage as Ulysses and amongst field agents he's something of a covert legend.

'To strive, to seek, to find, and not to yield,' Srinivas quotes Tennyson. The final line of his poem 'Ulysses' has been informally adopted as our unofficial credo. He then continues in a different vein. 'These are uncertain times, requiring courage and vigilance, whoever may be the captain of our ship.'

'Are you in danger?' I ask.

'Not physically, at least I don't think so, but politically, yes,' Srinivas explains. 'You can never tell what may happen. The Brits might decide that I know too much and throw me into jail using the Official Secrets Act. Of course, I have my contacts in the Congress party but many of them treat me with suspicion too. Some call me a traitor for having worked as a British spy.'

'Well, most of us have compromised allegiances,' I say.

'Exactly, but I need to know if I can trust you?' he asks, pointing a finger at me. 'Personally, I mean.'

I look at him and nod. 'Yes, of course you can,' I say.

'If anything happens to me, I want you to protect the Durbar Archives,' he says.

'Can you be a little more specific?' I ask.

'You see, I've broken every protocol by bringing you here and showing you this room and these documents, but I needed a third person, a disinterested party, to know of its existence because there will be a lot of powerful people who will want to destroy these files and the information they contain. No matter what happens, I want you to ensure that doesn't occur.'

'And how the hell am I going to do that?' I ask, with exasperation.

'I don't know, but you're a resourceful man,' he says, with a knowing smile.

Baffled, I look at him and shake my head in disbelief. 'I thought I was meeting you tonight because I have information to pass on regarding a conspiracy to disrupt the transfer of power. But now you're asking me to help you protect a mountain of files that contain all of the dirt on India's maharajas.'

'Yes, that's right,' Srinivas agrees. 'But there's a connection between the two. Conspiracies are never simple. As I explained, Joubert helped us establish a link between German efforts to woo India's princes and Britain's Nazi sympathizers. Now, please go ahead and tell me what you've learned.'

If there was ever a moment when I needed a cigarette, it's now.

As I begin to narrate an account of my meeting with Sir Denys followed by my conversation with Major Stapleton, Srinivas listens intently, fingers steepled under his chin. He shows no emotion when I describe their plans to bomb the Congress rally at Edward Park and kill Nehru as well as other freedom fighters. For a moment, I wonder if Srinivas already knows about this plan. After I finish, he questions me carefully and thoroughly.

'This man, Major Stapleton, he met with you alone? Was there anyone else in the room?'

'No, just the two of us,' I reply. 'As I said, the Brigadier excused himself before I was briefed. He made it quite clear that he could not discuss the details with me. In fact, he said that I should never meet him again.'

'Do you think they actually trust you, or are they just testing your resolve?'

'They were very concerned that I should keep the whole thing secret. My instincts tell me that I have gained their trust, such as it is,' I answer.

Slowly and deliberately, Srinivas makes me repeat everything I've told him, questioning me about the most mundane details, from the address of the bungalow on Cornwallis Road to the furnishings in the room where we met. For at least an hour, I answer him patiently, though I'm itching for a smoke. The interrogation feels as if I'm being tortured.

'So, he asked you to recruit a Muslim to collect the bomb and place it at the site, is that correct?' Srinivas confirms.

'Yes, exactly.'

'Did you suggest any candidates for the job?'

'I did,' I respond. 'I told him that I have a faithful sirdar, who accompanied me on my expeditions and will do whatever I ask of him.'

'Did Stapleton say anything about who is building the bomb?'

'Just that he's a Madras Sapper, obviously an officer,' I reply. 'No name. No rank. No other details.'

Though he's not taking notes, I can tell that Srinivas is mentally jotting it all down and cross-referencing it in his mind. For a while, he falls silent, his eyes fixed on the floor. Finally, I interrupt him with a question of my own.

'What do you think?' I ask. 'Suppose they are able to pull this thing off and kill Nehru. What would be the response? Would the handover be forestalled?'

Srinivas looks up at me with a wary expression.

'I really don't know,' he says. 'It's hard to predict what might happen, except that there would certainly be a wave of communal violence. You can be sure of that.'

'Maybe it would force the British to quit India even sooner than planned,' I suggest.

'Could be. Most of them are eager to get out of here,' says Srinivas. 'I just hope that in their haste they don't leave too much of a mess behind.'

Again, he lapses into a thoughtful silence. My hand searches my pocket for the pack of Cavender's and I wonder how much longer Srinivas will keep me here.

'What would you like me to do next?' I finally ask, intruding on his reverie.

Srinivas hesitates for a moment, and I can tell that he's been calculating what he plans to do, several moves on ahead.

'Well, you've set up the dead drop, which is good. I suggest you keep checking that. As soon as they contact you, let me know. From what you've told me, I have a feeling you'll have to meet with Major Stapleton at least one more time. Right now, we don't have enough evidence to act upon but if we can catch someone handing over the bomb, that would be ideal,' says Srinivas. 'We need to nab them red-handed, to ensure a successful court martial.'

'Whatever happens, they'll know I'm the one who betrayed them,' I tell him. 'It will be obvious.'

'Yes, that's why we'll have to ensure that our evidence is watertight,' he says. 'And at a certain point, we'll have to make you disappear.'

'That sounds ominous,' I respond.

'No, I didn't mean it that way.' Srinivas laughs.

'There's one more thing,' I tell him, taking an exposed roll of film from my pocket and placing it on the table in front of him.

'What's this?' he asks.

'I put my camera to good use,' I explain. 'The morning after my meeting with Sir Denys and Stapleton, I went back to the bungalow on Cornwallis Road. The property is poorly guarded and there's a ficus tree conveniently located next to the main entrance. Just before dawn,

I climbed over the garden wall at the back and took up position in the tree. The foliage was dense enough to keep me hidden, though I found a gap in the branches that gave me a clear view of everyone who was coming and going. During the course of the day, Sir Denys had quite a few visitors and I was able to photograph most of them. You'll probably recognize a few familiar faces.'

'Aren't you a little old to be climbing trees?' Srinivas says with a grateful smile.

19

After purchasing two more rolls of Agfa film at Kinsey Bros. Studio in Connaught Place, I set out for a bit of sightseeing. My first stop is the Jantar Mantar observatory, where I take a few photos of the eccentric structures built more than two centuries ago to study the stars and calculate their astrological significance. After that, I wander further down Parliament Street until I come to the Imperial Bank, where I need to withdraw some cash to help cover my expenses. MacNeil has deposited funds in a savings account in the name of Gordon Morris, an alias I use for anything that requires a signature.

Writing a cheque for three hundred rupees, I hand it over to the manager, who inspects the identity card I produce with a suspicious squint. After approving the cheque, he hands me a brass token and I step across to the cashier's window where I join a short queue. While waiting my turn, I wonder where MacNeil got the money from. After receiving his telegram ordering me back to Lahore, I responded by explaining that I couldn't leave immediately without arousing suspicion. He didn't reply and I suspect he's angry with me. Hopefully, by the time I return to Lahore his temper will have cooled.

Once I've got my money, I continue down Parliament Street to the building where Srinivas and I met last evening. There is nothing particularly photogenic about the old structure, which looks as if it has been neglected for years, the plaster peeling and the shutters in disrepair. Nevertheless, I snap a couple of photos surreptitiously, with the camera at waist level, hanging from the strap around my neck. Nobody seems to be around, and the front door is locked.

From here I carry on to the circular parliament building where the Imperial Legislative Council is debating India's future. Beyond this, Kingsway's broad central avenue stretches from the Viceregal Palace and Central Secretariat to the All-India War Memorial. The sun is bright overhead and I walk in the shade of a line of young jamun trees that border the lawns and reflecting pools. A few motor vehicles pass by but there is very little traffic other than the bicycles that seem to proliferate in this city, a mechanical swarm of spokes and sprockets.

It takes me a good twenty minutes to walk the length of Kingsway. By the time I reach the memorial, I am sweating and after snapping a photograph of the grand arch, I step up onto the plinth and into the shade. Two soldiers are on sentry duty, while George V's statue presides over the memorial in its own sandstone pavilion.

The names of the war dead are carved into the pale granite walls and I run my eyes over the long list of Indian Army casualties from WWI. Many of them were killed in Europe, others in Mesopotamia, Gallipoli, and Persia. Most of the names are of Indians with a few English, Irish, Welsh, and Scots amongst them. There is also a section dedicated to those who died during the Third Anglo-Afghan War in 1919. Scanning the chiselled names, I soon find what I am looking for, six inches above eye level.

Lt. Kimball O'Hara

Though I have been here many times before, it still gives me a strange feeling of remorse and guilt, seeing my name on the wall. More than likely, nobody else has ever recognized that name or taken any notice of it. This monument honours the memory of men who died in battle or, as the eulogists like to say, 'made the ultimate sacrifice'. For me, however, it signifies the anonymity of death in war regardless of the individual identities of those mutilated corpses buried in far-flung fields. Raising my hand, I trace the letters cut into the stone and then, impulsively, I open my camera and focus on my name before pressing the shutter release.

I am a ghost. Or at least I think of myself as one. This is something I have seldom admitted, even to my closest friends. Part of the reason for keeping it secret may be that I am ashamed of what I did because it was dishonourable, but more than that I attempted to erase my identity and became one of the dead. Whenever I come to Delhi, I visit this site to be reminded of my fateful decision, so many years ago.

During the Third Anglo-Afghan War, I was assigned as intelligence officer with the 12th Frontier Force. We were sent up from Peshawar to Jamrud to retake the Khyber Pass soon after hostilities began. The Amir in Kabul, Habibullah, had remained neutral during WWI but his sympathies were with the Turks and the Germans. Immediately following the Armistice, he tried to take over British territory along the North-West Frontier. It was a short but brutal coda to the Great War and ended with the Treaty of Rawalpindi that established the Durand Line, which remains the de facto border between British India and Afghanistan.

I was in my early thirties. Until then, I had never seen a battle before. Though I knew how to fire a rifle and was a reasonably good shot, I didn't much like the idea of being ordered to march into slaughter. I had no intention of sacrificing myself for a dubious cause, but there I was lined up with dozens of other young men, preparing to do combat with the Afghan hordes. Just because I was an intelligence officer didn't mean I could safely skulk about behind the front lines. A few days after our detachment reached Jamrud, we were ordered to proceed towards Landi Kotal. Within a few miles we came upon an Afghan force that had dug themselves in along a barren ridge overlooking the ancient caravan track that leads up to the Khyber Pass. They had some artillery as well as small arms and we came under heavy fire. Our commanding officer immediately ordered us to take cover, though there was little protection, other than a few boulders and a low parapet wall along the roadside.

I found shelter behind a rock about the size of an ox. Bullets were kicking up dirt all around me and I lay still, keeping my head down and expecting to die. Artillery shells landed nearby, and the sound of explosions was deafening, the air full of dust and smoke. When I finally looked up, I could see bodies strewn about and a wounded man flailing his arms and pleading for help. He was about twenty yards to my right. Crouching and running forward, I reached him in a few seconds and was able to hoist him over my shoulder. But as I ran back towards the rock where I'd been hiding, I felt him shudder and knew he'd been hit again. By the time I got the wounded soldier to safety, he was dead.

After another twenty minutes, which seemed like an hour, one of the officers began to shout for us to fix bayonets and then ordered us to charge. It was a senseless, stupid command but I did as I was told and stumbled out from cover with the rest of them. I don't know how I survived because the bullets were buzzing around me like an angry swarm of wasps. Just below the ridge on which the Afghans had their position, lay a deep ravine that cut laterally across the slope. I ran for it, along with another junior officer who was about ten steps ahead of me. Just as he reached the ravine, an artillery shell exploded and cut him in half. Though I wasn't injured, the blast knocked me to the ground.

As soon as my head cleared, I scrambled for cover in the ravine and found myself lying next to the dead man's legs, which were intact, his trousers still belted at the waist, though above this there was nothing at all. His torso and head had been blown to bits and there were pieces of him scattered all around. Though I was in shock, I realized that our futile bayonet charge had been repulsed and most of the soldiers were either dead or wounded, while those that survived had retreated. The Afghans kept firing from above, but I was hidden in the ravine and they showed no inclination to descend from the security of the ridge. For several hours, I lay where I was, trying not to look at the gruesome remains of my comrade in arms, whose name I never knew. Eventually, the gunfire subsided, and I could tell that what was left of our detachment had turned back to regroup. My only chance of escape was to wait until dark.

As I lay there, the horror and brutality of what we had experienced, and the utter pointlessness of this battle over barren ground consumed my thoughts. I was intent on escaping, but I was equally determined not to go back to the Frontier Force. By the time the sun dropped behind the ridges to the west, my mind was made up. I removed the identification tag from around my neck, an aluminium disc on a chain, which bore my name, K. O'Hara, my temporary service number and rank as a lieutenant. It was also inscribed with the letters

RC, which indicated I was Roman Catholic. Crawling forward, I placed my dog tag and chain next to the pair of truncated legs.

After that, I crept along the edge of the ravine and, as lengthening shadows stretched down the eroded slopes, I was able to disappear into the Khyber Hills. Altogether, it took me three days to reach Peshawar, by which time I had traded my rifle and uniform for the clothes and turban of a congenial Pathan whom I befriended in a small settlement at the foot of the hills. Speaking Pashto, I was able to reassure him that I meant no harm. He also fed me and explained what route I should take to avoid British patrols. In Peshawar, I met my old friend, Mahbub Ali. He gave me shelter and advice as I tried to decide what I should do next. Having relinquished my identity and deserted the regiment to which I'd been attached, I felt a strange sense of freedom as well as moments of doubt and regret.

Soon enough, however, I realized that it made little difference whether I was dead or alive. Now that Kimball O'Hara was officially deceased, I could assume whatever name and antecedents I desired. Mahbub Ali helped smooth things over with Colonel Creighton and others in the secret service. Though they were alarmed at first and expressed outrage regarding my actions, even threatening a court martial, these were eminently practical men and they soon realized there might be certain advantages to having me both dead and alive. My codename, as well as my true identity, were struck from the rolls of the secret service but those rolls are some of the best kept secrets in India, seen by only a few select pairs of eyes. Once the war was concluded, my superiors were able to confirm that my plan had succeeded. The identity tag had been found amidst the unrecognizable remains of a British subaltern killed by an Afghan shell. I have never known whose corpse was buried instead of mine in the British cantonment cemetery in Peshawar, but I have seen my headstone there and paid my respects.

Those who once knew me as Kim, still call me by that name while none of my fellow Freemasons at the lodge in Lahore, including MacNeil, has ever raised a question. If one of them did, I could easily argue that more than one Kimball O'Hara must have walked this earth, and the grave contains his bones, not mine. But more than that, the ease with which I shed my service number and rank confirmed that death in battle is an ambiguous fate and the senior officers who give orders to advance or retreat, care little about the men who obey their commands, while those who tally up the casualties have no real awareness of who we are.

Since that violent day in June 1919, I have lived a strange, discomfiting afterlife, though I content myself in the knowledge that when I do eventually die, the anomaly of my presence on earth will finally be resolved. Until then, perhaps I am one of those fortunate few that has been released from what the Holy One, the Lama, used to call the wheel of existence. Neither my sins nor my virtues affected my rebirth. It is only when I come to this War Memorial and trace the chiselled letters of my name that I wonder if my motives at that moment were driven by cowardice or simply a will to survive.

*

Though I check for a signal every day, there is no chalk mark to indicate that a message has been left for me at the dead drop and over the next week I receive no word from Srinivas. Yaqzan and I spend our time reminiscing about more peaceful days and trying to sift through the rumours that swirl through the lanes of Old Delhi like dust storms blowing in from Rajasthan. I idle away the hours playing Snakes and Ladders with Yusuf and drinking the cool, sweet almond sharbat that Tamanna serves us.

From time to time, I go out and buy rations and vegetables, as well as whisky, exploring the city which now lies in a summer torpor, which seems to have stilled even the most vengeful communalists. Several varieties of mangoes are available in the market and every time I go out, I bring back a seer or two. Yaqzan is a connoisseur of mangoes, and he can wax eloquent for hours on the relative merits of a dasheri or a langada aam. One day, when I am dispatched on a quest to find a particular variety of safeda from the orchards near Saharanpur, which Yaqzan claims are the sweetest of all, I wander past the haveli where Champa and the girls now live. While I am tempted to go upstairs and knock on their door, I know I must not intrude. Loitering near Ajmeri Gate, I catch sight of Munia and Kamla hanging laundry on the roof and am reassured by this pantomime of domesticity.

Only another week remains until I must travel up to Simla to receive the Kaiser-e-Hind award from the Viceroy. I now wish that I hadn't asked MacNeil to pursue it with the Governor but there is nothing to be done. If Major Leslie Townsend does not show up for the ceremony, suspicions will be aroused. Meanwhile, Anastasia has already migrated to the hills. While I am in Simla, she has invited me to stay with her in her cottage on Jakho Hill. If I do not get a signal from Stapleton soon, I will have to ask Srinivas to assign someone else to check the dead drop in my absence.

On the fourth of May, a Tuesday, while sauntering through the arcades at Connaught Place, I notice the diagonal chalk mark on the window frame at Wenger's. Without pausing, I continue around the inner circle going clockwise and eventually take the radial road to Empire Stores. The spacious, high-ceilinged premises are well stocked with a variety of foodstuffs from India, America, and Britain, though the shortages caused by the war have depleted some of the shelves. Nevertheless, there are plenty of tins and bottles full of everything from strawberry jam to mango chutney. A tall pyramid of Golden Syrup tins is on display as well as an assortment of biscuits and chocolate. During the war, Empire Stores catered to American GIs stationed in barracks nearby. Now that most of them have left, its clientele is mostly Britons as well as wealthier Indians. Against the innermost wall is a refrigerated case full of hams and sausages, as well as other cured meats and cheeses.

Ignoring all this, I go across to a set of shelves at the back, where a young man on a stepladder is restocking a depleted supply of Bronco lavatory paper. I pretend to inspect a selection of soaps and detergents nearby, until he is finished. As soon as the stock boy removes the ladder and departs, I slip across the shelves beneath the toilet tissues and select a box of boric acid, which advertises its effectiveness for eradicating household pests like cockroaches. Ten feet ahead is a set of shelves laden with packets of tea—Ceylon, Assam, and Darjeeling. As casually and quickly as I can, I reach into the narrow gap between the shelves and find the folded sheet of paper tucked at the very back, where nobody else will find it. Putting it into my trouser pocket, I go across to the cashier and purchase the boric acid. Tamanna has been complaining that cockroaches are invading her kitchen from the drain every night. Hopefully, this will put an end to their nocturnal intrusions.

Returning counterclockwise around the circle to Wenger's, I order a cup of coffee and a chocolate eclair, as if I have something to celebrate, though the typed message on the piece of paper fills me with a sense of dread. It is brief and to the point:

> Congress Rally at Edward Park
> 2:00 pm 8th May
> Collect the necessary items from
> 4 Battery Lane, 10:00 am sharp.

Until now, the plot seemed an abstraction, but the message leaves no doubt in my mind that Bromley-Pugh's men are serious in their intentions, though I still wonder if it might be a trap. Whatever it is, I must be cautious.

Anastasia has left instructions with her servants at Lunagarh House to allow me to use her telephone whenever I wish. From Connaught Place, I go directly there and ring Srinivas. An anonymous switchboard operator somewhere in the main telephone exchange connects us and I recite my prearranged response when Srinivas picks up at his end of the line.

'Good afternoon, this is Aslam Ahmed at Regency Tailors, calling for Mr Charles Blackstone.'

'I'm afraid he's not in,' Srinivas replies. 'May I take a message?'

'Mr Blackstone's suit is ready for fitting.'

'Thank you, I'll let him know but he won't be back in the office until six.'

The only relevant piece of information in this exchange are the last three words, which indicate that I should meet Srinivas at the Records Room on Parliament Street, at six o'clock this evening.

Stealth is something I learned as a boy, the ability to move about unnoticed in a city. If I had grown up in a forest instead, I might have stalked deer and other animals or camouflaged myself behind a curtain of leaves to hide from predators. However, my feral instincts were honed in an urban landscape, giving me an ability to slip through crowded markets with the anonymity of a phantom. Growing up in Lahore, I had to be wary of the police who suspected me and my companions of petty crimes and other mischief. I learned to avoid taking obvious routes and seldom retraced my own tracks, preferring back gullies and rooftops by which I made my way from place to place. I also had to keep a sharp eye out for missionaries and other do-gooders who felt that a white orphan needed to be captured and locked up in a charitable institution.

Only once was I taken prisoner by a Pentecostal minister, who wanted to save my soul from damnation, living as I did amongst the heathen masses. He was an Australian with a red, weather-beaten face and tufts of hair growing out of his ears. I had noticed him watching me several times near Taxali Gate, where he preached on the street, his Urdu and Punjabi unintelligible, as if he were speaking in tongues. He always drew a crowd because he was such a grotesque sight, over six feet tall in his white drill suit, wielding a Bible in one hand while haranguing the throng of idlers about 'Yesumassih' and 'Khuddahbaap'. I listened to him once or twice but I knew better than to get too close. The evangelist's huge hands looked like grappling hooks as he mopped the zealous sweat from his brow with a wrinkled handkerchief. But then, one day, as I was lurking near a cartload of guavas, with the intent of pocketing one, his hand reached out and caught me by the shoulder. Though he addressed me in English, I hardly understood a word he said because of his accent.

While I was tempted to squirm free of his grip, I hadn't eaten for the past twenty-four hours, and the missionary promised me a free supper. Leading me to his car, a battered Model T, he drove me to his home, which lay on the outskirts of Lahore, a large bungalow surrounded by a walled compound. A derelict brick dormitory stood at the back, where an assortment of foundlings were housed. My antennae had already picked up warning signals, but I let him coax me inside, confident that I could easily break out of the compound if I wished. Though I had imagined a delicious meal, the food that was placed before me was a tasteless stew ladled over a cold lump of mashed potatoes. It had no spices at all, and the only flavour was a hint of boiled cabbage and mutton broth. If I hadn't been as hungry as I was, I would have left it untouched on my plate.

After supper, I was directed to the dormitory, where a grim-looking matron with hair like steel wool, handed me a well-worn lozenge of soap and a coarse towel, ordering me to strip off my clothes. At this point, I made a run for it and would have been able to vault over the compound wall, if the missionary's dog hadn't cornered me, a vicious Airedale that barked and snarled until its master came and dragged me back to the dorm. While I bathed under a hand pump, the matron supervised me with a bamboo switch in hand, striking me several times on the back of my thighs and leaving raw, red welts. After this, I was given a grey cotton smock to wear like all of the other unfortunate inmates. Over the years, I've been locked up in prison several times but never under such dismal conditions as that dormitory with its hard steel cots and coir mattresses on which three of us lay together, sharing a single blanket.

Early the next morning, I made my escape, climbing out of the window and creeping across the weedy lawn in the half-light. The dog was asleep on the veranda, and I was careful to stay downwind of him, finding a bougainvillea vine that bore my weight, as I scrambled up and over the wall. Still wearing the smock, I ran as fast as I could. This part of the city bordered fields of mustard and wheat, though I ran in the opposite direction. Stealing a pair of shorts and a shirt from a laundry line, I discarded the smock. A passing tongawallah gave me a lift, though I hopped off near the Railway Station when he demanded I pay him, ducking into the switchyards in search of my friends.

After that, I hid whenever I saw the evangelist coming down the street, though I eventually got my revenge when I poured a bottle of lemon squash into his petrol tank. Nevertheless, I still feel a sense of panic when I think of that missionary stalking my every move. Even now, at this age, his malignant shadow pursues me and I am constantly aware of the urgent need to outwit him.

Following Srinivas's instructions, I make my way to the office building on Parliament Street, though I approach from a different angle this time, cutting through a construction site on the far side of a service lane that runs parallel to the main street and provides access to the rear entrance of the building. As dusk fades into darkness, I wait behind a shed that contains a transformer. Warning signs are posted, displaying a skull and crossbones, with the words Danger 880 Volts.

After a short wait, I see a car approaching, a Morris Minor still equipped with blackout lights from the war. As it pulls over, Srinivas steps out and glances around before the car drives off. A few bicycles are passing along the street but otherwise there is no traffic. As I begin to step out of the shadows, I see another figure approach from the opposite side, a European by the look of him, though it is too dark to know for sure. Srinivas turns around, as if surprised by the stranger's presence. Seconds later, I see the man extend his right arm and fire a pistol. The report is sharp, like the crack of a whip. As Srinivas drops to the ground, the man runs off in the direction from which he came. All of this happens so suddenly, I am transfixed in horror, then rush forward to help Srinivas who lies on his side, arms pulled in and his knees drawn up.

By the time I reach him, he is dead. The bullet has struck him in the chest and his blood has flowed out like a small, dark delta in the dust. I look up to see if there is any sign of the shooter, but nobody is around and the building behind us lies in darkness. Srinivas's spectacles have fallen off and his eyes are open, staring at me with the impassive vacancy of death. I know I must leave him like this for others to find, but in a final gesture, I reach over and lower his eyelids with my fingertips. Then I reach into his trouser pocket and find the set of keys for the front door and the padlocks to the records room upstairs. Rising to my feet, I retreat into the darkness, as if I am the assassin and Srinivas is my victim.

More than ever before, Delhi feels menacing now, a city full of fatal secrets and hidden threats. As I make my way through the dark by-lanes and half-constructed buildings, I lose all sense of direction, disoriented by fear and guilt. All I want is to get away, though I can hear Srinivas's words from two days ago, asking me to protect the information in those files, a haunting sense of premonition in his words. He knew he was in danger, yet he agreed to meet me. Now, I am alone.

Eventually, I find my way back to Chandni Chowk, after taking a roundabout route and switching tongas twice to make sure I'm not being followed. By now the adrenaline in my veins has been diluted though my mind is still churning, trying to sort through my options. I have no idea why Srinivas was killed and whether it had anything to do with me, though someone obviously knew he was coming to the records room tonight. If anyone is aware that he was here to meet me, I will be the prime suspect in his murder.

Yaqzan takes a while to open the door when I knock, and I can see that he had already gone to bed. Though he does not ask me where I have been, he can tell that I am distraught.

'Shall I make you some tea?' he asks, though it is almost midnight.

'No, thank you,' I answer. 'I'm sorry it's so late.'

'You must have been savouring the pleasures of Dilli,' he says with a wink.

'If only that were true, I would have come back at dawn,' I reply, trying to smile.

'Are you all right?' he asks with concern.

'Yes, I'll be fine,' I assure him, placing a hand on his arm. 'Goodnight.'

Once I am in my room, I open the whisky and put the bottle straight to my lips. My hands are shaking. I can still see Srinivas's dead eyes staring at me and the wet, warm blood staining his shirt. Mixed with a sense of grief and despair, I feel a knot of fear tightening in my chest. Taking the key ring out of my pocket, I turn it over in my hand, as if somehow one of these will unlock the answer to the questions in my mind.

※

Teshoo Lama, my guru, used to tell me that death does not release us from the eternal wheel of existence but only spins us in a new direction. On the other hand, Mahbub Ali always reminded me that I would face God's judgement after departing this life, and if I remained an unrepentant infidel, I would be denied entry into paradise. The priests at Xavier's reinforced this message with frightening stories of purgatory and hell, as well as the saintly pleasures awaiting the faithful in heaven. Each of these visions of the afterlife left me confused. Whatever I have seen of death, it is a final, irredeemable thing. Whether it was my father whose emaciated body was consigned to an unmarked grave in one corner of the Gora Kabristan or the anonymous soldier who died in my place along the Khyber Road, there was no evidence of any residual existence beyond their demise. I do not know what Srinivas believed. Though he was a Brahmin from Madras, he seemed a rationalist in most of his views and I can't imagine him reborn as anything else once the flames of his funeral pyre have consumed his flesh. For his sake and for the sake of others, I hope I am wrong, but for myself I doubt if there is any form of salvation.

Searching for the sacred River of the Arrow, which washes away all sins and brings an end to suffering, the lama's goal was to escape the relentless cycle of rebirth. Yet, even the most violent death delivers the same result. A corpse cannot sin; neither does it suffer, even as it rots. By saying this, I do not mean to mock my teachers' beliefs but as I grow older, I've spent a considerable amount of time thinking about my own mortality and there doesn't seem to be any way around it. Whether we're damned or not, all of us are certainly going to be dead one day.

About twenty years ago, I remember meeting a clairvoyant in Murree. For the price of ten rupees, she claimed she could speak to the dead. People flocked to meet her at Cecil's Hotel, where she'd set herself up in a suite, with the lights dimmed and candles burning in all corners of the room. A girlfriend of mine, Rehan Dastur, persuaded me to go with her. She wanted to speak to one of her past lovers who had committed suicide, but she was too afraid to go alone. I told her that I didn't believe in that sort of thing though she insisted on taking me along. The medium was a middle-aged woman with blowsy features and auburn hair that was grey at the roots. Her breath smelled of gin. Madame Sophia was her name and she claimed to be a descendant of Marie Antoinette. Her fingernails were painted silver and she wore an evening gown that would have been out of fashion fifty years ago, frilled with black lace. In addition to the candles, incense sticks were burning in the room, emitting a smoky jasmine perfume.

The whole thing would have been farcical except that Rehan was so nervous she was trembling and clutched my arm as tightly as a torniquet. Madame Sophia began with a series of vague comments about a male presence and hearing the voice of a man, unsure if he was young or old. He spoke of a tragedy, which immediately made Rehan shudder. She then asked the clairvoyant a number of questions, which were conveyed to the departed soul. Eventually, Madame Sophia explained that the spirit wanted to reassure her that she was not to blame. Tears immediately began flowing down Rehan's face and I realized that this was exactly what she had wanted to hear. Whether it be a suicide or not, we often feel some sort of guilt about the death of a person who is close to us. Madame Sophia exploited those uncertain emotions. Rehan was convinced that she had contacted her dead lover and admitted afterwards that she had always worried that he had killed himself because she had been unfaithful to him. Nevertheless, this didn't stop her from abandoning me for someone else a few months later.

Though I'm a sceptic, if I had the opportunity to speak to Srinivas, now that he is gone, I would have a number of questions to ask him. First and foremost, I'd want to know what he wants me to do next. Though he made me promise to protect the files in the records room, he gave me no hint as to how he expected me to do this. I would have also wanted to know the answer to the question that led me to ask for a meeting with him. How am I supposed to proceed with the instructions from Major Stapleton? And if I do collect the bomb, what am I to do with it?

21

Ask any spy and he or she will tell you that most intelligence work is a waiting game. Patience is not just a virtue but a necessity in espionage and I have learned these lessons from the best of them. As Colonel Creighton used to say, 'Emulate the spider, not the fly,' while Lurgan Sahib, that old wizard of skullduggery, put it more precisely: 'Sometimes the best course of action is to do nothing at all.' Having spent half a century in this business, I've often succeeded in gathering the required information by simply marking time, allowing my opponents to make the first move.

But there comes a point when I cannot sit still any longer and I am forced to take matters into my own hands, not because it is the wisest decision but simply because it would drive me mad if I didn't. The day after Srinivas was shot, I remained indoors. Yaqzan understood that I was upset but he allowed me the solitude and privacy I required. Knowing there would be alert eyes on the street looking for me, I waited until darkness fell before going out.

The disguise I choose is the same one I wore on the train from Lahore—the muslin turban and loose garments of a Punjabi merchant, recently arrived as a refugee. For identification, I have a ration card in the name of Lala Jagat Kapoor, in case it is required. My face is darkened with make-up and tucked into my waistband is my revolver, the hard steel digging into my skin. In the pocket of my kurta is the set of keys that I took from Srinivas. Before I leave the house, Yaqzan studies me with a bemused expression, though he knows better than to ask the purpose of my transformation.

'What will the neighbours think when they see a Hindu leaving my home?' he wonders aloud.

'You can tell them I came here to repay a debt,' I reply.

'More than likely, they'll think you have murdered us,' he answers bitterly.

Fortunately, nobody observes me as I descend the staircase and soon enough I have merged with the passers-by on the street. To help clear my thoughts and ease the tension in my limbs, I walk for a ways. The night is warm and the air is still. Inhaling the smells of the bazaar, I make my way through the crooked by-lanes of the old city, which reminds me of parts of Lahore. Stopping to drink a cup of tea and eat a kachori at an open stall, I keep an eye out for anyone who might be following but there is no one on my tail. Emerging from the warren of gullies near Ajmeri Gate, I pass the building where Champa and the girls are living. Once again, I feel an impulse to knock on their door, but resist the temptation.

From here it is a short rickshaw ride to Curzon Road. Instead of following the route I took last evening, I circle around in the other direction, turning right along Lytton Road and passing the Freemason's Lodge. Though I have been welcomed here many times before, on this trip to Delhi I have avoided entering the temple. Lighting a cigarette, I squat down under a neem tree to watch for any suspicious movements nearby. While nobody seems to be about at this hour, my sixth sense tells me that I am being watched.

Slipping through the shadows and avoiding the pools of light under lamp posts, I reach the spot where Srinivas died. The building looks as empty as it did last night and there is no sign of blood on the ground. I wonder briefly if I imagined the murder but the sound of the pistol shot still rings in my ears and I can't erase the image of Srinivas's crumpled form on the ground. Reaching under my kurta, I pull out my revolver and check to make sure all six chambers are loaded, before flicking off the safety catch.

The first key I try opens the front door, and I quickly enter, pulling it shut behind me. The staircase is unlit and I can see barely anything at all. Reaching out with my left hand, I feel my way along the wall to the first step and from there I climb slowly, turning at the landing and then proceeding to the first floor. The only window is a roshandan high above me, just below the ceiling. My fingers come in contact with the grille, and I can feel the padlock. Needing both hands, I place the revolver carefully on the floor by my right foot. Everything I do is by feel. Finally, I find the right key and the tumblers inside the lock give way with a rusty snap, after which I pull the steel grille aside. The second padlock gives me more trouble but eventually, it also opens. Each sound is amplified in the stairwell though the building is completely silent.

Retrieving my revolver, I push open the door. The room inside is somewhat brighter, as the distant glow of streetlights enters through the windows and reflects off the whitewashed walls. My eyes scan the space for any sign of movement, or the silhouette of a killer crouched in the shadows. Though my attention is directed at any possible threats, I immediately realize that the room is empty. All of the files and papers have disappeared and even the steel cabinets are gone. The only furniture left are two chairs and a wooden table, which was piled high with documents the last time I was here. Now there isn't a scrap of paper on it. Reaching into my pocket for a box of matches, I put my revolver on the table and strike a light, the yellow flame briefly illuminating the room, which is as bare as a squash court. All of the dossiers and folders have been removed. For a moment, I wonder if I may have entered the wrong room, but remind myself that both of the keys worked.

After the match goes out, I am blinded for several moments. At the same time, I hear the door creak open behind me and I reach for my revolver.

'Don't move, please,' says a man in English, speaking softly. 'I won't harm you.'

To turn and fire would require no more than a second or two, but I know that before I am able to pull the trigger, I will certainly take a bullet in my back. Strangely, though, the voice isn't threatening, even as his words startle me.

'Hello, Kim,' he says. 'You don't know who I am. We've never met.'

I remain frozen in place, my fingers no more than an inch from my weapon, as I try to visualize exactly where the man is standing, about two yards behind me and a few feet left of the door.

'Of course, I know who you are. I know all about you.' He sounds as if he might be Welsh, though I can't say for sure...not a proper English accent.

'Actually, you're a bit of a legend.' He laughs quietly to himself. His tone is casual and confiding. 'Are you aware of that?'

I do not respond, trying to stay focused and not be distracted, waiting for the moment when I can turn and fire.

'Some would call you a hero, while others claim you're loyal only to yourself, a bit of a lone wolf. A maverick like your father.' Again, a soft chuckle.

He isn't taunting me but there is a note of irony in his words.

'I know your codename. Q15.' His voice drops to a whisper. 'I know all of the scars on your body. Two toes on your left foot were lost to frostbite. Your right forearm was cut to the bone by a Dogra sabre and badly stitched by a drunk surgeon in Pathankot. The knuckles on your hands still bear the marks of a brutal interrogation in Kandahar. Then there's that bullet hole on your left side that looks as if you had your appendix removed the wrong way around. And of course, a fresh wound on your right thigh.... Would it surprise you if I told you that I also know about your death and resurrection?'

I do not recognize the voice and have no idea who this might be or how he learned these things, though I'm beginning to have suspicions, even as I hold my tongue.

'You see, I've heard so many stories about you, Kim. Some of them are true, I'm sure, but you'll admit that a lot of it is exaggeration, the kind of lore that accumulates around a man like you. Myths and rumours....'

He pauses, as if expecting me to answer, though I remain mute.

'There's one particular tale I recall,' he continues, 'from the Great Game. 1915. You'd been sent to Kabul undercover, dressed as a Pathan. As usual, you had no trouble passing yourself off as an itinerant trader buying dried apricots and raisins, as well as walnuts and almonds, to carry back with you to Peshawar. During the course of your visit, you learned that a group of Tajik tribesmen, under the influence of the Russians, were planning to kidnap the British Principal Secretary. They'd timed their raid to coincide with an audience he had scheduled at midday with the Amir. After alerting your contacts, you climbed the hill overlooking the city of Kabul and successfully fired the noon gun an hour early. When the Tajiks swarmed out of hiding, they were quickly routed.'

'Who told you that story?' I ask, finally breaking my silence.

'I heard it from Creighton himself,' comes the reply. 'Is it true?'

'Mostly. Except they weren't Tajiks but a group of Uzbeks and it turned out that the Germans had paid them off.'

By now most of my tension has eased, though I am still on guard.

'You can turn around now,' says the man. 'Please leave the pistol where it is.'

Slowly, I rotate my head and take a step back, then turn to face him. All I can see is a blurred figure in the darkness. He is much shorter than I expected, a stocky man in a shapeless summer suit with a golfing cap on his head. He has one hand in his pocket. In the other, he holds a cane. By now, I've guessed who he is. As the man comes towards me, I can see that he walks with a limp, using the cane to support himself. Taking his hand out of his pocket, he extends it for me to shake, without introducing himself. I can't see much of his face, though he has an untidy moustache and a double chin. I'd say he is about my age, maybe a year or two older.

With a wave of his hand, he signals for us to sit in the same two chairs that Srinivas and I occupied three nights ago.

'I'm sorry to have surprised you like this,' he says, resting his cane against the table.

'How did you know I'd be here?' I ask.

'We've been keeping an eye on you,' he says with a smile, 'as best we can, though I'll admit it hasn't been easy. When I found that the keys were missing, I thought you'd probably come back.'

'Did you think I killed Srinivas?'

He shakes his head. 'No. Poor chap was shot by someone else. Very sad to lose him. A terrible tragedy. He was a fine man, one of the sharpest minds in the secret service. India will miss him.'

'India?' I say.

'Yes, he was a tremendous asset for the British empire, but he would have become an even greater intelligence officer for independent India.'

After a brief pause, I ask, 'What happened to all of the documents in this room?'

'They've been removed for safekeeping,' he says. 'Did Srinivas explain their significance to you?'

'Yes, in a general sort of way,' I reply, not wanting to confirm too much.

'What did he tell you?'

'He said there were people who wanted to destroy those files,' I answer. 'Powerful people.'

'Indeed,' he replies.

'Srinivas asked me to protect them. That's why I came back here tonight.'

My anonymous companion nods in the dark.

'I know. He told me that he'd spoken to you and revealed more than he should have....' the voice hesitates, as if fighting a stammer. 'Of course, I don't blame him. He was deeply concerned that the files might disappear or fall into the wrong hands. The truth is that he didn't trust any of us....'

'Did you have him killed?' I ask, my suspicions aroused.

'No. Absolutely not. I disapproved of his decision to involve you. I told him this plainly when we met, only yesterday morning. It was our last conversation,' he says.

'And why should I trust you?' I ask.

'Because I want to make sure that Srinivas didn't die in vain,' he replies.

'I don't even know who you are,' I tell him, reaching into my pocket for a cigarette. 'Though you seem to know a great deal about me.'

'I suspect you've probably got some idea of who I am, though I'm not as much of a legend as you are....'

I quote Tennyson: 'To strive, to seek, to find, and not to yield.'

He laughs but says nothing, neither denying that he is Ulysses, nor confirming it.

'May I smoke?' I ask.

He waves a hand, as if granting my wish. I offer him a cigarette, but he refuses.

In the flare of matchlight, I can see his face clearly for several seconds, his features lined with age but a boyish look in his eyes. The cap covers a bald head. In some ways he reminds me of a classmate from Xavier's, an impish lad we called 'Puck'. He knows that I am studying him, but he doesn't turn his face away and I can tell he is looking at me with the same discerning gaze.

'I'm glad to see you in costume,' he remarks. 'It's very romantic. With modern technology our work has lost much of it charm, don't you think?'

'If you say so,' I agree.

'As I told you earlier, Kim, we've never met before,' he says. 'But I wanted to speak to you face to face because there isn't much time and matters have reached a critical juncture.'

'Please go ahead, I'm listening.' The cigarette smoke fills my lungs and I hold it in for as long as I can, as he continues.

'Srinivas briefed me on your conversations with Sir Denys and his associates. As I'm sure he explained, we've been keeping an eye on them for some time but it's a tricky situation because of his influence with the powers that be. I understand that they are going to hand over an explosive device tomorrow morning, which is to be detonated at a Congress rally in the afternoon. Is that correct?'

'Yes,' I reply.

'And are you sure that this isn't some sort of trap or diversion?'

'No, I can't be sure,' I respond.

'What are their motives?' he asks.

'They want to forestall the transfer of power,' I say. 'Whether they will succeed is another matter. But they are willing to kill people in their attempt.'

'Mr Nehru, specifically?'

'Yes. Didn't Srinivas explain all this to you?' I ask impatiently.

'He did. I'm only confirming.' His voice remains calm.

'Do you want me to go ahead with the plan?' I ask.

'If you think you can do it, yes,' he replies. 'It would give us irrefutable evidence of a conspiracy. That would be very helpful, indeed.'

'What do I do with the bomb once I get it?' I demand. 'Surely, you don't want me to plant it at the rally.'

'No, of course not. We'll arrange to collect it from you and defuse the bomb.'

'But when there's no explosion, they'll suspect I betrayed them,' I say.

'Hopefully, by then we'll have been able to apprehend the conspirators and the government will be forced to lodge a case against them.'

'Including Sir Denys?'

'It all depends on how much his associates are willing to talk... and, I hate to say it, but also how far the government is willing to pursue the matter.'

'If we can't implicate him, the whole effort will be pointless,' I say, with frustration.

Ulysses shakes his head.

'I have to caution you, Kim,' he says. 'In our line of work, we do not interpret or enforce the law. Our job is simply to provide as much information as possible to those who govern the empire, so they can make the right decisions. No matter how compelling the evidence we provide, the final outcome is never in our hands.'

'It sounds as if you're already making excuses for the higher ups,' I complain. 'Sir Denys is the kind of privileged toff who can never be held accountable.'

For almost a minute our conversation stops, and I wish I could see the expression on the face across from me, though the glowing nib on my cigarette is too dim to expose his features. Finally, he answers me with a question.

'How much did Srinivas tell you about the files that were stored in this room?'

Exhaling a cloud of smoke, I realize there is no point in holding back the information I was given. Speaking slowly and as precisely as I can, I explain everything I know about the Durbar Archives and Srinivas's intentions of using the contents to persuade India's royals to concede their power and territory to the new government. When I finish, Ulysses shifts in his chair and leans forward.

'All of that is true,' he murmurs, 'but there is more to it than you've been told. Each of the political officers assigned to the native states have kept confidential files on their respective charges. As you can imagine, this amounts to a voluminous record of royal mismanagement, incompetence, and moral turpitude, not to mention legal jeopardy. The Council of Princes convened by the Maharaja of Patiala is negotiating with the government and the Congress leaders to try and secure their sovereignty following independence. On the other hand, the socialists in London don't have any time for the privileges and prerogatives of native princelings. Meanwhile, within the Viceroy's staff, there are several senior civil servants who are in favour of allowing the princes to keep their kingdoms, though this would be an untenable situation for them and for India as a whole. It's one of the Viceroy's thorniest problems. He is, of course, a member of the British royal family and first cousin to the king.'

I listen closely until the ash from my cigarette drops on my clothes. Tossing the butt on the floor, I crush it beneath my chappal.

'The Congress party has asked the Viceroy to intervene with the princes, knowing that Mountbatten is probably the only person who can coerce them into signing an Act of Accession. The compromise that has taken shape is that the princes will be allowed to keep their titles and personal property. They will also receive generous privy purses from the government to compensate them for the loss of revenue. In addition, they will not be subject to most forms of legal prosecution. Essentially, they hold onto the trappings of power though they surrender their authority as independent rulers. At this point, nobody knows if they will accept the proposal.'

'And all of them will have to agree,' I add, when he pauses.

'Exactly. The challenge of forcing the princes to hand over power is, perhaps, even greater than persuading Britain to quit India. And it all has to happen at once, in concert with Partition. They will be given the choice to join India or Pakistan, but only if their kingdoms are contiguous with the territory of each country, as it is divided. If nothing else, they can delay the entire process for years, squabbling over the terms of accession.'

'Sounds like a nightmare,' I mutter.

'In and of itself, this whole operation would be difficult enough, but the civil servants who are working behind the scenes are an unpredictable lot. Even the Viceroy's own Political Secretary, Sir Conrad Cornfield, a staunch conservative who doesn't hide his prejudices, is determined to let the princes decide their own fate and he has been encouraging them to demand independence. Recently, he made a secret visit to London and met with the top brass in the Colonial Office including the Secretary of State for India and Burma. He was able to extract permission to destroy all of the files pertaining to the native states.'

'But what about the files that were in this room two days ago?' I interrupt him.

'The Durbar Archives are the property of the ISS and do not come under the purview of the Political Secretary,' he says. 'Much of what they contain duplicates the documents that Cornfield has already started to burn. Very few people know of their existence, though somebody must have got wind of it and Srinivas paid with his life.'

'Where did you move them?'

He shakes his head. 'You know I can't tell you that, Kim, but I can assure you they are safe and secure.'

'Will you hand them over to the new government after independence?'

'We'll negotiate an appropriate agreement,' he says. 'Nobody really wants to go rummaging through that mess. It's a distasteful business and the archives compromise not only the princes but a lot of other important people as well. The truth is, there probably won't be any need to expose the information those files contain. Just the fact that we have them in our possession, is enough to help influence important decisions.'

'But I still don't understand why Srinivas was killed,' I say.

'Unfortunately, he had his enemies in the secret service. Many of my countrymen, sad to say, couldn't stand the idea of a native intelligence officer, especially someone in an influential position with access to highly classified information. The same people who want

India to break up into a jigsaw puzzle of independent kingdoms are closely allied with your friend, Sir Denys, and his Brotherhood of Courage. They saw Srinivas as a threat. The conspiracy is much larger than we thought. I confess, I didn't believe it myself until Srinivas laid it out for me, in no uncertain terms. He also showed me the photographs you took of the men who visited the bungalow on Cornwallis Road, which revealed an all-star cast, as they say in Hollywood! It proved that several senior British officers and civil servants are in league with Bromley-Pugh. And if they can't stop the handover, they're determined to destroy India forever. Instead of just one partition, there will be dozens all over the country.'

22

I've always had an aversion to using false beards and moustaches, partly because they seldom make a convincing disguise but also because they have an awkward habit of coming unstuck. Today, however, I have no choice. As I apply spirit gum to my cheeks and chin, the chemical odour is unpleasant and makes my eyes water. For much of my adult life, I've had a natural beard, which I've trimmed and shaped to suit my various personas, but being clean-shaven at present, the only option is an artificial beard, dyed orange with henna.

Yaqzan assists me with my costume, searching through his wardrobe to help me dress up as a venerable Mohammedan, donning a grey silk waistcoat over a loose cotton kameez and baggy salwar with cuffs that end an inch or two above my ankles. It is a simple costume, but often the best disguise is the least. Of course, there is the obvious risk that Stapleton or one of his men might recognize me. However, I don't know anyone else I can trust to carry out this task. Should something go wrong, I'll be able to improvise a solution, rather than depending on a novice who might panic. Though I've never been a stage actor, I do know that the most important part of a dramatic performance is to project a confident sense of self-awareness, which is as vital as any costume or make-up.

When I have finished dressing myself and take a last look in a mirror, I can see Yaqzan studying my reflection. He gives me a smile and raises one hand in salutation.

'Wah!' he says. 'Now Kim has finally become Qasim!'

∽

Battery Lane is a quiet cul-de-sac that dead ends on the edge of a forested tract along the northern end of Delhi's Ridge. A dozen or more bungalows and other single-storey buildings are arranged on either side. Most of them are the residences of junior civil servants and municipal officials. Getting down from a cycle rickshaw on the corner of Rajpur Road, I walk the last hundred yards to the address

I've been given. At 10 a.m., it is already hot, and the bristling beard glued to my chin is uncomfortable. A tightly wound turban shields my head from the sun and I use the loose end of it to mop the sweat from my brow, noticing that some of my skin colour is coming off.

Though there is no guard at the gate, two large dogs are chained to the posts on either side and they set up a loud barking as soon as I approach. Moments later, a servant appears from inside the house. He grabs one of the chained brutes by the collar, so I can squeeze past, bared teeth only a few inches from my calf. The servant does not ask the purpose of my visit and he has obviously been told to admit anyone fitting my general description. Escorting me past a line of empty flowerpots and up the three front steps, he asks me to wait. Standing in the shade of the veranda, I can hear a telephone ringing and voices inside. After several minutes, a young Englishman appears at the door and squints at me suspiciously.

'Who sent you?' he asks in English.

'Townsend Sahib,' I reply.

Scanning the front yard, the man makes sure I have come alone.

Though he is out of uniform, I recognize the Englishman as one of the officers who accompanied Sir Denys at the Gymkhana. Gesturing for me to wait, he disappears back inside, leaving the door slightly ajar. My revolver is securely tucked in at my waist, held in place by the knotted drawstring on my salwar. After a good five minutes, the door opens again but this time I am greeted by the twin muzzles of a twelve-bore shotgun, pointed at my chest. A different Englishman, slightly older and stockier, holds the weapon and glares at me.

'Git' inside,' he says, under his breath.

Doing as I'm told, I step into the entry hall of the bungalow, which is bare, except for a couple of trophies on the walls, the antlers of sambar and chital deer. Nudging me with the shotgun, the man directs me through the first doorway on the right, into a sparsely furnished drawing room with split bamboo blinds covering the windows. A single ceiling fan is turning overhead but the lights are off. On a writing desk in one corner of the room sits a black telephone. The Englishman who spoke to me first is standing to one side, next to Major Stapleton, who is also dressed in civvies. They look me over with sceptical expressions, as if they were expecting someone else, though I am relieved to see no hint of recognition in their eyes.

In bad Hindustani, Stapleton asks my name.

'Qasim Khan,' I answer.

'Do you speak any English?'

'Some,' I say. 'Kuch kuch.'

He then demands to know my profession. I answer him in a mix of Hindustani and broken English, explaining that I have worked as Major Townsend's head syce for fifteen years, looking after his horses and accompanying him on expeditions in the Himalaya. Despite the twelve-bore's muzzle pressing into my lower back at about kidney-level, I try to convey the noble dignity of a loyal retainer, who knows that he is indispensable to his sahib. Since I use a thick accent when I utter an English word or phrase, it's unlikely that they will recognize my voice.

'What did Townsend Sahib tell you to do?' Stapleton asks.

'Sahib boley…come here, get bag,' I reply. 'Take to Dangal Maidan and leave next to stage where haramzade Congresswallahs are speeching.'

He smiles for the first time.

'You don't like the Congress party, do you?' he says.

'No.' I shake my head. 'Only Muslim League. Mohammed Ali Jinnah Zindabad?'

The Englishmen exchange satisfied glances, convinced that I am the person I say I am. Stapleton nods to the young man beside him, probably the sapper who built the bomb.

'All right, give it to him and get him out of here!' he commands.

The young man steps into the hall and returns a minute later with a brown leather gladstone bag with sturdy handles. It looks innocuous, though he holds it gingerly, as if it were full of eggs. The man with the gun takes a step back as I reach out to accept the bag, acting as if I have no idea about the combustible contents.

'Khabardar!' says Stapleton. 'Don't drop it.'

I look at him and nod, touching the fingers of my right hand to my forehead in a gesture of farewell. Turning towards the door, I hold the bag in my left hand as I slip my right hand under my shirt tails and grip my revolver. Swinging back to face them, I am relieved to see that the shotgun is now pointing at the floor.

'Stay where you are,' I say, in English, holding the bag in front of me. 'If you fire at me, this goes off and we'll all be dead.'

Pointing the revolver at the man with the shotgun, I tell him to lay his weapon on the floor and take two steps back. He glances at Stapleton, who nods.

'Slowly,' I warn him. 'Very slowly.'

Once the twelve-bore is safely on the ground, I wave them to one side and the three men retreat to the far end of the room.

'Is anyone else here, in the house?' I ask.

'No,' says Stapleton, his voice tense. 'Only the three of us.'

'I hope you're not lying,' I tell him. 'Because if anything happens to me, I'll lose my grip on this bag and your bomb will go off.'

'There's a servant, that's all,' he says.

'Call him,' I say, stepping forward and kicking the shotgun under the desk, so it's out of reach.

Stapleton hesitates, then summons the servant by name. 'Atma Ram!'

As I guessed, he must have been waiting outside, in the hallway. The servant immediately enters with an anxious expression. Seeing the revolver in my hand, he almost bolts, before I speak to him in Hindustani.

'Nothing will happen to you, unless you try to run away,' I assure him.

He looks as if he doesn't believe me but stays where he is, glancing across nervously at the others.

'Do you have a knife?' I ask him.

He shakes his head.

'What about the three of you?' I repeat the question in English. 'One of you must have a pocketknife.'

The young man who gave me the bomb nods his head.

'Take it out slowly and toss it to him.'

He does as he is told but the servant fails to catch the pocketknife, which falls to the ground with a clatter. Waving the pistol, I direct him to pick it up.

'Now, do as I say,' I tell him. 'Those cords on the window blinds, cut them loose.'

For a moment, he doesn't seem to understand. I repeat the command, with greater emphasis and urgency, after which the servant goes across to the nearest window. Prying open the knife blade, he cuts the sturdy cotton cord, which is used to roll up the blinds. It slips free and falls to the ground.

'Two more,' I tell him, and he complies, moving across to the other windows.

'Shabash,' I say, then address the three Englishmen. 'Now, gents. I want you on your knees.'

I can see that Stapleton has guessed who I am, though he isn't completely sure. None of them moves.

'Down!' I shout, an insistent twitch of the revolver punctuating my words.

The three men lower themselves to the ground and I instruct the servant to tie their hands behind each of their backs.

'Quickly,' I insist. 'And make sure the knots are tight.'

At first his efforts are half-hearted but after I threaten him, he does a better job, trussing up the three sahibs, firmly and efficiently. Each length of the cord has several feet to spare.

'Now, close the knife and throw it under the desk, next to the twelve-bore,' I instruct him, patiently. 'After that, I want you to go and sit over there, facing the wall, with your hands covering your eyes. Stay there and don't move, or else I'll put a bullet through your brain.'

After he crouches down, I finally lower the leather gladstone to the ground while keeping a sharp eye on Stapleton and the others, who appear very unhappy and uncomfortable. Going across to them, I test the knots at their wrists and satisfy myself that they are securely bound.

Lifting Stapleton to his feet, I walk him across to the middle of the room and make him sit on the carpet, facing away from the bomb. Taking the loose end of the cord, I slip it through the handles on the bag and tie a double knot about six inches from his wrists. Then I do the same with the other two men, so they are all seated on the floor, with their backs to each other and tethered to the bomb.

'What time is it set to go off?' I ask.

'Half past two,' says Stapleton, then adds with a grimace, 'I should have known it was you, Townsend. You're a traitor to your country and your race.'

Ignoring the comment, I look at my watch.

'Ten minutes to eleven,' I say, 'which means you have three hours and forty minutes until it explodes. Plenty of time to consider your options.'

'You'll pay for this with your life, you know,' says Stapleton.

'Fucking swine,' the man who was holding the shotgun curses, while the third member of the group remains silent and morose. The servant in the corner hasn't moved.

'I suggest you don't try to stand up or make any sudden movements,' I warn them, walking across to the telephone. Calling the operator, I recite a number I was given last night. It takes more than a minute before I hear a ringing on the other end of the line. Someone picks up without saying hello. I too remain silent but wait a full sixty seconds before hanging up, so this number can be traced. Then picking up the phone, which has a long cord, I take it across to Stapleton and place it in front of him.

'What do you want from us now?' he asks in a surly but defeated tone.

'I want you to call the Brigadier,' I say.

'Who?' he says, pretending that he doesn't understand.

'Sir Denys Bromley-Pugh,' I prompt him.

He shakes his head. 'I won't.'

Smiling at him, I stroke my false beard.

'That's a shame,' I say. 'I was going to suggest you tell him what's happened and ask him to send help. But if you'd rather not,

I'll lock up the house and be on my way. It's now eleven o'clock.'

'You wouldn't dare!' Stapleton hisses. 'That would be murder.'

'Perhaps. But I'm not the one who built the bomb. Nor did I set the timer.'

The young man finally speaks. 'Please!' he begs me. 'Don't leave us like this. I can tell you how to disarm the bomb.'

'Shut up, Colebrook,' snaps the third man. 'Don't be a coward.'

'Three and a half hours is a very long time,' I say. 'Especially, when you know how suddenly it will end…. Boom!'

'Bastard!' the man yells.

'I don't think anyone will hear you outside, even if you shout,' I caution him.

'Show some mercy, for God's sake!' Colebrook begs.

'I'm offering you a simple way to save yourselves. One phone call to the Brigadier and I'm sure he'll send some of your chums around here straightaway to untie you,' I suggest, looking Stapleton in the eye. 'You do have his number, don't you? I'm sure he's waiting by the phone, expecting you to call and tell him that I've taken the bomb and I'm on my way to the Congress rally, just as we planned.'

Stapleton knows that he's trapped. Though he still has a glare of hostility in his eyes, I know that sooner or later he will choose to save his own skin, rather than dying for a lost cause. This was one of several calculations I made when I persuaded Ulysses to let me try to turn things around. Though I didn't explain my plans in any detail, largely because I had none, except for a clear intention of exploiting whatever opportunities arose, Ulysses reluctantly agreed to let me strike back at the Brigadier's men, as long as I didn't endanger anyone else. I also got him to agree to have a surveillance team ready at the telephone exchange to monitor and record any calls I might send their way. This was my only hope of implicating Sir Denys in the plot, a desperate ploy that was more likely to fail than succeed.

For a few minutes more, I engage in an unproductive debate with Stapleton, trying to persuade him that it's in his best interests to speak to the Brigadier. Eventually, I lose my patience. Grabbing the servant by the arm, I haul him to his feet. The poor fellow is so terrified I can feel him trembling, as I head for the door.

'Well, you can't say I didn't give you a chance to save yourselves,' I remind them. 'Don't blame me when the bomb goes off. They'll have to scrape you off the walls.'

Colebrook gives a low wail of despair, as I step out into the hall. 'Wait!'

I keep walking towards the front door.

'Come back! I'll do it, goddamn you!' Stapleton's voice has a plaintive tone.

Returning to the room, I say nothing, pointing the servant back to his spot by the wall and then kneeling down in front of the squat black telephone with its steel dial. Picking up the receiver, I dial '0' and a moment later, a woman's voice answers, remarkably cheery.

When I hold the phone to his mouth, Stapleton gives her the number, while I keep the muzzle of my revolver an inch from his ear. I'm close enough to hear it ringing three times before a man's voice answers.

'May I speak to Sir Denys...urgently, please,' Stapleton responds.

'Who is this?' the man asks. It's a poor connection, with a buzz of static.

'Major Derrick Stapleton.' The sweat is now pouring down his face.

'Hold on, please....' A long, crackling silence follows but then I recognize the Brigadier's voice, with his haughty upper-crust accent.

'Hello, Stapleton. What news?' he asks brusquely.

'Sir....' the Major begins, then pauses as if unwilling to carry on before finally stammering out a confession. 'Sir, there's a problem. We're in a bit of a fix.'

'Why? Didn't they collect the bomb?' I can hear Sir Denys's irritation over the hum of interference on the line.

'Yes...I mean, no, sir. It's Townsend! He's betrayed us! Colebrook, De Vigne and I are being held hostage here at the house. He's tied us up and attached us to the bomb.'

'What the hell are you talking about?' the Brigadier shouts.

'I'm afraid, he turned the tables on us, sir,' Stapleton continues.

'Held us at gunpoint, then threatened to detonate the bomb. Now, he's saying he'll leave us here. Unless you send someone to release us, sir, we'll be blown to bits.'

'Are you mad! Why would you call me? They'll trace this number,' the enraged voice is abruptly cut off as Sir Denys ends the call, knowing full well that I've got him.

'What did he say?' Colebrook asks. Even De Vigne, whose name I've just learned, looks puzzled and anxious.

'He hung up,' says Stapleton.

'Is he going to send someone?' I ask, replacing the receiver and returning the phone to the desk.

'I don't know,' says Stapleton in a weak voice. 'I don't think so.'

A silence follows and I let each of the three men consider their fate. Though I have no sympathies for any of them, they are a pathetic trio, bound together by the consequences of their own actions and the arrogance of their political beliefs.

'Well, if it's any consolation, you'll obviously be martyred for the noble principles of the Brotherhood of Courage,' I say, trying not to sound as if I'm gloating.

Just then, I hear the two guard dogs begin to bark at the gate, making a ferocious row. Lifting the servant to his feet again, I tell him to go and see who is here. As soon as he leaves, I catch Stapleton's eye for the last time.

'You're in luck,' I tell him. 'If I'm not mistaken, the military police are here with a bomb squad. A lucky reprieve!'

With that, I slip out into the hall and find my way to the back of the house, where Qasim Khan makes a quick exit and climbs over a low garden wall, disappearing into the dense forest of Delhi's Ridge.

23

The steam locomotive pulling our miniature train huffs and puffs at every turn, labouring up the steep ascent. I have travelled on this line so often, I know each of the eighteen stations after we depart from Kalka—starting with Taksal; then Gumman (where a cart road takes you to Kasauli); then Koti (also known as Jabli); after which comes Sonwara, where students of Lawrence School get down in a noisy, restless swarm; then Dharampur; then Kumarhatti, after which the train passes through the longest tunnel before Barog; beyond this halt lies Solan; and then Salogra, where Dyer Meakin's brewery and distillery turns the clean, clear waters of Himalayan springs into bitter beer and heady whisky. These stations are followed by Kandaghat and Kanoh, between which lies the highest bridge, spanning a gorge more than seventy-five feet deep; Kathleeghat is next, where I buy tea and cutlets from a platform vendor, before we proceed to Shogi, Tara Devi (sacred to the goddess), and Jutogh, a military cantonment just short of the penultimate station—Summer Hill, where the turrets of the Viceregal Lodge protrude above the treetops and finally...finally Simla!

Coming up the hill from the plains, the air grows gradually cooler and fresher. Now, as I step out onto the platform, I can smell the resinous fragrance of deodars, mingling with the sour, sooty tang of coal smoke. A sturdy hillman ties my duffel bag and suitcase onto his back and we set off on foot for Jhako Hill. It's a two-mile walk to Anastasia's cottage and a section of our route follows the Mall Road. There was a time when natives were not permitted to promenade here but that has changed for the better and I see several honeymoon couples from the Punjab in rickshaws pulled by four coolies. Without a disguise, I feel self-consciously European as I make my way past Christchurch and other familiar landmarks. The only place I break stride is when I pass the shop where Lurgan Sahib used to sell his curiosities and antiques. Though the premises are closed, the building hasn't changed much, a low, pitched roof with fretted gables and a wooden façade, painted dark green. Chequered windows reveal only shadows inside and the main door is locked. It was never an inviting place, poorly lit and cluttered with brass urns and salvers of unknown vintage, decrepit furniture, and strange objects like Tibetan masks and thangkas, ornate Chinese vases, and assorted statuettes of Buddhist and Hindu deities or demons cast in copper, bronze, and brass.

I spent a summer here, in this building, quartered in one of the musty rooms that I shared with another boy, a young Hindu who was fiercely jealous of the attention Lurgan paid me. Sleeping on a lumpy cotton mattress, spread over a frayed Bukhara carpet, I wrapped myself in a Kullu shawl to ward off the chill at night. We ate whatever Lurgan fried up on his paraffin stove or ordered meals from the Sardarji's dhaba on the lower Mall. I would be sent to fetch it in a battered tiffin carrier. Though I learned to read and write at Xavier's in Nucklau, it was here that I got my true education. Lurgan was a dedicated and experienced master and I his eager pupil. More than anything, he taught me skills of observation and the ability to memorize details, from the gleaming colours and names of semi-precious stones, to the faces of those we passed on the Mall, when he took me along for his evening constitutional. He also taught me the subtle art of disguise, how to change the colour of my skin and wear appropriate costumes, while speaking obscure dialects.

But beyond all that, Lurgan conveyed more important lessons and philosophical truths that were almost as profound, and certainly more practical, than the teachings of Teshoo Lama. Lurgan was an amateur ethnologist, a scholar of human traits, traditions, and temperaments. First and foremost, he made me understand that the distinctions between races, castes, and creeds are not always what they appear to be on the surface. Someone like myself, with a white face, an Irish name, and a baptismal certificate that defines me as Roman Catholic, can slough off that identity as easily as a serpent sheds its skin. It is a simple matter of exchanging one disguise for another...and then, another and another. After a point, there is no way of knowing which mask is real and which is not. 'Metamorphosis is not the monopoly of moths and butterflies,' he would say. 'It is a human quality as well. Nobody is the same person he was yesterday and tomorrow you are bound to be someone else. It is similar to what your lama calls "the web of illusion", though instead of leaving it to predestination, Kim, I believe we have agency over our fates. Human beings possess the power to transform themselves, though few men use it and fewer still understand what it means.'

Another fundamental lesson Lurgan taught me was that when a person speaks, you must listen not only to the words but also to the harmonies and dissonance in his voice. 'A man's gestures and facial expressions can reveal much more than his vocabulary. You will know whether he is telling the truth from the flicker of an eyebrow or a slip of the tongue. You're a glib young lad, Kimball, my boy,' he would mumble into his black beard as he chewed on a stinking pipe, 'but never forget that language is more than just talk. Listen for the silences between consonants and vowels, the intake of a nervous breath or the exhalation of a lie.'

Though I am not nostalgic by nature, seeing the old building on the Mall, I feel a sad, queer longing for those lost days, when I was still green and compliant, learning this trade. My reflection studies me from the cobwebbed windowpane, and I wonder, if Lurgan were still alive, would he recognize me now? I'm certainly not a boy any more but, as he would have been the first to remind me, neither am I the same man I was yesterday. Lurgan Sahib was a great illusionist, a sorcerer who played games with a confident sleight of hand, but also an enigma himself. I never understood his relationship with the jealous Hindu boy, who once tried to poison me and crouched in hiding behind the antique furniture in the shop, slinking through the shadows like a cat. Or was he a catamite?

These thoughts and memories continue circling in my mind as I reach the eastern end of the Mall and begin to climb under the tall, straight cedars, crooked oaks, and many-limbed rhododendrons with their blood-red blooms. A bridle trail circles the hill and leads to a viewpoint halfway up while a network of footpaths connects the scattered buildings on the hill. After the first three switchbacks, I am out of breath, feeling my age and unacclimatized to the altitude. It will take a week or two, at least, for me to get my hill legs. Slowly, slowly, I tell myself, letting the coolie carry on with my luggage. He knows the way. We pass a dandi coming downhill carried by four men, bearing a young memsahib wearing a yellow felt hat with an egret plume. She ignores my glance and turns to look in the other direction. Following her are two gentlemen in casual dress, out to take the air. They look like bureaucrats, recently arrived with their files from Delhi. We nod to each other coldly.

At one of the turns in the trail, I stop to have a cigarette, lingering for a while on a view of distant ranges fading into haze. The high Himalaya are hidden today by clouds and dust that has blown up from the plains. Though I am not a mountaineer, only a pretender, there is always a moment of elation when I arrive at these heights, which makes me forget the gross, grim realities of cities on the plains. A quiet smoke takes away the lingering agitation I felt when peering through the windowpanes of Lurgan's shop. I realize that I am a good deal older now than he would have been, when I was a boy. Lurgan died about ten years ago, of a self-inflicted gunshot wound. I got the news in Lahore and later learned that he was buried in the Sanjauli cemetery at the eastern edge of Simla, in one of the unsanctified plots reserved for suicides.

Stamping out the smouldering butt of my cigarette on the path, which is covered with dry deodar needles, I carry on to Swinburne, Anastasia's cottage. A stone staircase leads from the path up to the garden gate. The princess is standing outside, surrounded by irises, larkspur, cornflowers, and primroses, a floral palette of vivid colours.

'Ah, there you are, mon chevalier!' she cries.

Anastasia is holding a trowel in one hand, wearing gardening gloves.

'The flowers are beautiful,' I say.

'It's a complete jungle!' she cries, in frustration. 'I'm going to sack the mali! He doesn't have any sense of how to organize a garden. I leave for the winter and when I come back, he's forgotten everything I told him!'

'Well, it looks like a perfect English garden to me,' I say.

She waves me indoors. 'Your luggage has been put in the back room. Go on in. You know the way,' she says. 'I'll finish here and then we'll have tea.'

The coolie is waiting by the kitchen, and I pay him off, then let myself inside. One of the women who works for Anastasia greets me with folded hands and points me to my room. I've stayed here several times before and there's a comfortable familiarity about the place. Two cats are curled up on the couch in the drawing room. On the mantelpiece are photographs of Anastasia's husband and their son, as well as several portraits of the princess herself as a young woman, wearing silk saris, with her long hair plaited in an elegant braid. Back then, she was acknowledged to be the most beautiful woman in Simla, turning heads at every party, her dance card filled with the names of viceroys, governors, and major generals, all of whom vied for her attention.

After washing up and changing, I wander outside again and find Anastasia sitting under a wisteria arbour. The cottage faces southwest. A section of the town is visible, spread out along the ridge below us.

'So, you got your work done in Delhi?' she asks with a pointed look.

'As much as I was able,' I tell her, kissing Anastasia's cheek, then taking a seat across from her in the shade.

Moments later, the maid emerges with a tea tray and places it on the wicker table between us.

'I suppose you still can't tell me what mischief you were up to, Kim?' she asks.

'I was saving India,' I reply.

She snorts and rolls her eyes. 'Are you still consorting with that awful Brigadier and his fascist goons?'

'No, I think I'm done with them,' I say, watching her pour us each a cup of tea and helping myself to a biscuit from the plate.

'And what's this medal you'll be getting from the Viceroy?'

Anastasia continues to quiz me. 'Did you do something very brave?'

'It's not for me,' I explain. 'It's for the man I'm impersonating, Captain Leslie Townsend. He's being awarded a Kaiser-e-Hind.'

She squints at me suspiciously. 'For what?'

'For performing good deeds on the frontier,' I say.

'Kim, you are impossible!' she complains. 'Why can't you respond to a simple question without turning it into some sort of a riddle?'

'Because there isn't a simple answer. You should know that better than me,' I reply, taking the cup she hands me, then adding three lumps of sugar.

'So, am I still supposed to call you Captain Townsend?' she demands. 'Such a boring, English name. It makes you boring too!'

'I hope we're not going to be socializing much,' I reply. 'I'd be happiest just staying here at home with you and being myself.'

'Oh, Kim, my darling,' she exclaims. 'You pretend to be such a saint, but I know you better than that. Why didn't you and I ever fall in love when we were young?'

'Because it would have ended very badly,' I say. 'And then, we would have been enemies instead of old friends.'

'Old friends!' She laughs, as if it's a joke. 'Don't worry. I seldom go out any more, though I get invited to every do in Simla. I'm too old to walk very far or ride a horse and I've never liked being carried in a dandi or pushed around in a rickshaw.'

'You must get lonely up here,' I say.

'Sometimes,' she answers. 'But I have visitors like you from time to time and I've come to cherish my solitude. Besides, Simla has changed so much. It's not the same happy place it was, when I first came here....'

'On my way up from the station, I passed Lurgan's shop,' I tell her. 'Or what's left of it. The building looks deserted.'

'It was bought by a Jain moneylender, but he's done nothing with it,' says Anastasia. 'Poor Lurgan! He recruited me, you know.'

'Yes,' I say. 'What happened to all of his antiques?'

'The new owner got rid of them. One of the kabadiwallahs carted everything away, though I salvaged a few things, for sentiments' sake, like that brass begging bowl over there. Lurgan said it belonged to your lama. It makes a nice flowerpot for my begonias, don't you think?'

Looking across at the bowl, which sits on a stand with other potted plants, I recognize it straightaway.

'How did Lurgan get it?' I ask.

'He said that once the lama found his sacred river and he was released from the wheel of existence, he didn't need it any more,' Anastasia replies.

'May I have it?' I ask her.

'Of course,' she laughs. 'Are you planning to become a monk?'

'Who knows?' I smile.

'I'll repot the begonia and ask my maid to clean it up and polish it for you.'

A bird lands in the flower bed near us—black with grey wings and a yellow beak.

'Do you know why Lurgan killed himself?' I ask.

She sips her tea before responding.

'It had something to do with that wretched boy,' she says. 'He grew up to be a wicked, wilful young man.'

'Can't blame him, I suppose,' I mumble.

'Who, Lurgan?' she asks.

'No, the boy,' I say. 'Did he have a name?'

'Lurgan called him Jackie,' Anastasia recalls. 'But he must have had another Hindu name.'

'I can't imagine the boy enjoyed a happy childhood, being kept like a pet or a plaything,' I say. 'And who knows what Lurgan made him do. I never thought about it much before but looking back, their relationship seems cruel and perverse.'

'Well, we don't know for sure if Lurgan was a pederast,' says Anastasia. 'Did he ever make a pass at you?'

'No, not really,' I say. 'He fawned over me sometimes, but it never went any further than that.'

'The man with a million secrets,' Anastasia muses, 'and only one that really mattered. It must be dreadful having to hide your desires!'

'He was an inspiring teacher and I admired him,' I concede.

'But it often happens, doesn't it? Someone you respect, suddenly crumbles before your eyes.'

'Perhaps,' Anastasia replies, 'though I always found Lurgan much more interesting than Creighton. They were two opposite personalities—the stiff, military surveyor who did everything by the book and the subversive bohemian, twisting the truth as if it were a corkscrew. Both of them lived for the Great Game and once it was over, I think they lost their way.'

'It happens,' I agree, then change the subject. 'By the way, do you know of a good tailor here in Simla?'

'Yes, there are several excellent darzis. What do you need to have stitched?'

'A suit for the ceremony at the Viceregal Lodge. It's only three days from now and all I've got are a few tattered shirts, khaki shorts, and my salwar-kameez.'

'I think you should go in disguise,' Anastasia teases me. 'Dressed up as a wily Pathan, like your horse trader, Mahbub Ali!'

Smiling, I shake my head. 'No, sadly, I must pretend to be an Englishman for a little while longer.'

'Hang on!' Anastasia exclaims. 'There are two old suits in the cupboard in my dressing room. They belonged to my late husband, tailored on Jermyn Street in London. I've never had the heart to give them away. They might just fit you.'

Within a few minutes, the maid has fetched the suits, both of which smell strongly of mothballs. One is a fine grey tweed, the other a dark blue flannel, double-breasted. The tweed seems more in keeping with my character, so I shrug on the coat. It's a little long in the sleeves, but close enough. Anastasia insists that I try the trousers, which are a couple inches too long, though the waist is comfortably snug.

'We'll have the cuffs taken in,' Anastasia decides, 'and the suit dry-cleaned so you're not smelling of naphthalene. What about a tie and shoes?'

'I have a pair of black Oxfords,' I tell her, 'which can be polished up.'

'There are several of Manjeet's old ties in the cupboard,' Anastasia says and disappears inside, returning a few minutes later with a selection in hand.

'They're all a bit wide, don't you think?' she says.

'No problem,' I assure her, choosing one with red and grey stripes. 'Captain Townsend is at least twenty years out of date.'

Anastasia studies me for a moment.

'I remember that suit,' she says. 'Manjeet and I had gone to London and we were staying at the Savoy. He and I spent a whole morning choosing the fabric. Manjeet wanted a rougher tweed but I told him he wasn't going to use it for shooting. Though he agreed with me in the end, I think he was disappointed and seldom wore that suit. I thought he looked very smart in it, as do you!'

'How many years ago was that?' I ask.

She thinks for a moment, before answering. '1903, the year after we got married. Imagine! Forty-four years ago.'

'Do you miss him?' I ask, feeling a twinge of unease, knowing that I'm wearing her dead husband's clothes.

Tilting her head to one side and keeping her eyes on me, she replies, 'Sometimes, yes. He was a dear, sweet man. I never heard him utter an angry word.'

'When did he die?'

'Nineteen oh nine, the year after Pratap was born. We were married for only six years. He was three decades older than me,' Anastasia says.

'And you never thought of remarrying?' I ask.

'No,' she says decisively, then gives me a coy smile. 'I preferred to remain a merry widow. Besides, what more did I need? I inherited this cottage and a share of the home in Delhi, as well properties in Lunagarh, all of which will go to Pratap, after I'm gone.'

'You've done pretty well for a penniless girl from Odessa!' I tease her.

'God knows it hasn't been easy,' she says. 'I was never meant to live an idle life. Thankfully, Lurgan offered me an escape from the pampered privileges of petty royalty. I would have gone crazy living in the palace at Lunagarh with my sisters-in-law and the rest of them, performing the rituals of a princely household. They disapproved of my headstrong nature but if they'd known I was a spy, it would have scandalized them!'

24

The Viceregal Lodge is an enormous Victorian pile, supposedly modelled on castles in Scotland, though I wouldn't know if that's true, never having been there. All I can say is that on first impression, the building is a forbidding structure with red tiled roofs, heavy walls of roughly dressed stone, and broad balconies with splayed arches. It rises three storeys above an expanse of manicured lawns and gardens, framed by stately deodars and oaks. A hexagonal tower on the left is surmounted with a weathervane shaped like a rooster. The grand entrance is ornately sculpted out of pale grey granite, embellished with the royal crest. Above and behind the main building is a second tower, with square walls that ascend two levels higher than the rest, like the uppermost battlements of a fortress. Atop this flies the Union Jack, its red, white, and blue crosses fluttering in the afternoon breeze.

Arriving on foot, half an hour before the ceremony is scheduled to begin, I feel an immediate impulse to flee back to Anastasia's cottage and hide. Two of the Viceroy's Bodyguard, in red uniforms with blue facings, stand sentry at the gate. After I present the invitation card I received in Delhi, they allow me to proceed along the paved driveway that curves up to the main portico. Approaching the lodge, a strange, unsettling sensation overcomes me, as if I am no longer in India, transported in a dream, to some faraway land that I vaguely recognize but have never seen before.

The Viceroy's staff receive me at the door. With polite mumblings that I barely register, they usher me inside the main hall, a grand, vacuous space with a ceiling three floors high. The walls are panelled in Burma teak, polished to a rich russet hue that reflects the amber glow of chandeliers and other lamps. Skylights high overhead admit an opaque aura that creates a mosaic of shadows on the tiered balconies and staircases that surround us.

Twenty or thirty chairs have been arranged at one end of the hall, facing a large stone fireplace. The scale and grandeur of the architecture, as well as the lavish décor and furnishings, have the desired effect of reducing me to humble insignificance. The Viceroy's personal secretary, Michael Dunbar, introduces himself and casts a tolerant eye over the cut of my suit and the knot in my tie, which Anastasia struggled for half an hour to get right. I invited her to come to the ceremony, but she declined, insisting that her petunias needed transplanting. Dunbar, who is a restless, eager man with a full moustache, introduces me to a pair of elderly women from the Zenana Mission. They are receiving Kaiser-e-Hind medals for their charitable good deeds in the villages of the United Provinces. The missionaries are chatty with Dunbar, though they obviously sense in me a lost soul who has gone too far astray.

After a few minutes, once a small audience of officials and other guests have assembled, we are asked to take our seats and a prolonged silence follows, broken only by the two miss sahibs whispering to each other on my left. Then, all at once, without any fanfare, Lord Louis Mountbatten enters the room from a door to our right, accompanied by her Ladyship, Edwina, in a stylish summer dress. She has a long face and thin lips, her features beautiful in a plain sort of way. The Viceroy is dressed in his white naval uniform, with a loop of gold braid on one shoulder and a fair share of medals on his chest. He is about twenty years younger than me, in his early forties. I've seen plenty of photographs of him in the papers, with his chiselled good looks and dark hair combed back from a noble brow. Someone told me that his family name used to be Battenberg, in keeping with his Teutonic roots, but it was changed to Mountbatten during WWI because of anti-German sentiments in Britain. The Viceroy is also closely related to the Russian royal family, most of whom are now dead, killed during the revolution. More importantly, he is the first cousin of King George VI. Mountbatten has the suave, slightly high-strung manner of the British upper classes. If it wasn't for his dark hair and sombre eyes, he might even look quite similar to Sir Denys Bromley-Pugh, though the Brigadier is shorter and has a haughty manner, while the Viceroy seems a congenial man, confident in his own superiority but happy to make small talk with lesser mortals.

Thankfully, the ceremony is brief and the two zenana missionaries, Miss Thorpe and Miss Carter, receive their Kaiser-e-Hind silver medals before me. The Private Secretary reads a citation for each, and his lordship offers a few unscripted remarks after pinning the medals to their pious bosoms. When Captain Leslie Townsend's name is called next, I almost forget to stand up but then do my best to straighten my shoulders and look like someone who deserves a medal, rather than the charlatan I am. Dunbar reads a highly fictional account of my heroics in Chilas, digging survivors out from under the debris of an earthquake and offering assistance to the local tribesman in the aftermath of a seismic disaster. For this, Captain Townsend is commended by his Majesty's government and awarded a bronze Kaiser-e-Hind. The Viceroy takes the medal from a silver salver held by his ADC and pins it above the breast pocket of Kanwar Manjeet Singh's suit. Then he shakes my hand vigorously, looking me straight in the eye while offering a few platitudes about courageous deeds in remote places, after which I bow gratefully and retreat to my chair. The entire event takes no more than fifteen minutes, following which we are invited to a reception on the lawns outside, where tea will be served.

As I rise from my chair and congratulate the two missionaries, Dunbar comes up behind me and places a solicitous hand on my arm.

'Captain Townsend,' he says, under his breath. 'Would you mind coming with me? His lordship would like a private word in his study.'

Surprised, I nod, wondering what's going on. Perhaps they know I'm a fraud and they'll take the medal back.

When we enter Mountbatten's study, which is lined with bookcases containing more volumes than any man could read in several lifetimes, I begin to understand what's going on. The Viceroy is standing with his back to me, speaking to a bald-headed gentleman with round spectacles, wearing a tweed suit, somewhat shabbier than mine. He is leaning on a Malacca cane. I recognize Ulysses immediately, though the only time we've met was in the dark. He catches my eye and gives me a tentative smile, as the Private Secretary retreats and closes the door behind him.

'I believe you know each other,' the Viceroy says, turning towards me with a casual wave of his hand.

'Yes, yes of course,' says Ulysses, stepping forward and shaking my hand. 'How good to see you again.'

'I've been hearing all about your exploits, Townsend,' Mountbatten interjects. 'It seems we owe you a profound debt of gratitude for your actions. Quite a remarkable feat! Of course, I've always admired you chaps in the Secret Service, though I seldom know what you're up to with all of your cloak-and-dagger operations. Must be terribly exciting and unnerving. On the Burma Front and in Malaya, we relied heavily on our intelligence officers. How the deuce they kept an eye on the Japs, I haven't a clue, but the information they gave us was invaluable, absolutely critical to our victory.'

Ulysses nods appreciatively.

'As I was saying, your Lordship, Captain Townsend has been working undercover for some time. He's one of our finest, most experienced agents....'

The Viceroy smiles at me, then winks. 'And I understand that Townsend isn't your actual name.'

I shrug and smile. There doesn't seem to be any reason to contradict the most powerful man in India. He's obviously been briefed on what happened in Delhi.

'Single-handedly, Townsend uncovered a conspiracy that would have rocked the empire to its core,' Ulysses declaims, his manner and voice reminding me of one of my teachers at Xavier's, who always kept his hands clasped behind his back when speaking and rose up on his toes to emphasize a point. 'If that bomb had gone off as intended, Mr Nehru and many of his associates would have been killed. God knows what the consequences would have been....'

'Horrific!' Mountbatten agrees. 'All of the plans we've set in motion for the handover of power in India would have been decimated in an instant.'

'Have the perpetrators been arrested?' I ask, politely.

'Yes, of course,' Ulysses confirms, though I can see a flicker of hesitation in his eyes, as if he doesn't want to take the conversation in that direction.

'Treason!' the Viceroy exclaims. 'To think that men who took an oath to serve their King Emperor and uphold the honour of their regiments, could have plotted something like this. It's incredible! Shocking! Unthinkable....'

Ulysses coughs into his fist.

'If I may, your Lordship,' he interrupts. 'Perhaps we could proceed.... I'm sure her Ladyship is waiting for you to join her outside.'

'Yes. Yes,' Mountbatten agrees, turning towards his desk. Ulysses helps him retrieve a blue velvet box that sits by an inkstand. 'It's such a shame, we can't do this in public. If you weren't in the secret service, I'm sure they'd put up a statue of you somewhere in London.'

When the box snaps open, I see another medal, this one much grander than the bronze Kaiser-e-Hind pinned above my coat pocket. A silver cross with a circular insignia at the centre, it is suspended from a royal-blue ribbon. Clearing his throat, the Viceroy speaks in a formal tone: 'On behalf of his imperial majesty, King George VI, we are pleased to confer on you Great Britain's highest civilian award for gallantry—the George Cross.' Mountbatten positions it to the right of the Kaiser-e-Hind and pins it in place. 'This medal recognizes acts of the greatest heroism or of the most conspicuous courage in circumstances of extreme danger.'

For once, I am entirely speechless, having never imagined that I would receive an honour like this. I wonder what Creighton, Mahbub Ali, Lurgan Sahib, and Hurree Babu would have thought to see their pupil adorned with this imperial bauble. An inexplicable lump begins to form in my throat, but I control myself and take a deep breath as the Viceroy shakes my hand again, with an earnest, heartfelt grip.

'Congratulations, Kimball O'Hara. I know I'm not supposed to utter your name, but at a moment like this....' The Viceroy claps me on the shoulder.

'Thank you, your Lordship,' I finally get the words out, then exchange a glance with Ulysses, who blinks at me through the thick lenses of his spectacles. 'I am deeply honoured and thoroughly surprised, so please forgive me if I can't find the appropriate words of gratitude. But may I ask a question?'

'Fire away!' The Viceroy insists, beaming with pleasure.

'Has Brigadier Sir Denys Bromley-Pugh been arrested? I hope he'll be court-martialled along with the rest of them.'

Immediately, the two men's expressions waver. They continue smiling but an awkward tension contorts their facial muscles, what Lurgan called 'the fatal twitch'.

'Ah, yes....' says the Viceroy, hesitating. 'He's been ordered back to London. Flew home two days ago. You can be sure that India has seen the last of him....'

At this point Ulysses steps in and explains, 'Given the sensitive circumstances surrounding this conspiracy, it's been dealt with in a strictly confidential manner. You will appreciate that arresting a senior British military officer for an act of terrorism would have serious political consequences, both here and in Whitehall. The Government of India feels that under present conditions, with the country experiencing unprecedented turmoil, even the hint of what was being planned would undermine any efforts for a peaceful transfer of power.'

'So, you're letting him off the hook,' I blurt out, my mouth dry as chalk.

'Not at all,' says the Viceroy. 'At this very moment, the Ministry of Defence in London is setting up a special investigative committee to review the case. Bromley-Pugh will undoubtedly suffer the consequences of his rash actions....'

'I understand, your Lordship,' I reply, not wanting to hear any more.

'Good man! Now, if you'll excuse me, I'll leave the two of you alone. I'm afraid I'm expected to make an appearance at tea. Congratulations, once again!'

With that, Louis Francis Albert Victor Nickolas, the First Earl Mountbatten of Burma takes his leave, opening the door for himself before exiting the room.

'You've got some cheek, berating the Viceroy,' says Ulysses, though he maintains the benign look of a schoolmaster who has just reprimanded one of his students.

'I didn't want a damned medal,' I complain. 'I wanted that bastard to go to jail.'

'Of course, I understand,' Ulysses nods. 'But as I told you, it isn't our job to make decisions, only to provide the evidence and information that government requires.'

'So, Srinivas died in vain?'

'No, not at all. The Durbar Archives are secure. More than anyone, his lordship recognizes the significance of those files, and you can be sure that they will be used exactly as Srinivas intended, to keep the native princes in line.'

'What about Stapleton and the others?'

'They'll be court-martialled, no question.' Ulysses blinks and tucks his arms behind his back, then chuckles. 'You literally tied them to the bomb.'

'What about the recording of Sir Denys speaking on the telephone?'

'Yes, we have the tape, but the Adjutant General didn't feel it was sufficient to bring formal charges.' Ulysses rises up on his toes. 'And, frankly, these days nobody has the stomach for a scandal.'

'They'll always save one of their own, won't they?' I shake my head in disgust.

'Indeed,' Ulysses agrees.

'What if I give testimony?' I suggest. 'As a witness to Sir Denys's culpability.'

'As Captain Townsend?' Ulysses asks. 'Remember that's your alias, Kim. They'll never accept testimony from someone who doesn't exist.'

'Then what if I testify as myself?' I say, throwing up both hands. 'At this point I don't care if my cover is blown.'

Ulysses gazes down at the parquet floor, silent for several moments.

'You're forgetting something,' he reminds me. 'Kimball O'Hara is no longer alive. He was killed in action in the Khyber Agency in 1919. I don't think any court-martial is going to accept evidence from a ghost.'

'Are you serious?' I blurt out.

'Quite serious,' he says. 'The George Cross that's dangling from your coat, I had to pull a lot of strings to get them to award it to you, because I felt you deserve it more than anyone I know. But, Kim, the only way I could make it work with the red tape-wallahs in Delhi, was to have it awarded posthumously.'

Glancing down at the medal, I have to laugh at the absurdity of it all.

'Did the Viceroy realize he was pinning it on a dead man?' I ask.

'I made him aware of the special circumstances,' Ulysses answers cautiously. 'Being in the secret service allows us some room to manoeuvre and his Lordship chose not to ask too many questions.'

'But you told him my name,' I say.

'I did,' he replies, unfolding his arms from behind his back. 'I felt it was only appropriate that he should know exactly who it was that saved the day!'

Glancing around at the walls full of books, I shrug my shoulders.

'I suppose it doesn't matter, does it?' I concede. 'Who I am and who I'm not.'

Ulysses extends his right palm.

'Goodbye, Kim. And thank you for all you've done.' He shakes my hand with a gentle but resolute grip, before pointing to the door. 'I'll let you go out first.'

⁂

In no mood for small talk, I skip the tea party and by the time I reach the main gate both medals are safely tucked away inside the pocket of my coat. Though I can still feel an agitated pulse in my ears, it has slowed by now and a fatalistic sense of resignation dilutes my anger and bitterness. There was no need for Ulysses to honour me, as he has done, and I am moved by his gesture, even if the George Cross itself means little to me.

Before heading back to Jhako Hill, I decide to take a detour along a quiet path that leads away from town towards the Sanjauli cemetery. I remember walking here as a boy, whenever I grew bored with Lurgan's games and lessons, needing to get away and be on my own for a bit. The path leads through an oak forest and then crosses a grassy knoll from where I can look southward across the foothills that extend towards the plains. Lighting a cigarette, I inhale the fumes from the fragrant weed and let my mind wander across the pleated contours of the landscape.

But all at once, my sixth sense warns me, and I look around to see if I am being followed. Nobody else is on the path behind me though there are a couple of hillmen on ahead, carrying loads of firewood on their backs. Just above the knoll is a grove of rhododendrons, some of which are blooming. Instinctively, I climb towards them and stoop beneath the lower branches, taking shelter in their shade. Hidden from view, I finish my smoke, seated on a soft cushion of dry leaves. A griffon vulture circles above the valley, on outstretched wings.

Just as I stub out my cigarette, a lone figure appears around a bend in the path. He pauses for a moment, scanning the slope ahead before continuing in my direction. As the man passes below the grove where I am hiding, I recognize him straight away. His pale blonde hair and brutish features are unmistakable—Lieutenant Craven, the Staffordshire Bull Terrier, who beat me at billiards. Sir Denys praised his talent as a marksman and in his right hand, the killer cradles a pistol.

25

When I arrive at Swinburne, out of breath and very red in the face from having rushed up the path, Anastasia is busy watering her fuchsias, which are just coming into bloom. Their delicate, tassel-like flowers always remind me of Chinese lanterns. She waves as I step through the garden gate at the top of the steps.

'How was it?' she cries, then seeing that I am panting and sweating, looks at me with alarm. 'Good God! What happened to you, Kim?'

'Someone's on my tail,' I explain. 'I need your help.'

'Of course,' she responds, putting down her watering can. 'I thought you were getting a medal.'

'I did. In fact, I got two,' I answer. 'But come inside for a moment and I'll explain what I need you to do.'

Earlier, hidden in the rhododendron grove, I evaded my assassin. After that, it took me three-quarters of an hour to get here. Once Craven realized I'd given him the slip, he obviously turned around. Halfway up the hill, I spotted him following me again. I've got less than a thirty-minute lead. Though the lieutenant is much younger than me, I doubt if he's got his hill legs yet and he certainly doesn't know all of the shortcuts up Jhako Hill.

Twenty minutes later, Anastasia resumes her watering, humming the opening bars of *Peer Gynt Suite*. If anyone can act calm and unflustered, even in the most dangerous circumstances, it is the princess. As she refills her watering can at the tap, Anastasia scolds the old mali, who is weeding a flower bed full of sweet William and phlox, berating him for having left the garden in such a neglected state. He ignores her, crouched barefoot at the edge of the flower bed, with a dishevelled turban and a shawl draped over one shoulder.

As I expected, Craven arrives a few minutes later, appearing at the gate like a dog that's lost his bone, irritable and restless. By now the sun has set beyond the treetops and the garden lies in shadow.

'Hello!' Anastasia calls out in a cheerful, disarming voice. 'May I help you?'

He eyes her with suspicion then answers. 'I'm looking for someone.'

'Oh! Who's that?' she enquires.

'Townsend. Is he here?' Craven's manner is blunt and rude.

'Yes, of course, Leslie's my guest. He went to the Viceregal Lodge this afternoon for a ceremony, but he hasn't come back.' She pauses and smiles. 'You look thirsty. Would you like to come inside and have a glass of water?'

Craven nods and unlatches the gate, then leaves it open. He follows Anastasia into the cottage. Though his pistol is hidden under his jacket, the bulge is visible.

As she pours a glass of water for Craven, the princess explains that Townsend was planning to visit a friend after the ceremony, at a cottage called Ravenshead, on the other side of Jhako Hill. Craven drains the glass while eyeing the interior of the cottage with a predator's gaze. Anastasia's performance is utterly convincing, babbling on like a voluble spinster who has nothing to hide.

'Where's Ravenshead?' Craven demands, as they step back outside onto the veranda.

Anastasia begins to explain, then stops herself with an apologetic laugh.

'So sorry. I'm afraid I'm useless when it comes to giving directions and I'm sure I'll get you thoroughly lost, especially since it's growing dark. Why don't I send my mali with you to show you the way? It's about twenty minutes' walk from here. You might even meet Leslie on the path.'

Craven glances around him with a look of sullen uncertainty.

'Or you could come back tomorrow,' Anastasia suggests. 'Have lunch with us, perhaps. I'm sure he'll be delighted to see you.'

'All right,' Craven mutters and points to the mali. 'Tell him to take me there.'

Ignoring the lieutenant's uncouth manner, Anastasia simpers then speaks in a memsahib's Hindustani. 'Chet Singh. Take the sahib to Ravenshead. Jhat Phat!'

The old mali gets up stiffly and straightens his back, then greets Craven with a deferential salaam. Shoulders stooped, and his head bowed, he turns towards the gate. The bull terrier follows without thanking Anastasia, looking back over his shoulder one last time before descending the stairs. The princess waves and smiles.

Under the deodars, the shadows have blackened where the trail zig-zags downhill. Ten minutes later, they reach a fork in the path, where the old mali gestures for the sahib to follow him to the right, along a level path that circles the hill. Passing above another cottage, they see lamps burning in the windows. Nobody else is on the unlit trail. After another hundred yards, the forest opens out into a clearing, from where the lights of Simla are visible far below. Their route then passes beneath a stand of mixed oaks, conifers, and barberry bushes. A troop of langur monkeys leaps across a gap in the branches overhead. Silhouetted against the twilit sky, they look almost human except for their long tails.

The mali curses them roundly in his rustic hill dialect, telling the sahib how the bhainchud langurs destroy the garden at Swinburne, uprooting plants and eating the flowers. Understanding nothing of what's being said, Craven only grunts in response before urging the mali to walk faster.

'Get a fuckin' move on, you old turd.'

Ordinarily, I would take offence to a remark like that but I carry on along the path without reacting, my head still bowed and shoulders hunched. No cottages lie along this section of our route and at this hour nobody else is about. As we come to a narrow ravine, the trail bends sharply to the left and a steep cliff falls away about forty feet into a tangle of thorn bushes below. Taking two quick steps forward, I cross over to the other side of the ravine. Craven is about five yards behind me, as I reach into the folds of my shawl and pull out the Webley .38. It takes him a moment to register what's happening, after which he immediately draws his pistol. But before he can fire, my revolver barks twice, the flare from the muzzle flashing in the shadows and the smell of cordite mingling with the mountain air. Craven falls backwards against the slope of the hill and then rolls sideways, still gripping the pistol. His mouth opens but no sound emerges, and I can see blood seeping from the wounds in his chest.

Keeping my revolver trained on him, I wait another thirty seconds, then cross back over the ravine and nudge Craven's leg with my bare foot to make sure he's dead. In the gathering darkness, his face looks even whiter and uglier than before. Using my foot again, I push him off the side of the path and he tumbles down the cliff before disappearing with a crash into the underbrush below.

∽

'It will be at least two or three days before his body is found,' I reassure Anastasia. 'Once he begins to stink. We didn't meet anyone on the path, and nobody saw him coming here. There's nothing to trace him to you.'

'I'm not worried,' she says, petting one of the cats that is nestled in her lap. 'I'm just glad that he's dead, not you.'

Swallowing the dregs of my whisky, I get up to pour myself another drink.

'I had a feeling somebody would come after me,' I say. 'Obviously, they must have learned about the Kaiser-e-Hind. It was no secret and after what happened in Delhi, they clearly wanted revenge.'

I have told Anastasia the whole story, about the bomb and the plot to kill Nehru. There is no reason to hide it from her anymore. I also told her about the Viceroy presenting me with the George Cross and that Sir Denys will not be court-martialled.

'How long has it been since you killed a man?' she asks.

My hand shakes as I pour the whisky.

'Quite a few years. Maybe eight or ten,' I say. 'One never gets used to it.'

'No. Not even if it's the most vile and evil person in the world,' she says. 'I've only shot three men and each of them deserved to die. That was more than thirty years ago, yet I can still see their faces, as if it were yesterday.'

'Do you keep a weapon in the house?' I ask.

'I have one of Manjeet's old shotguns, which he used for

partridge-shooting, and there's a Browning pocket pistol that Creighton gave me.' The cat is purring in her lap. 'You never know when you might need it.'

We sit in silence for several minutes.

'May I light a fire in your bukhari?' I ask, pointing to the wood stove in the far corner of the room

'It's not that cold, is it?' she replies, puzzled.

'No, but I need to burn some things,' I say.

'Go ahead,' she agrees. 'There's split wood in the godown behind the kitchen, and pine cones for kindling.'

The maid has gone home and neither of us is hungry. Setting my drink down, I go and fetch an armload of wood and two pine cones. With some crumpled paper to get it started, the fire catches easily and I listen as the stove begins to roar, while I sip my whisky. Then I carry the duffel bag and suitcase in from my room. One by one, I begin to burn my clothes and other belongings.

'Where are you planning to go?' Anastasia asks me, after watching for a while.

'Back into the hills,' I reply.

'How far?'

'I don't know. As far as I need to go,' I say.

'When will you leave?' she asks.

'Tomorrow morning,' I tell her, as I stuff two of my shirts into the bukhari. 'I'll be gone before dawn.'

Anastasia says nothing for several minutes, then asks, 'Will I see you again?'

I look up at her and try to smile. 'Probably not, but you never know....'

'Well, don't expect me to stick around much longer,' she says. 'I'm getting older by the day, you know, and my heart's not what it used to be. The doctor says I have arrhythmia. I felt it skip a couple beats while I was charming your assassin.'

'You were magnificent today,' I compliment her. 'Absolutely brilliant!'

'So were you,' Anastasia says. 'Will you pour me a drink? A

small whisky with just a splash of water.'

I get it for her, placing the glass on the side table beside Anastasia, who touches my hand with a grateful gesture.

'How many of them do you think there are?' she asks.

'Who?' I say, tossing my black Oxfords into the blaze.

'The Brotherhood of Courage,' she says.

'Probably not more than a hundred core members, though I'm sure they have plenty of sympathizers. Fascism never seems to go out of style.'

'What did they really hope to achieve?' she asks.

'Obviously, the brotherhood wants to undermine the handover of power, but beyond that their real ambition was to persuade some of the princely states to remain autonomous kingdoms, rather than siding with India or Pakistan. In that process, they hope to exert influence over the maharajas and nawabs, promoting their fascist principles and politics.'

'Many of the princes would have probably found that an attractive proposition,' Anastasia muses. 'I'm sure they aren't particularly happy about Gandhi and Nehru's socialist rhetoric.'

'You're right,' I agree. 'In fact, I've been told that Sir Denys actually held several rounds of talks with the Maharaja of Kashmir's top advisers, offering to raise an army for him and recruit ex-civil servants to help run his kingdom. They promised to turn Kashmir into the Switzerland of Asia.'

'It could happen, couldn't it?' Anastasia nods.

'Yes, and if they succeed in Kashmir, the rest of India will fracture too, breaking up into dozens of independent states,' I explain, recalling my last conversation with Srinivas. 'You might even find yourself crowned queen of Lunagarh.'

Anastasia laughs. 'Pratap and I call it Looneygarh. It would be madness! But you've put a stop to that, haven't you, Kim?'

A couple of my old turbans join the burning remains of my shoes, while I add a few more pieces of wood to help keep the fire going.

'I'm not sure if I've accomplished anything at all,' I tell her. 'With Sir Denys out of the picture, even if he isn't court-martialled, the government has a better chance of holding India together, but it will be a delicate process and a fragile union. I'm sure that Mr Jinnah would be delighted if he gets Pakistan for himself while the rest of the subcontinent fragments into disarray.'

'You should have been a politician, Kim,' the princess teases me.

'No, it's a dirtier business than even espionage.' I shake my head.

'Let's not talk about the present, it's too depressing' she says, holding out her empty glass for me to refill. 'I'd much rather remember the past. We had a lot of adventures, didn't we? And good times too!'

After I get us both another drink, I sit cross-legged on the carpet, feeding the last of my clothes into the bukhari. Anastasia reminisces about our visits to Kashmir in pursuit of Russian provocateurs, both real and imagined. Her mood grows increasingly nostalgic, which is unusual for someone as practical and pragmatic as her. Recalling the time in 1917, when she and I camped on the meadows above Pahalgam, posing as White Russian émigrés who had escaped from the Bolsheviks and taken refuge in Kashmir. We were trying to lure a Czarist agent out of hiding, though it turned out he had already left Kashmir and was on his way to Australia. While we were in Pahalgam, Anastasia tried to teach me a few Russian phrases, the only one of which I could remember was, 'Mozhno mne stakhan vodki?' which means, 'May I have a glass of vodka?' Whenever anyone came to our camp, I kept repeating this phrase to them like a parrot, though they had no idea what I was talking about. After a while, every time I said it, Anastasia would burst into laughter.

'A stupid, silly joke,' she says. 'I don't know why I found it funny.'

By now, most of my clothes have been consigned to the bukhari and I take my Leica out of the suitcase, handing it over to Anastasia.

'What's this?' she asks

'A camera,' I say.

'I know that,' she responds. 'But why are you giving it to me?'

'I won't need it any more and I thought you might be able to use it,' I say.

She opens the case and examines the Leica, adjusting the settings.

'Is there any film inside?' Anastasia asks.

'Yes, I took a few pictures in Delhi, nothing important, but there must be a dozen frames left on the reel,' I tell her.

Raising the camera, she points it at me, then snaps a picture.

'What are you doing?'

'Taking your photograph, what do you think?' she says. 'If you're going to be leaving me forever, I'd like to have a picture of you.'

She takes another shot, though the light is poor and without a flash, it will probably be underexposed.

'Come on, Kim, give me a smile,' she says, clicking the camera again. 'You look so glum!'

Though I don't feel like smiling, I try my best, as Anastasia takes a couple more shots, focusing on my face.

'Mozhno mne stakhan vodki?' I say, as the camera clicks, after which both of us break down in a fit of uncontrollable laughter, until the tears flow from our eyes.

26

Departing at first light, he steals quietly out the kitchen door, so as not to wake Anastasia. After passing through the garden gate, which he closes carefully behind himself, he makes his way like a shadow down the stone steps to the footpath below. Instead of turning left, as he did last night, he heads in the opposite direction, around the north side of Jhako Hill, until he comes to a mule track descending into the valley. This route leads away from Simla, towards villages further back in the hills. At this hour of the morning, nobody else is moving about and the only sounds are birdsong and the scuffling of leaves as small, nocturnal creatures retreat into hiding.

Today, the snow peaks are visible as faint blue shadows against the brightening sky. He pauses for a moment to trace their profiles, trying to recall the names of each summit, though his memory fails him. The air is cool and still. Dressed as a mendicant, he wears an unstitched cloth of reddish hue wrapped about his loins, and a thin cotton shawl of the same colour draped over his shoulders, covering his upper body. On his feet are a pair of sandals. In one hand he holds the begging bowl that Anastasia gave him. The only other possessions he carries are tucked into a cloth satchel slung over his right shoulder. His face and the rest of his skin is smeared with ash, which was taken from the bukhari stove and mixed with a little water to make a grey paste. A frayed turban covers his hair, hiding one ear.

He walks slowly and deliberately down the dusty track without looking back. The expression on his face is impassive, revealing no emotions, yet hinting at a sense of quiet resolve. This is not the beginning of a journey, it would seem, but the continuation of a lifelong quest. As an ascetic sanyasi, he has renounced the world, casting off all material desires and personal relationships or attachments. He no longer has a name and has absolved himself of the past. The pronoun 'I' has been shed along with his ego, lineage, race, and caste. He has no home and will survive on the charity of those he meets during his wanderings.

The sun rises to his right and gilds the high mountains, which gradually turn from blue to gold and then to white. From his satchel he takes a rosary of rudraksha seeds and fingers the rough beads while he walks. The rumpled contours of the mountains unfold in front of him, corrugated with terraced fields. When he reaches the foot of the valley, the sanyasi wades across a shallow stream and begins to ascend the opposite slope. Hours later, as daylight fades into darkness, he takes shelter in a wooded glen, near a spring where Bhotia traders are camped with their pack animals, both sheep and ponies. Fierce dogs bark at him menacingly but the nomads bring him food, parched barley flour mixed with butter tea, which he receives gratefully in the lama's begging bowl. The traders also offer him chang, a cloudy millet beer, poured into a dented brass tumbler that he produces from his satchel.

Lighting a twig fire, he smokes a chillum of tobacco laced with ganja before falling asleep on the grass. Exhausted from the day's exertions, he wakes hours later in the darkness to a sky full of stars. The faraway constellations and galaxies spread over him like spindrift in the heavens. He feels every pinprick of light piercing his soul. Lying awake until dawn, he listens to the soft hooting of owls and feels the dew moistening the ash on his skin.

His legs ache and his feet are sore, but he rises with the sun and continues on his way, climbing to the top of the ridge and following the crestline until it dips down to a pass, where another trail leads on to the next valley. In a village of a dozen homes, he is offered amaranth cakes and buttermilk, as well as apricots ripening on a crooked tree that leans over a stone wall. He rests in its shade for a while before moving on.

In this way, the days pass slowly, as he climbs higher into the Himalaya, crossing over meadows above the tree line and traversing forested slopes where the paths he follows disappear in the tangled gloom of giant oaks with broad-leafed domes and tall fir trees that tower above him like green minarets. For days he eats nothing but wild raspberries, hazelnuts, honeycombs, and mushrooms that he gathers in the forest. By now the sun has burned his skin a walnut brown and a grey beard bristles on his chin. Disillusioned and depressed, he craves solitude and seeks no human company, except when strangers feed him.

Reaching the highlands of Kinnaur, the sanyasi arrives on the banks of the Sutlej, which flows from the far side of the Himalaya in Tibet, its source near the sacred mountain, Kailas. The great river is too swift and deep to ford. Following its course downstream, he comes to ropeway strung over the roiling current. A rickety jhoola is suspended from wooden pulleys greased with sheep fat. Seated in the cramped gondola, he pulls himself across. Halfway to the other side, he takes the revolver from his satchel and tosses it into Sutlej along with a handful of bullets.

Next day, the monsoon breaks, engulfing the mountains with clouds, rain falling in sheets. Thunder echoes across the ridges and jagged streaks of lightning rent the sky. His path becomes a fast-flowing stream and sections of the slopes wash away in landslides. Ascending through a torrential downpour, he takes shelter in a cave beneath a pile of limestone boulders, shivering with cold as the rain turns into a fusillade of hailstones. He has nothing with which to light a fire and huddles against the hard, unyielding stones. Convinced he will die, he folds himself into a ball and kneels on the ground. The next morning, when he finds himself alive and sunlight enters the darkness, he sees a rude shrine at the back of the cave. It is nothing more than an uncarved shard of granite propped on a narrow ledge, where a few dry flowers have been sprinkled as an offering. Reaching into his satchel, he takes out the two medals he carries, one silver and the other bronze. Placing these in front of the stone icon, he offers them here as a gesture of gratitude to propitiate the nameless spirits that haunt this mountain cave.

After crossing a cragged ridge littered with scree, he descends into the Kullu Valley where the mighty Beas flows through deep canyons, the second of the five great rivers of the Punjab that have their source in the high mountains. Here he finds lush fields and orchards surrounding prosperous, slate-roofed villages, where the inhabitants ply him with rotis, lentils, and curd. With the rain still falling and mist cloaking the mountains, he remains in the valley for several weeks, living in an abandoned hut near a watermill.

The villagers, especially the young children, are curious about this old man. They call him Baba and watch him as he sits in meditation on a flat rock overlooking the valley, while the clouds unfurl around him. He accepts their generosity with gentle words of blessing. Eventually, as the monsoon storms continue, the villagers invite him into their homes to sit beside a smoky hearth, serving him sweet tea and asking questions about his journey. At first, he is reluctant to speak, shrugging off their inquisitive chatter with a benevolent smile. But the hill folk of Kullu charm him with their rustic manners and the innocence of their queries.

Soon enough, he begins to tell stories, not of himself but of cities like Lahore and Dilli, of bustling markets, where caravans unload their precious cargo. Knowing a few words of the hill dialect, he uses these to embellish his Hindustani. He speaks of Peshawar and the Kissa Kahani Bazaar, where traders from every corner of Central Asia converge on the walled city with its sixteen massive gates, recounting the legends and lore of distant places—Bukhara and Samarkand. There are stories of Sikander and Babur, Genghis Khan, and Nadir Shah. He recounts the parable of a beggar who sits by Kabuli Gate, accepting only offerings of pebbles instead of coins because he hopes to use them to build a palace and become a king. Then, one day, a tiny stone is dropped at his feet, which turns out to be a nugget of gold and the beggar's dream is fulfilled.

The villagers listen to tales of strange places and strange men, legends of fierce battles on the frontier—the cruel intrigues of warlords and the bravery of those who challenge their rapacious rule. At times, he grows philosophical and shares the teachings of Teshoo Lama and the secrets of the wheel of existence. The villagers ask him what gods he worships, and the sanyasi replies with enigmatic answers. He claims his faith takes inspiration from the Jataka tales of Bodhisattvas and moral fables about wild animals that perform righteous acts of compassion. He calls himself a bhikkhu and recites prayers in the Bhotia language. At other times, he suggests that he is a Sufi fakir, a follower of a holy tariqa that traces its teachings to a venerable dervish in the Persian city of Isfahan. When the mood strikes him, he also sings the Qawwali verses of Baba Farid and Bulleh Shah, tapping his fingers on his thigh to set the tempo and then lifting his hand to the heavens as he cries out with a wail of ardent adoration. At the same time, he offers obeisance at each of the temples and shrines in the village, the stone images of Hindu deities and the local guardian spirits, who live at the edge of the forest, sheltered by ancient trees.

And then, as abruptly as he arrived in the village, the sanyasi disappears one day, crossing a footbridge that spans the Beas. Walking into the mist, he travels westward, along mossy, overgrown paths, where the monsoon has thrown up green barricades of nettles and creepers. Now that he is well rested and has regained his strength, he walks with the vigorous stride of a man half his age. From Kullu, he descends through the kingdom of Mandi and skirts the high ramparts of the Dhauladhar range that rises above the Kangra Valley. Most of the paths are level here, broad cart tracks, passing through fertile gardens and fields of rice and corn. His begging bowl is seldom empty, and he finds shelter in temples and dharamshalas built by wealthy benefactors for the convenience of pilgrims. He visits shrines like Jawala Mukhi, where an eternal flame burns for the goddess, fuelled by natural gas that escapes through a crack in the rocks.

One day, the ascetic finds himself in the princely state of Lunagarh, and he asks the way to the palace. Presenting himself with his begging bowl at the gate, he recites a couplet in praise of the royal household. The palace is a sprawling mansion with a belfry modelled on Tom Tower at Oxford, where one of the former scions of the state was a student. An officious guard tries to shoo the sanyasi away, but a young princess walking her lap dog in the garden intervenes. She instructs her servant to fill his bowl with rice and curried vegetables from the royal kitchen. The sanyasi blesses her and blesses Anastasia too.

Ascending into the mountains again, he passes through the hill station of Dalhousie, which is smaller and less pretentious than Simla. Though he has ignored the news of the world and made no effort to read a paper or listen to the radio, odd scraps of information have come his way—rumours and conversations overheard along his journey. Riots continue, especially in Bengal as well as the Punjab. Unable to control the violence, the British have advanced the date for the handover of power to 15 August of this year. At a dry goods shop in the market, where he begs for a tola of tobacco, he finds a discarded copy of *The Tribune*, which has been used to wrap a loaf of bread. Spreading the newspaper open across his knees, he reads the narrow columns of English print, as he smokes his chillum. By the time the tobacco has been consumed, he is as well informed about the latest political developments, as anyone might be. The date on the paper is 18 July 1947.

Until this point, his wanderings have seemed aimless, without any fixed destination. But now, his objective has become clearer, as he crosses the third great artery of the Punjab, the Ravi, which has its source in the mountains north of Kangra and then flows out onto the plains near Pathankot. This river leads to Lahore and, for a moment, the sanyasi forgets his vows of self-abnegation, remembering the city of his birth, recalling the Shalimar Gardens irrigated by the Ravi. As a boy, he learned to swim in this river and fished in its waters for the great mahseer. A ferryman poles him across in a leaking boat and he dangles his hand in the current, feeling the pull of the river, tempting him to follow the Ravi downstream.

But as soon as he reaches the opposite bank, the mendicant continues on his way. The mountains rear up in front of him like waves of rock and he fears they will never end, his feet blistered and bleeding. From a high hilltop, where the wind cuts through his thin garments, he spies yet another river, coiling its way through the rugged terrain. Though he has never been here before, he knows it is the Chenab, which cuts a course from the high deserts of Lahaul and Spiti, through these forested gorges. Arriving on its banks, he despairs, for the cold, glacier-fed current is broad and swift, its waters milky with silt. He sleeps by the riverside, in the ruins of a goatherd's hut, on a pile of dead leaves under rotten timbers.

In the morning, the river remains impassible but as he is about to turn back and find another route, the lonely ascetic sees a raft of logs floating towards him. Tall trees have been felled upstream and the timber is being carried on the current. Three men with inflated buffalo hides dislodge the logs where they are trapped by rocks in the stream or wash up on the sandy shoreline. Seeing the sanyasi, and recognizing his plight, one of the men beckons to him and offers to take him across. Clutching the balloon-like hide, he and the man swim out into the current. Immediately, they are tossed by the rapids, struggling to avoid whirlpools and submerged rocks. The Chenab grapples with him, twisting his limbs and dragging him under. He feels sure he will drown as the satchel with his few meagre possessions, including the begging bowl, are swept away by the river. Finally, after they reach a less turbulent stretch of water, the sanyasi swims to the other side. All he possesses now is his loincloth; even his shawl and sandals have been lost.

Yet, he does not give up hope, knowing that the only obstacle ahead are the blue-green ranges of the Pir Panjal, each ridgeline stacked upon the next like a pile of books. Half-naked, he climbs a winding path carpeted with soft pine needles, hearing the cackle and crowing of pheasants. On the first hill he crosses, he meets a group of shepherds grazing their flocks. Taking pity on the elderly sanyasi, they make space for him by their fire. The graziers brew tea for him and give him a bowl of kheer made with rice and cream, which he scoops into his mouth with his fingers, having fed on nothing for the past three days. They also give him a torn blanket to cover himself. Though full of lice, its warmth allows him to sleep.

From the shepherds, he learns that three day's walk from here is the Banihal Pass, beyond which lies Kashmir, the paradise he seeks. His body is gaunt, and his grey beard, now mostly white, falls to his chest, while the hair on his head is matted. The sanyasi takes leave of the shepherds and continues slowly across the mountains. At one place, a bear stands up out of a bush and startles him as he fords a stream, but the animal runs away. The rain has finally eased, though the mist continues to hide the hills on ahead, and he stumbles forward as if possessed by trance.

At last, he reaches the final pass and for once the clouds have parted. Far below him, he sees the Vale of Kashmir spread like a quilt of green, creased with streams and patterned with fields and orchards. To the north lies an arc of snow-clad peaks that frame the valley in rugged symmetry. Suddenly, the air is easier to breathe and the ache in his legs is soothed. That evening, when he reaches the valley, dusk settles over the willows by a stream where he lies down to rest. The fragrance of woodsmoke is carried on the breeze though he is too exhausted to seek its source. An hour later, he wakes in the dark to find a young man holding a lantern and gazing into his face.

Though he hasn't spoken the language of Kashmir for years, the words tumble out as he answers the boy's questions. Soon, he is led to a wooden house by a shallow brook, where he is fed leavened bread and stewed turnip greens, after which he falls asleep on a soft pallet of straw.

The following morning, the young man's family gives him a woollen pheran to cover himself. The loose cloak falls below his knees. It is patched in places and one sleeve has unravelled at the hem. They also provide him with an old salwar-kameez to wear under the pheran. When asked where he is headed, the mendicant says he hopes to reach the Jhelum, the last of the five great rivers that flow into the Punjab before merging with the Indus. The young man explains that tomorrow he is going to Srinagar in a bus that will pass through their village and offers to take the old man with him.

For the first time in weeks, the dark shadows in his soul have lifted and he is grateful for human company and conversation. The family asks where he has come from and he tells them of his adventures, the mountains and rivers he's crossed, while they listen in amazement and wonder at his tales of the road. After days of dejection and despair, he feels once again, that truly, he is a 'Friend of all the World'.

27

Srinagar. 20 August 1947. The street barber in Lal Chowk, who cuts my hair and trims my beard, is a loquacious man, with strong opinions. Though Pakistan and India gained independence a week ago, he claims that nothing will change in Kashmir until the maharaja is removed from his throne.

'That kambakht Hari Singh is a worthless ruler,' he says, speaking in Hindustani, though he is a Kashmiri. 'He cannot make up his mind and dreams impossible dreams of holding onto power.'

'What do you think he should do?' I enquire. 'Accede to Pakistan or to India?'

'Neither,' says the barber, his scissors snipping fiercely near my ear. 'He should turn over power to the people and let them decide their fate.'

'Don't you support the Muslim League?' I ask. 'Or are you a Congresswallah?'

'I am a member of the Communist Party,' he says proudly. 'Jinnah is no better than Nehru. Both of them are pampered aristocrats, out of touch with the masses. This Lal Chowk, Red Square, takes its name from our agitations.'

'So, you want to replace the British with the Russians?' I suggest.

'Of course not,' he replies, pausing and leaning back, as if offended by my remark. 'The British are not the only enemy. We have been fighting to overthrow the Dogra monarchy for decades. Revolution and freedom should be for all humanity, not just one country or people. Duniya ke mazdooron ek ho. Workers of the world unite!'

I am seated on the pavement, overlooking the busy square, while people pass back and forth around us. The barber squats beside me. Earlier this morning I bathed in the Jhelum and rinsed away the sweat and toil of my journey, determined to return to society and retract my ascetic vows.

'They can still throw you in jail for being a communist,' I remind him, as he crops the matted hair on the back of my neck.

'Who cares?' he says, brandishing his comb and scissors as if they were a hammer and sickle. 'Inquilab Zindabad!'

I have to smile, wondering what Creighton and Lurgan would have thought of his slogans. Maybe the Russians will win the Great Game after all.

'Have most of the British left Kashmir?' I ask.

'No, not at all!' the barber answers, rising in a crouch to circle around to my other side. 'Haven't you seen them? The houseboats on Dal Lake are still full of the English. They continue to drive about in their motor garries as if nothing has changed.'

'What about the police and the army?' I ask.

'The goras are still giving orders. Mountbatten is now Governor General instead of Viceroy. Toba toba! Imagine! India and Pakistan claim to be free, yet their soldiers are still commanded by British officers. They say it is only until the transition is completed, but who knows...'

'Has there been much violence in Kashmir?'

For a minute or more, he doesn't reply, examining the length of my hair and evening it out on top.

'There have been riots,' he says. 'Right here in Lal Chowk, two men were killed by a mob last week. Haven't you seen it for yourself?'

'I only arrived a few days ago,' I explain.

'From where?' he demands.

'Lahore,' I reply.

He eyes me with a sharp, inquisitive look.

'Outsiders are the ones who cause trouble,' he says, as if issuing me a warning. 'Most Kashmiris want to live in peace.'

His scissors now set to work trimming my beard.

'Not too short,' I instruct him. 'Just even it out.'

He nods.

'What is your name?' the barber asks.

'Qasim Khan,' I reply.

'From Lahore, you say?'

I wait a couple of beats before explaining. 'Yes, but originally my family comes from Nowshera.'

'Naushera in Kashmir or Nowshera near the Khyber?' he asks.

'Near the Khyber,' I answer. 'On the Indus.'

'So, you are a Pathan?' he declares, with a note of disapproval.

When I nod, he falls silent again, then takes a straight razor and shaving brush from the leather attaché case that lies open on the pavement beside him. He fills a tin cup with warm water from a metal flask, then sharpens the razor on a leather strap that he has hung from a streetlamp beside us. Setting the razor down, he produces a cake of soap and works up a lather. Being on the street, he has to juggle his implements.

'Pathans are said to be fierce warriors,' he says, lifting my chin with his thumb and brushing the white foam on the lower half of my neck.

'Not all of us are,' I reply.

The razor scrapes away soap and hair, as the barber expertly sculpts the underside of my beard with a few deft strokes.

'Have you come to Srinagar on business?' he enquires, wiping my face with a well-used towel before admiring his handiwork.

'Yes,' I acknowledge, 'I am a horse trader.'

'Do you buy them or sell them?' he asks, with suspicion.

'It depends,' I tell him. 'Usually, people ask me for a particular breed, and I do my best to locate what they want. I have contacts in many cities, from Karachi and Quetta to Peshawar and Lahore.'

He says nothing but holds up a pocket mirror for me to see what I look like. The face that stares back at me is much thinner than it was when I left Simla. My shorn hair and beard are now a respectable length, no longer the wild, dishevelled look of an ascetic. When I nod my approval, the barber sets the mirror down and gives my head a vigorous massage, his fingers kneading my scalp, as if he is exorcising the demons from my brain. After he finishes the champi, I pay the eight annas he demands, which amounts to most of the baksheesh I've been able to beg, since I arrived in Srinagar.

Now that I'm no longer a sanyasi, I will have to earn a living instead.

From Lal Chowk to the Polo Grounds is a ten-minute walk and I make my way to the stables, which are located at the back, beneath a line of stately chinar trees. Over the years, I have spent a good deal of time here and the sweet smell of fresh fodder and horse dung is familiar. Two uniformed syces are exercising a pair of polo ponies, which are tethered to long ropes. Handsome, sturdy animals, they circle the handlers at a slow canter, heads held high, manes flowing in the breeze.

Loitering near the stables are half a dozen men of different ages, all of whom appear as disreputable as I, though none is a familiar face. Greeting them with a heartfelt 'Salaam Alaikum!' I join their circle, squatting down in the dappled shade. Years ago, Mahbub Ali taught me the conversational art and etiquette of horse traders, especially the small talk they make amongst themselves, to disguise their true intentions. Questions are exchanged about the price of feed or the condition of routes between distant places, without any hint of a trader's real motives—the search for a thoroughbred Arab stud or a high-spirited Marwari mare. Hours are spent discussing the merits of a turmeric and iodine poultice to treat a lame leg, or a decoction prepared from the roots of bitter gentians that is used as a purgative for qabaz—equine constipation. Under Mahbub Ali's tutelage, I learned the best methods of trimming a hoof and shoeing a horse. After I share my thoughts on this subject with the group, one of them offers me a bidi and asks where I hail from.

Being a practised liar, I concoct an autobiography not unlike the one I told the barber but with added details regarding my expertise in judging the pedigree of a pure white Nukra or the untainted bloodline of a Kathiawari stallion. The tobacco smoke helps loosen my tongue and I am soon welcomed into this equestrian fraternity.

At a certain point, our conversation turns to the political and practical changes now that independence has been achieved. Kashmir remains undecided territory, neither India nor Pakistan, a no man's land. Yet, for the horse traders, the most pressing question is how they will source and bring horses into Kashmir once new borders are created and what taxes or other levies will be introduced after the British are gone. I can tell that my companions are anxious that with the departure of the sahibs, their business will suffer a serious decline.

As we are talking, out of the corner of my eye, I see a group of three Europeans approaching from the far side of the Polo Grounds. They are all dressed for practice, wearing jodhpurs, polo shirts, boots, and helmets. We watch as they advance upon a cluster of syces, squatting next to the stables. Seeing the sahibs, the grooms stand up quickly and assume a respectful demeanour.

The horse traders and I are seated about fifty yards away and our conversation tapers off as we watch the proceedings. One of the stablehands fetches a selection of polo sticks and balls. After a brief discussion, three of syces open the stalls and bring out the mounts requested. Amongst our group, a few remarks are passed on the merits and demerits of each horse as it is being saddled up for its master. One of the sahibs mounts his steed with practised ease and gestures for his stick. I can tell he is about my age and not as agile as he would have been in his youth. The second horse, a young chestnut stallion with a white blaze on its forehead, is jittery and gives his syce some trouble as he tightens its girth. Minutes later, when the second of the three sahibs tries to put his boot in the stirrup, the horse rears up. The rider tumbles backwards onto the ground. Shouts of warning erupt amongst the onlookers and the toppled Englishman curses loudly, as he dusts himself off.

Anticipating more entertainment, two of the traders and I get to our feet and stroll across to take a closer look at the action. The Englishman who fell is very red in the face and seems reluctant to try again, while his syce struggles to calm the horse. The older man, who has already mounted, is giving instructions. To my surprise, I suddenly recognize who it is. More than his features it is the South African accent that makes me freeze. There is no mistaking Victor Joubert, the veterinarian, though I haven't seen him since 1941, when I escaped from his Vauxhall and took a bullet in my back before jumping into the Upper Jamuna Canal.

'Your bloody syce didn't exercise him properly this morning,' Joubert tells the rider who fell, while the third Englishman successfully climbs into his saddle.

Another attempt to mount the chestnut stallion is unsuccessful, as it shies away from its master, the inexperienced groom barely able to control the agitated horse.

The Englishman looks as if he is about to take a whip to both the animal and his syce. Meanwhile, each of the men who have gathered round offers advice as the horse grows increasingly restless. Having recovered from my astonishment at seeing Joubert, I sense an opportunity to earn a few rupees. Calling out respectfully in Hindustani to the Englishman, I offer my services.

'Huzoor, if you wish, I can calm your horse down so that you will be able to ride him,' I propose. 'It is only a matter of soothing his nerves and releasing the tension.'

Joubert turns to look at me, with an arrogant expression.

'What would you know, old man?' he says, derisively. His Hindustani was learned in stables across the Punjab, and he adds a couple choice abuses. 'Does a bastard like you, who commits incest with his mother, know how to mount this beast?'

'I will ride him and show you,' I reply, ignoring the insults.

'What did he say?' The unsaddled Englishman asks.

'He claims he can control your horse,' says Joubert.

Several of the syces begin to laugh, chiding me with their own taunts.

'Let him have a go, Thornton!' says the third sahib. 'It should be amusing, if he doesn't get himself killed. Besides, your man is useless.'

Stepping forward into the circle, I reach for the stallion's reins and relieve the hapless syce of his charge. The horse eyes me with a wild-eyed expression, like a mustang that's never been ridden. Placing one hand on his neck, I speak to him in Pashto, invoking the blessings of various frontier saints while returning in kind the compliments that Joubert has paid me. Then I lead the horse away from the others to a distance of about thirty yards.

The veterinarian is still smirking at my audacity, but he can see that I know how to handle a horse. Several minutes pass, as the stallion grows accustomed to my voice and the words I whisper in his ear. He snorts, flaring both nostrils, but his hooves are no longer as agitated as before and I can hear him exhale, his flanks shuddering, as if he has accepted his fate. Keeping the reins taut with just enough tension on the bit so the animal feels the assurance of my grip, I stroke his shoulder and neck, still speaking to him like a lover being coaxed into an ardent embrace. Then, once I have gained his confidence, I reach down and adjust the girth, which is too tight.

The pheran I wear is an awkward garment for riding and the sandals, which I stole from the threshold of a mosque this morning, are a size too large. But with as much agility as I can muster, I slip my left foot into the stirrup and launch my body atop the saddle. For a moment, it feels as if the stallion will throw me, but I keep the reins taut and maintain control, still murmuring sweet endearments in Pashto. Mahbub Ali would have been proud.

Turning the horse towards the polo ground, I let him trot forward. Within a few strides he breaks into a canter, after which I give him his head and let him gallop, flying across the green expanse of open grass, as if set free. No longer troubled by my weight, he races around the field, while I keep low in the saddle like a good Chitrali horseman who has competed against the best of them on the polo fields near the Shandur Pass.

After completing a chakkar, I slow the horse down, easing his pace with a firm but gentle hand on the reins. He responds to my commands, a combination of words and other sounds, as he obediently walks in a broad circle, ears erect. I stroke his mane and direct him back to the waiting group of men. The rest of the horse traders have joined them and even the sahibs eye me with respect.

Dismounting, I whisper a final blessing to the horse and then gesture for his master to climb into the saddle again. This time the stallion doesn't flinch and after taking the reins, the sahib reaches into his pocket and hands me a five-rupee note.

'Where did you learn to ride?' Joubert asks me in Hindustani.

I avoid his eye but answer with a vague gesture. 'Here and there.'

He is holding his horse steady, standing about ten yards away, looking down at me from under the brim of his helmet.

'You look familiar,' he says. 'Have I met you before?'

I shrug my shoulders. 'Perhaps, perhaps not.'

His eyes study me with intensity and I remember how tiny his pupils appeared, like cinders, when I saw him last, in the back seat of the Vauxhall.

I return his gaze with an impassive expression, stroking my beard and adjusting the turban on my head.

'What is your name?' he asks.

'Qasim Khan,' I reply.

'Would I have met you in Lahore?' he persists.

The crowd disperses and the other two sahibs have moved off to practise their forehand strokes, knocking the balls across the field.

'Huzoor, I have been to Lahore but please forgive me if I do not recognize you,' I answer, with a courteous gesture, though I can feel the bile rising in my throat.

He begins to turn his horse aside, preparing to follow the others and then looks back with a sudden flash of recognition. Joubert's eyes narrow and his mouth tightens into a scowl.

'Goddamn you, O'Hara,' he says, under his breath, as I walk away.

28

While I have several old friends and acquaintances in Srinagar, I do not contact them, preferring to remain a stranger here. Qasim Khan is a name I've often used in the past. Neither MacNeil nor Srinivas was aware of his existence, which has allowed me to disappear from time to time. Instead of being an alias, I like to think of Qasim as the person I become when I'm not myself. Perhaps he represents my second self. Yaqzan, who gave me the name years ago, claimed that Qasim Khan suited me better than Kimball O'Hara, and sometimes I think he might be right. I often feel more comfortable as a Pathan horse trader than a country-born Irish malcontent. Whenever I take on Qasim's identity, I find myself completely at ease, as if there is no need to invent a personality or story for myself. I am who I am. It's not a role I play as an actor, but instead a reflection of my true character, if such a thing exists.

Most of the five rupees that I was given by the Englishman whose horse I tamed, was spent last night on a sumptuous meal and a quarter bottle of rum. The owner of the hotel where I ate and drank, let me sleep on a balcony overlooking one of Srinagar's many canals. This morning, I wake up to the mutterings of ducks swimming by in the scummy green water. Though the woollen pheran kept me warm during the night, I know that the first thing I need to do is procure a new set of clothes. This is accomplished by visiting the main Dhobi Ghat on the banks of the Jhelum. A young washerman, with whom I strike up a conversation, is using a heavy brass iron, filled with burning charcoal, to press a pile of clean laundry. When he turns around to pick up a wrinkled shirt, after putting the iron down on a crude metal trivet, I distract him by clumsily knocking it over. As he gathers up the burning embers with a pair of metal tongs, I apologize profusely, while helping myself to a freshly pressed set of salwar-kameez that I tuck beneath the voluminous folds of my pheran.

Of course, I feel a twinge of guilt, for I know the dhobi will have to answer to his irate customer, but I'm sure it isn't the first or last time he'll need to make up excuses for missing laundry. After changing into my new clothes, in a deserted alley behind the Palladium Cinema, I head across to the main Post Office. Buying a stamped postcard for half an anna, I borrow a pen from one of the men in the queue and write Dr Victor Joubert's name on the front of the card. After that, I approach one of the postal clerks, who is seated at a desk outside the sorting room. Explaining that I need to send Dr Joubert an urgent message, I ask the clerk if he can help me find his address. At first, he is brusque and waves me aside impatiently, though when my eyes well up with tears and I explain that my son, who worked for Joubert sahib, has died, the man squints at the name.

'Do you know which part of Srinagar he lives in?' asks the clerk.

'I think on a houseboat,' I reply.

'Dal Lake or Nagin Lake?' he demands. 'Or on the Jhelum?'

'I'm not sure,' I reply.

With an irritated frown, the clerk gets up from his desk and goes into the sorting room where a group of postmen are waiting to collect the day's mail for delivery. Through the open door, I can see the clerk speaking to one of them and showing him the card. The postman shakes his head, then calls out to another mail carrier, who shuffles across and looks at the name. He seems to recognize who it is and glances up at me briefly from a distance, then says something to the others.

Returning to his desk, the clerk picks up a pen and fills in the address:

> Buckingham Palace
> Nagin Lake,
> Srinagar, Kashmir

Wiping the tears from my eyes, I thank the postal clerk and head outside where a line of professional letter-writers, with their pens, papers, and bottles of ink, are seated in the shade of a jacaranda tree, composing messages for those who cannot read or write. Walking past them, I remember how, as a boy, I dictated cryptic missives for Mahbub Ali, informing him of the secrets I'd uncovered.

Nagin Lake is about a four-mile walk from the Post Office but compared to my recent journeys through the mountains it is an easy stroll, along quiet by-lanes north of the city. Most of the route is shaded with poplars as well as chinars. Crossing bridges over canals, I watch men paddling shikaras with heart-shaped oars. Many of these small skiffs are laden with vegetables from the floating gardens or other produce and supplies. Some of the shikaras, which are brightly caparisoned, ferry tourists through the maze of waterways. Srinagar has sometimes been called the Venice of the East, though I can't say if that's an apt comparison, never having been there. All I know is that Kashmir is as close to paradise as I will ever get, though it's never been a place where I felt I belonged.

A narrow channel connects Nagin to Dal Lake, which is a much larger waterbody. As I cross the bridge that spans this conduit, I stop to look out over the liquid mirror of blue that reflects the sky. Water lilies are blooming near the shore and a heron is poised in the shallows waiting to spear a fish. Off in the distance, I can see the layered profiles of purple ridges. Just beyond the bridge, I turn left and proceed along the shore of Nagin Lake. Each of the houseboats, moored at the water's edge, have whimsical names—Cleopatra's Barge, Cheerful Chippendale, Halleluiah Chorus....

Buckingham Palace lies at the far end of the lake, half-hidden behind a thicket of willows. The boat is not as grand as its name implies but it seems to be luxurious enough, with large, curtained windows. A spacious porch, at the prow, faces out into the lake, where guests can admire the sunset while reclining on cushioned divans. A wooden staircase descends to the water, so that passengers can board the shikaras that ply on the lake. Along both sides of the houseboat is a narrow walkway, a ledge about six inches wide, which allows the houseboys and other staff to access the front and back, without passing through the rooms inside. Over the years, I've stayed on half a dozen houseboats in Kashmir and they're all much the same, constructed of fragrant deodar wood that is carved into elaborate floral patterns. The floors, also made of cedar planks, are covered with Kashmiri carpets while the furnishings and décor reflect the handicrafts of the valley. From my experience, the food is usually bad and the water, drawn straight from the lake, will give you dysentery unless it's boiled twice over.

The only person I can see is a woman washing dishes on the shore, her head wrapped in a brightly coloured scarf. I keep my distance, not wanting to be seen, though I suspect Joubert has gone out for the day. Perhaps he's looking for me.

※

Several hours after sunset, the moon comes up, a cocoon of light, three-quarters full. A few stray clouds drift overhead but the air is still. Near the hotel where I spent last night, a shikara is tied up along the canal. Unlike the tourist boats, it is a simple craft, used for transporting goods. After eating a meagre meal of bread and yoghurt, which is all I can afford, I slip outside through the shadows and untie the shikara. Stepping into the stern and settling myself on the low seat at the back, I lift the paddle quietly and dip it into the canal, propelling the slender craft through the shadows.

One canal leads on to the next, a watery labyrinth. I do not know the way, though I keep the moon to my right and eventually, after more than an hour, I paddle out into an open expanse of water. A few lights glimmer along the shoreline, though most of the houseboats lie in darkness, their occupants asleep. A lunar sheen on the surface of Nagin Lake glistens like silver foil. I let the shikara drift for a while, resting the oar across my knees. Though I have no watch, it must be close to midnight now.

Gliding over the moonlit water, the shikara hardly leaves a ripple as I paddle slowly forward. Each of the houseboats has its name written above the prow and there is enough illumination for me to read these signs. Finally, Buckingham Palace comes into view, and I am relieved to see that no lights are burning, neither inside nor out. It looks deserted in the moonlight, a dark hulk anchored to the shore. My shikara slides towards the wooden steps that descend to the water and I grab one of the posts that supports a banister, then crawl crablike out of the boat. The hull of the shikara scrapes against the steps, where I crouch and listen, before tying up.

The main door is latched from inside. When I step onto the outer ledge, a plank creaks under my weight. Moving carefully forward, I test the windows one by one, each of them secure. The last window, however, is open and through the screen, I can hear someone snoring—a low, gurgling rumble. The butcher knife I stole from the hotel kitchen is in my right hand while my left hand pushes the screen. At first it doesn't budge but with a little more pressure, it swings inward as the snoring continues. There is just enough moonlight for me to make out a figure asleep in the bed, as I step through the window and across the carpet on the floor. Within seconds, my knife is pressed against his throat.

Joubert wakes with a start and tries to push me away, though I have one arm locked around his neck.

'Don't move,' I tell him, 'otherwise I'll cut you open like a fucking goat.'

He stops and lies motionless in my grasp. Both of us are breathing hard.

'Who else is here?' I whisper.

'Nobody,' he says.

'Don't lie to me,' I warn him.

'I am alone.'

We are so close I can feel the beating of his heart and smell the stench of his breath, the two of us clasped together in a violent embrace.

'Where do you keep your pistol?' I whisper in his ear.

He hesitates until I press the blade firmly into his larynx.

Joubert gasps. 'In the bedside drawer.'

With the knife still digging into his throat, I pull my other arm away and sit up beside him. He doesn't try to fight back, knowing that it would take one swift stroke of the blade to kill him. Reaching across to the bedside table, I fumble with the drawer and pull it open. At first, I can feel nothing inside but then my fingers touch the cold, hard steel. It's not a revolver but a compact semi-automatic that fits snugly into my palm. I cannot be sure if it is loaded, though chances are it is.

'Roll over, face down,' I tell him, as I pull the knife away. 'And keep both arms at your sides.'

He obeys my command and puts up no resistance. Quickly, I check the clip, realizing it must be the same Beretta that Joubert used five years ago, when he shot me—a small but lethal weapon. Pointing the pistol at him, I stand up and take a step backwards. It would be so easy to put a bullet in his back.

'Turn around,' I tell him.

Slowly, he rolls over and stares at the pistol.

'What do you want?' he asks me, still out of breath.

'Answers,' I tell him.

He laughs softly, though it sounds more like a cough.

With the pistol still aimed at his face, I switch on a lamp by the bedside table. Though it isn't very bright, the light makes Joubert squint. He is wearing green silk pyjamas. On his neck is a streak of blood where the knife sliced his skin.

'Sit on the floor,' I tell him.

He climbs slowly off the bed and lowers himself onto the carpet. Joubert and I are about the same age and size, two old men who should know better than to play these dangerous games. In one corner of the room is a chair, which I draw forward.

'What sort of answers?' Joubert asks, his voice full of resentment.

'Did you kill Srinivas?'

His eyes are dull, as if he's not fully awake. I can see his spectacles on the bedside table, resting on a book.

'No,' he says.

'Srinivas told me that he'd successfully turned you. Instead of working for the Germans you were reporting to him,' I say. 'Is that true?'

'Perhaps,' he responds, unwilling to concede too much. 'But I didn't kill him.'

'Who did?'

He sighs. 'I don't know who pulled the trigger, but it was one of your own people who gave the order that Srinivas should be shot.'

'My people?'

'An Englishman.'

'Sir Denys Bromley-Pugh?'

'Yes,' he says. 'It was his decision.'

'How do you know?'

'I was there when he gave the order,' says Joubert.

'What were you doing with Sir Denys?' I demand.

'I was meeting him on behalf of my employer, who needed to recover some documents that Srinivas had,' Joubert replies, touching his neck and noticing the blood on his fingers.

'Which employer?' I ask.

'The Maharaja of Kashmir,' Joubert explains. 'There were files that contained damaging personal information. With the British departing, he wanted them destroyed.'

'What kind of personal information?' I enquire.

'For many years he's been subjected to blackmail because of certain indiscretions in his youth....'

'How could Sir Denys help him?'

'He had connections in high places, as well as in most government departments,' Joubert answers, 'including the secret service.'

He touches his neck again, then wipes his fingers on the carpet.

'Did you warn Srinivas that his life was in danger?' I ask.

'I tried,' he claims. 'But it was too late. They got to him before I could.'

'You should have tried harder,' I tell him, then ask, 'Are you still working for the maharaja?'

'No,' says Joubert. 'I'm leaving India in another week. It's all over now.'

'You're not going to stay on and help Kashmir become an independent state, the Switzerland of Asia?'

'That's not going to happen, is it?' he says, shaking his head. 'Between Nehru and Jinnah, they'll carve it up. I'm afraid his highness doesn't have a winning hand.'

'What happened to the files he wanted destroyed?' I ask.

'I have no idea,' Joubert responds, then touches his neck again.

'By the way, I'm bleeding. May I get a handkerchief?'

'No,' I say. 'It's nothing serious, just a scratch, though it could have been worse. Will you be going back to South Africa?'

'That's my plan,' Joubert replies. 'I've got a passage booked from Bombay to Cape Town on the sixth of September. What about you? Are you going to stay on?'

I ignore his question. 'There's one more answer I need from you. Who was it that tried to shoot me in Lahore?'

Joubert shifts uncomfortably and then shrugs.

'It was me,' he says, after a pause.

I shake my head. 'That was the second time you failed to kill me.'

'Shouldn't you be grateful for that?' he says, attempting to smile.

'Grateful?' I laugh. 'Why? Because your aim is so poor?'

'Perhaps I should have tried harder,' he says.

I stay silent for a while, realizing how much I hate this man, for his politics and duplicity, as well as the snide, smug look on his face. I also have to admit that I hate him because, in some ways, he reminds me of myself. Though I came here with every intention of killing Joubert, I know that I can't. While I've shot men like Craven in self-defence, I've never been able to take someone's life just because he deserves to die.

'Where do you keep your money?' I ask him.

'In the bank,' he tells me, with an insolent scowl.

'No, I mean here on the boat,' I say. 'How much have you got in cash? Let's see if it's enough to pay for your life.'

'Are you serious?' he says. 'Is that all you want? My money?'

'It depends on how much you've got,' I answer.

His mouth curls up in a sneer. 'I always knew you were nothing more than a common thief, O'Hara. A dirty, fucking swindler.'

'Don't tempt me,' I say. 'I'll be happy to shoot you for free. Just tell me where you keep your money.'

In his eyes, I can see the calculations going on in his mind.

'How do I know you won't shoot me after I tell you where it is?' he asks.

'Because one way or the other, I'll find it,' I say. 'You'll just make it easier on yourself and me.'

'There's a key in my trouser pocket, over there on the chair,' he confesses. 'It unlocks that cupboard, the one on the right. There's a cash box inside, on the top shelf. Take what you want.'

Stepping across the room, with the pistol still aimed at Joubert, I find the key and open the cupboard. The metal cash box is where he said it was. Taking it out, I spill the contents on the bed. There's a wad of rupees, in large denominations, probably a thousand or more and a dozen ten-pound notes, not a fortune but certainly enough to take me wherever I choose to go. Putting the money in my pocket, I approach Joubert, the Beretta aimed at his head.

He looks worried now and says, 'I thought you weren't going to shoot me.'

I say nothing, my finger on the trigger, the muzzle six inches from his eyes, which are full of panic and fear.

'Please,' he begs me. 'I won't tell anyone who you are. I'm leaving India. Don't shoot me in cold blood…. Good god, O'Hara. Have some mercy!'

'It's what you deserve, you grovelling swine.'

With that, I lean forward, and gathering the full force of my anger, I slam the butt of the pistol into his right temple, halfway between his eyebrow and the top of his ear. Without making another sound, he falls on his side, eyes wide open.

Leaving him like that, I turn off the lamp and step through the window onto the ledge outside. Looking across the shimmering surface of the lake, I pocket the Beretta and then toss the knife into the water. It will be a while before Joubert wakes up and he'll have a headache to thank me for, along with his life. I make my way to the front of the houseboat and descend the wooden steps to the shikara. Untying the rope, I settle myself at the stern and then paddle out into the moonlight, across the silent water, before disappearing into the remains of the night.

Epilogue

Whenever I grew bored of sitting atop the great fire-breathing cannon, Zam-Zammah, and lording it over my friends, I would dismount from the tarnished bronze barrel, etched with inscriptions in Farsi, and cross the street to the Ajaib Ghar, 'the house of wonders', as we called the Lahore Museum. Ducking under the turnstile when the attendant wasn't watching, I would scramble inside that mysterious building, which had more domes than most mosques I've seen and more hidden chambers and sancta sanctorum than any temple I've entered.

Here lay the relics and treasures of Hindustan, Bhot, and Bactria, arrayed upon the walls, displayed atop pedestals and lodged within glass cases. My visits to the museum always began by paying obeisance to the Tibetan ritual masks, marvelling over the grim and grotesque visage of each demon or demigod. If only I could wear one of these, I'd be transformed into a wild, ferocious monster, feared by one and all. From here, I wandered into a gallery full of swords and polished armour, the weaponry of Ranjit Singh's fearless warriors and Mughal armies that fought to rule the Punjab. Just the sight of those steel blades and shields of rhinoceros hide was enough to carry me back in time to a bygone era of chivalry and conquest. After that, I drifted through a room full of Kangra miniatures, delicate paintings with luminous colours, the blue-skinned Krishna and his beloved Radha meeting in a garden of flowering trees, beneath dark monsoon clouds, pregnant with rain. As streaks of lightning flashed in the sky, I imagined that I could step into that scene, if only I knew the sacred incantations that would transport me there.

The museum's elderly curator, with his white beard and saintly brow, indulged my incessant questions and told me stories from the past, the lore and legends of various dynasties and invaders, from the great Mauryan emperor Ashoka to Sikander-e-Azam and his Greek armies, as well as Sultan Mahmud of Ghazni, who crossed the Khyber seventeen times to loot and pillage the land of five rivers and beyond.

When Teshoo Lama first arrived in Lahore and visited the Ajaib Ghar, he was overawed by the collection of Buddhist statuary, images of Shakyamuni carved out of Taxila's hard, grey stone. For a while, I listened to the Holy One discuss the mysteries of Shambala and Suchzen with the curator but soon I grew tired of their esoteric discourse. Seeking out an image of the starving Buddha, I studied his emaciated body, so clearly and intricately chiselled out of rock that every vein and sinew, as well as the bones of his skeleton showed through the skin. Surely, this was a divine soul who symbolized compassion and humility, rather than power and vengeance.

Seeing the many archaeological wonders and artefacts in the Lahore Museum, I recognized, even as a young boy, that the British empire, just like all the rest of them, could not last forever. Now that the Angrez are gone, and India has split apart, another chapter will be written in a language all its own. At times like this, I am convinced that I understood the world better when I was a child, rather than as an old man with tangled memories and tortured dreams. Who knows what will happen next, but as it's been said many times before—the present inevitably becomes the past, and all that remains are the tea leaves of history.

Acknowledgements

My sincere thanks to Jonathan Addleton, Steve Rasmussen, and Navtej Sarna, who read and commented on an early draft of this novel. Their insightful suggestions were invaluable and helped me avoid potentially embarrassing mistakes. However, any errors that remain are mine alone, as are the political, social, and historical perspectives expressed in this book. While translating the Urdu verses by Ghalib and Mir, which appear in this novel, I referred to Saif Mahmood's *Beloved Delhi: A Mughal City and Her Greatest Poets*, Gulzar's *Mirza Ghalib: A Biographical Scenario*, and Ralph Russell's *The Oxford India Ghalib*.